CW01208201

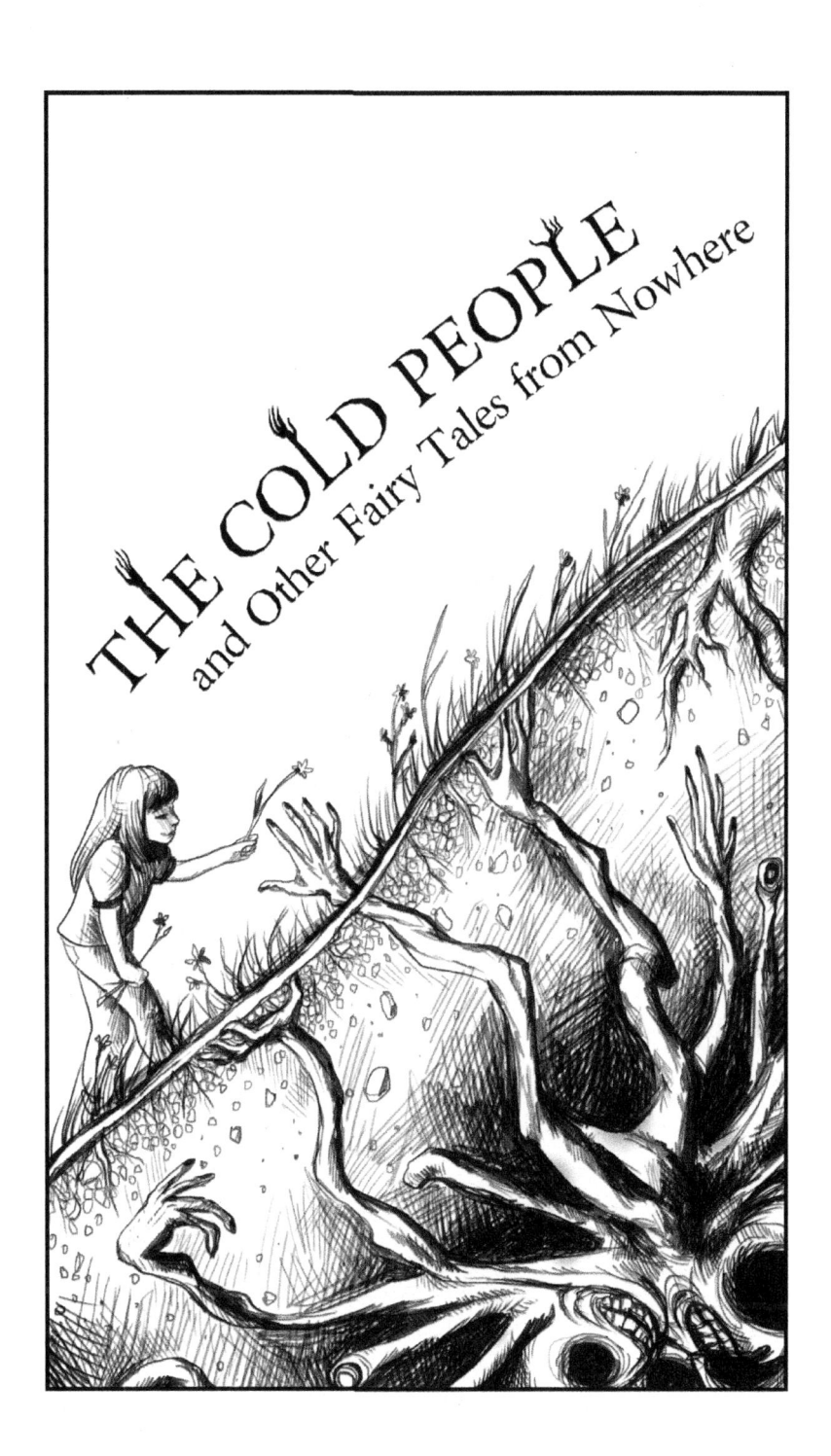

THE COLD PEOPLE
and Other Fairy Tales from Nowhere

The Cold People
And Other Fairy Tales from Nowhere

Copyright © 2016 by Felix Blackwell
www.felixblackwell.com

All rights reserved in all media. No part of this book may be used or reproduced without written permission, except in the case of brief quotations embodied in critical articles and reviews.

The moral right of Felix Blackwell and Colin J. Northwood as the authors of this work has been asserted by them in accordance with the Copyright, Designs, and Patents Act of 1988.

This is a work of fiction. All names, characters, locales, and incidents are products of the authors' imaginations and any resemblance to actual people, places, or events is coincidental or fictionalized.

All artwork by the brilliant LORINDA TOMKO.
www.lorindatomko.com

Published in the United States in 2016 with CreateSpace.

Copyright © 2016 Felix Blackwell
All rights reserved
.
ISBN: 1532854552
ISBN-13: 978-1532854552

The Cold People

And Other Fairy Tales from Nowhere

Felix Blackwell • Colin J. Northwood
artwork by Lorinda Tomko

Dedicated to Daniel, Keshav, and Chandranil

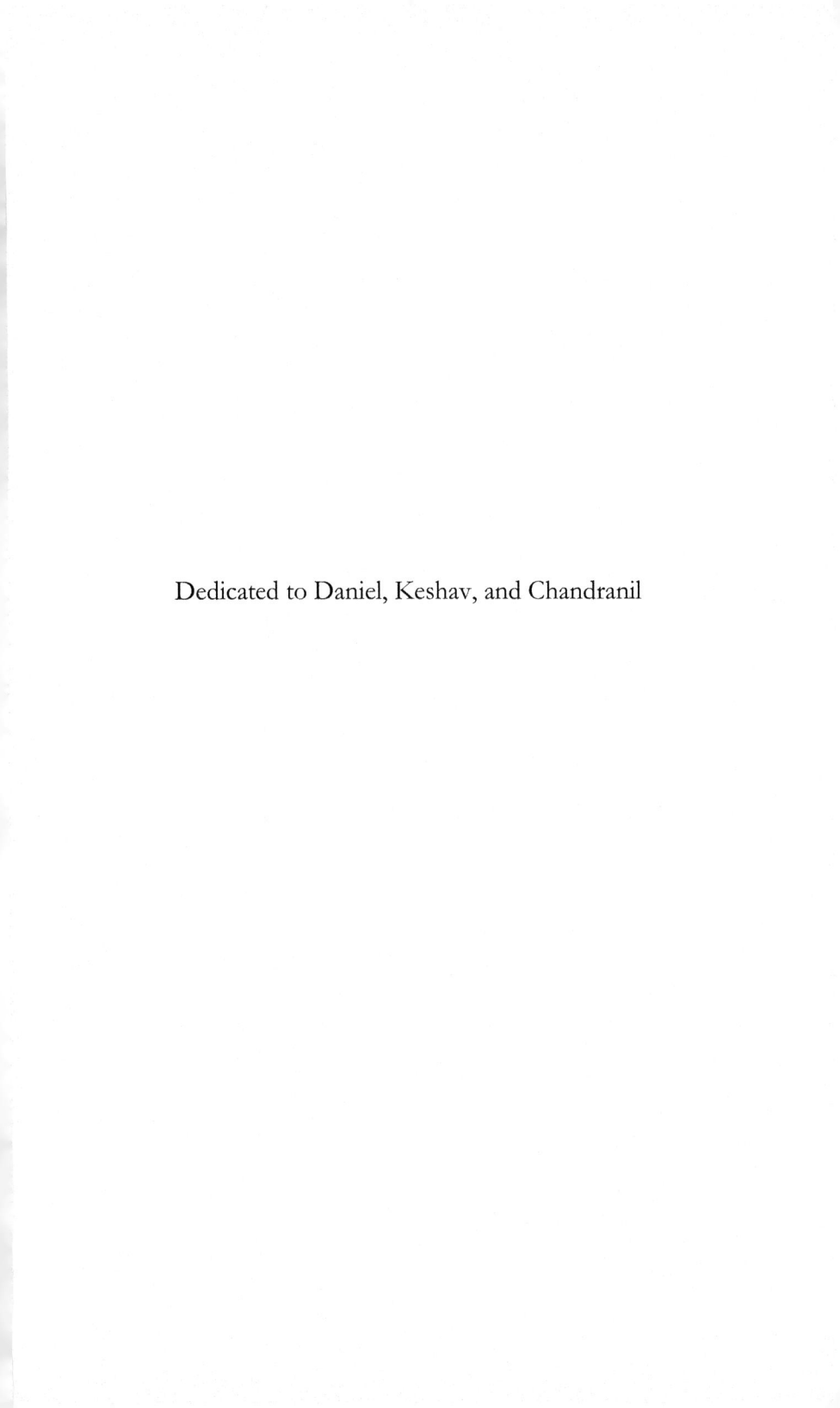

Table of Contents

World Behind the World · 1

Icebreaker, part I · 12

Clean · 22

Lily · 38

Spare Parts · 50

The Cold People · 66

Cubes · 82

The Bleeding Window · 90

Going Down · 94

Edwin · 108

Nothing Goes to Waste · 112

Motherbird · 123

Chocolate is Rocket Fuel for Nightmares · 135

Long Live the King · 148

Cold Shoulder · 155

inbetween · 160

Kismet · 164

Spike · 175

Six Steps Forward · 190

Poor Richard · 208

Maternal Instinct · 221

Icarus · 235

Icebreaker, part II · 240

World Behind the World
Felix Blackwell

The experience of many people with what we call the "paranormal" typically consists of uneasy feelings, unexplained sounds, objects moving. Sometimes it is a strange form, caught just in the periphery of one's vision, only to vanish when noticed. But these things are all mere shadows on the wall of our dimension. Since I was a child, I've had the curse of seeing through those walls. I have seen the ones who cast those shadows.

It was a rough breakup. I was a Junior in college with my whole life ahead of me, but I couldn't pick myself up. She was the one I had dreamed of for many years, and the one I thought I'd wake up to for the rest of my life.

And then she was gone. It was all my fault. I blamed myself every waking moment, and when I slept she haunted my nightmares. I was, as my friends put it, "in a bad place," and needed to find my way out. So they insisted I socialize more.

One night, my friends took me out to a movie. We romped around downtown Westmaple in the frigid winter air, bobbing in and out of the shops before the film started. When we couldn't take the cold anymore, we headed into the theater lobby. Christine and Kevin stood in line for snacks while Nathan and I went looking for the bathroom.

It was a Friday, and the whole theater bustled with young couples, professors, and generations of hippies.

It was one of those upscale theaters. The bathroom was decadent, lined with sparkling black tiles and ambient lighting. Even the sink counters looked like marble. We shuffled in with several other random guys, and Nathan took the last urinal. I found a stall.

I stood there, staring at the wall as I drained, almost hypnotized by the decorative metallic flecks in the tiles. Thoughts of my now ex-girlfriend surfaced in my mind from the depths where I tried to hide them. As I thought of her, the din of people and sinks and hand dryers all around me faded to silence. I shook off the thoughts and tried to flush, but the toilet did nothing. I tried again. The handle stuck.

"Nice place," I said, then turned and exited the stall.

The bathroom was now empty; the dozen people who were here just moments ago had vanished. I bent down and glanced under the long line of stalls. No feet.

"Nate?" I called out. He must have gone back to the lobby. I wasn't quite sure how everyone had left without a sound.

Breakup's makin' you a space cadet, I thought.

It was quiet enough now that I noticed pop music playing through the speakers on the ceiling. The wall lights flickered, then went out. For just a moment, I stood there in absolute darkness, and then they came back on.

I shrugged, headed to the sink, and tried to turn on the faucet. The tap was dry.

"*Real* nice place."

An ancient fear flickered inside me when the door to the lobby didn't budge. I instantly recalled the claustrophobia that I'd buried with my childhood, and the way it pressed down on my chest and throat. I rattled the door harder. It didn't open. It didn't even shudder under a spirited attempt. It was as though someone had affixed a useless knob to a metal wall where there had never been a door.

I sucked in a deep, slow breath, swallowing back the primal urge to panic. My phone had reception, but neither Christine nor Nathan answered my call. I texted them both:
Locked in the bathroom. Get me the hell out of here. Not joking.

Minutes went by. I bashed my fist against the door, issuing thunderous booms across the walls, but there was no response. Only the vapid pop songs kept me company.

There must be another way out, I thought.

The bathroom had six stalls, six urinals, five sinks, painted tile floors and ceilings, and one door. One locked door. Or rather, the semblance of a door on one part of the wall. I examined every inch of the place, and beneath the long sink counter I found a vent panel. Cool air poured out of it. With the corner of my debit card, I loosened the four screws that held it to the wall.

A twenty-foot metal vent shaft lay before me, with faint light glowing at the far end. I ran a finger along the inside rim of the vent and studied the dust that caked it.

Allergies be damned! I thought, trying not to imagine the legion of filthy bathroom germs I was about to wade through. I slipped into the duct headfirst, and propelled myself to the other side with my feet like a penguin on an ice sheet. There was not even enough room to crawl on all fours.

There wasn't a vent panel on the far end of the tunnel – instead there was a wall of stench that hit me in the face before I reached the light. The stink was indescribable. Having lived in an old dorm hall with one giant bathroom, I was no stranger to foul odors. But this smelled less like a rancid bathroom and more like rotting meat.

The room I emerged into was a mirror image of the

bathroom I'd just escaped. I reasoned that this must be the ladies' restroom.

"Uh, anyone in here?" I called out, hoisting myself off the ground and batting the dust off my shirt. "Sorry, I...uh...I was locked in the men's room..." I could almost taste the horrid smell as I spoke.

Nobody replied. The same music played in this bathroom too, but it seeped out of the speakers like mud. It almost sounded like I was hearing it underwater.

The rest of the place was a bit odd too.

Some of the lights were off, but even in the darkness I could see that mold had grown over half the floor and one of the walls. It crept all the way up to the ceiling and spiraled out in different directions. The air was cold and moist.

That claustrophobic flicker was blossoming into a robust fear within me. I went straight for the door, but as I approached, I noticed that it was completely overtaken by rust. The reddish-brown corruption took on the appearance of dried blood in the pale light.

I reached out and yanked the door knob. It snapped off in my hand and crumpled into little pieces.

"Fuck!" I shouted. I threw the pieces to the ground and watched them skitter under the line of stalls. They collided with something wet.

I knelt down and peered under the doors.

There were feet. A woman's. Bare.

The skin was gray and white, crisscrossed with purple veins. Long, putrid nails bent and curled away from the toes like the branches of a dead tree. Mold caked the spaces between the feet and the floor.

My breath died in my chest. I snuck back to the vent, wide-eyed with terror, and crawled back in. I propelled myself back into the men's bathroom at light speed, then quietly slipped the vent panel back into place and made sure those screws were on tighter than ever before.

But this bathroom was different now. Only one light remained on. It illuminated just a portion of the long room, whose floor was now stained with all manner of unspeakable filth. The one wall I could see had chunks torn out of it in the shape of nails or claws. The music that played was garbled, choppy, and completely off-key.

A voice rang out from far off.

"*Nuuhhhhnn...ah...ahhh...*"

It echoed all around me; I could not tell from which direction it came. It certainly didn't come from the speakers overhead.

"*Ehhhk- aaaaah...*"

It sounded like an animal waking up from hibernation.

"*Mm...*"

It was coming from the vent.

I squatted down and pressed my ear against the panel.

Something was stirring on the other side of the tunnel, from the women's restroom I'd just escaped. The feet immediately came to mind.

"*You,*" the voice croaked. It was a woman's voice. She laughed a weak, wet chuckle, then began to grumble indecipherably. Her voice crept up to a high-pitched strain, then dropped down to a much lower octave, deeper than a man's.

My intestines knotted up.

"*Yoouuuuuu...*" she groaned, enthusiasm building in her voice. The speech carried through the vent and bounced all around me. I leaped to my feet and tried the locked door again, to no avail, then ran to the stall I had pissed in. My intention was to stand on the toilet and hide, in hopes that whatever was on the other side of that duct would not crawl in here and find me.

I pulled the stall door open. The toilet was gone, seemingly ripped from the floor. In its place, a maw of

5

darkness yawned before me. It was so deep that I couldn't see the bottom, but sounds of dripping water echoed from within. I stood there at the edge of the broken tiles, staring deep into the void, wondering if I was meant to go in. Wondering if it had been opened up for a reason.

Soft, raspy breathing disrupted my ponderings. I glanced behind me, back at the vent.

The outline of a face appeared in the shadows, partly obscured behind the panel. Deep, dark eyes stared out at me. Watched me. But these eyes didn't study me; somehow, they already knew me.

I didn't have to jump. The sight of that face compelled me forward under the force of terror. I fell headfirst into the impossible abyss. My shoes squeaked across the tiles as I slid in.

The sensation of falling did not overtake me. No wind rushed up from below me. My stomach did not leap into my throat. I felt suspended, still, unmoving in the velvety black. I reached my hands out and discovered a metal surface before me. The hole I'd fallen into was gone, and the only light now was a line of pale white where my feet rested.

I felt around the metal surface until my hand fell on a knob. It was a door. I shoved it open and beheld another bathroom, just like the two before it. The second my brain processed this room, gravity caught up with me, and dragged me straight down. If I hadn't been holding the door knob, I'd have fallen deeper into the dark.

Instead I dangled there, yelling and cursing, trying to hoist myself up into the wretched bathroom. My legs flailed all around as I pulled myself up. There was nothing to step on; it was as if the bathroom itself hung in an empty void. The moment I flopped onto the dirty tile floor, the door slammed shut behind me, and a chorus of demonic screams rang out behind it.

I lay there on the floor, shaking violently, trying not to

cry. Water droplets trickled all around me. Above the sinks, a single lamp flickered, but its light didn't even reach the stalls a few yards away. Someone could very well have been in this bathroom with me.

I pulled myself up and hobbled to the sinks, rubbing my face with desperation.

You're having a psychotic episode, I thought. *You've completely lost it. Are you high? Did you drink anything that wasn't yours tonight?*

I stood under the dim light and checked my eyes in the mirror.

Pupils aren't dinner plates. That's a good sign.

I pried my eyelids open.

Healthy white. You aren't high. Mental breakdown it is.

While looking at my reflection, I noticed something different about this bathroom. Unlike the two before it, this one had another mirror on the wall behind me. Both mirrors faced each other, creating the appearance of an infinite succession of bathrooms all in a row. I saw hundreds of copies of me, trailing off into forever in either direction.

I studied the many copies of myself – how they grew dimmer and fainter as they withdrew into the apparent distance. The closer reflections of me were accurate, but the farther ones appeared more and more distorted. My eyes looked impossibly dark, my face grayed and sunken. Even my teeth yellowed in those wretched duplicates that stood far off.

Something else caught my eye.

Something moving.

I peered hard down the line of images. The endlessness of it dizzied me, but I distinctly perceived a figure moving around in one of the distant reflections. It was too tiny to make out. I spun around, checking the mirror behind me, and looked all around the room I stood in.

No one here.

My eyes returned to the figure, which was now close enough for me to see that it was a person – or something with a humanoid shape, at least. It bobbed up and down, periodically dipping beneath the threshold of the reflection that contained it. It got closer, and closer, and closer. There were hundreds of duplicates of me, but only one of it.

Finally, the person got close enough that I could get a better look. Only a few dozen reflections into the vast series of them, I could make out the form of a woman. She was crawling from one reflection to the next, crawling over their edges like a person climbing through a window on all fours. She moved like an animal, and periodically gazed straight at me.

She was coming for me.

I backed away from the mirror and bumped into the one on the wall behind me. I glanced over my shoulder. The woman was not shown in any of those reflections, only the one at the sinks. Now she was close enough that I could make out her features. Her skin was gray and bruised, and instantly reminded me of the feet I'd seen before. The head was partly bald; clumps of stringy brown hair drooped over her face.

"Youuuu...." she groaned, reaching for me with a shaking hand.

A scream exploded from my lips and echoed around the bathroom. The woman's dark eyes lit up with horrific glee, and her tongue slid back and forth across her jagged teeth. She was only a few reflections away now, and her gaze was fixed upon me. Those hypnotic eyes and the death within them drove me to the edge of madness. Tingling pain seared across my skull and down my neck. I tried to move, but my body barely responded.

There I stood, back against the opposing mirror. There was nowhere to run.

I'm going to die. She's going to eat my face.

Suddenly, an idea occurred to me. I pulled the cell phone out of my pocket and whirled around. With all my strength, I smashed it against the second mirror over and over until the glass shattered and fell to the floor. Then I turned around and faced the mirror at the sinks.

The infinite series of reflections fell away, and with it, the image of the crawling woman. After a moment, the mirror reflected only my own image and the bare tile wall behind me. I took a deep breath of the dank bathroom air and savored my small victory.

But my relief was misguided. The woman's voice cried out in the dark from far away.

"*I remembeerrr…your naaaame…*"

This bathroom was the same as the ones before it. It had the same layout, including the vent beneath the sink counter. When I looked at the steel panel that covered it, I recognized those same eyes from before, peering up at me from the shadows.

"*Felix!*" she shrieked, bashing her corpselike hands against the metal. It bent and squealed under her rage. A screw popped off.

I ran straight for the door I'd come in, not caring about the endless void on the other side.

Better to die out there than in here.

To my surprise, the door opened up into a hallway. Inexplicably, the abyss was gone. Without a second thought I bolted into the hall and slammed the door shut behind me.

The hall was so long that I couldn't see the end. The walls were perfectly straight all the way down, and so precisely constructed that the symmetry made me dizzy. A light fixture hung from the ceiling every few yards, illuminating the ground beneath it. Each was far enough from the next that the space between them was completely dark, giving eerie contrast to the scene. Dozens of small rusty pipes ran across the length of the ceiling, stretching into forever.

"*Feeeeliiiiix....*" the woman moaned behind the door. I was already twenty steps down the hallway. I came to a set of doors, one on each side of me, beneath the first light. Each was marked with a blue triangle that read MEN'S RESTROOM. I continued past them, hoping to find an exit up ahead.

The door I came out of crashed open behind me. My pursuer rounded the corner on her hands and feet, barreling toward me like a tiger. Pure terror fueled my muscles; I rocketed down the hall, screaming bloody murder. Doors rushed past me. Two, four, ten, twenty. Every single one of them was identical, right down to the blue sign.

"Where the fuck am I?!" I shouted in rage and fear.

The woman moved with terrifying speed. The clattering of her long toenails grew louder, and the smacking sound of her palms on the cold cement reverberated off the walls and deafened me. She was closing in.

The hall went on and on. There was no end. There was no way to tell if I had even gone anywhere – every light, every door, every length of pipe was exactly the same as the last. My body grew heavy with exhaustion.

I glanced over my shoulder. The woman had reared up onto her legs and was running after me with her arms dangling at her sides. Her legs bowed and flailed inhumanly as she moved. Her head was craned up and to the side like she was looking at the pipes above us, but her eyes were rolled all the way back as if she were in the midst of a seizure. The horrifying image of it all caused me to lose focus and trip over my own feet.

I lost balance and started to wobble all over the hall,

desperately trying not to lose speed. The woman was only five or six steps behind me, and was closing in. In a last-ditch effort to escape her, I grabbed the handle of a random bathroom door and plowed into it shoulder-first. My feet slipped out from under me.

That's it, I thought to myself. *You're dead.*

The door flew open under my weight, and I sailed through its frame completely airborne. My body landed in a heap on popcorn-littered carpet. Bright fluorescent lights blinded me. All around, I could hear gasps. Recognizable music played somewhere above me.

I instinctively covered my head and curled into a defensive ball, but when no cold hands fell upon me, I opened my eyes and looked around.

It was the theater lobby. Patrons stood all around me, amazed at my display. Their worried faces lined the room; even the teenager working the concession stand stopped scooping popcorn to examine me.

I looked behind me. The men's room door was open, and inside were three guys trying to get a look at me.

"Uh...you...alright there?" one of them called out. The light above him was bright and full. The walls around him were immaculate and free of the stains and mold I'd seen before.

It took me a long moment to compose myself. "Y-yeah," I replied, brushing myself off and clambering to my feet. "I'm good."

I dashed off to the theater to find my friends, trying to ignore the curious stares of two dozen onlookers. The movie had already started. As I stumbled to my seat in the dark, I couldn't help but think to myself, *I should have stayed home.*

There are "bad places" in this world – or perhaps between this one and the next – and I dreaded the conviction that this visit would not be my last.

Icebreaker, part I
Felix Blackwell

The darkness that plagues my life was not born with me, but rather transmitted down through the generations. It came from long ago, from far away, and chose my family for a reason I do not yet understand. It was my grandfather who first peered into that darkness. It peered back, and saw something it liked. Something it wanted. And so our suffering began.

It was 1968. My grandfather, Martin Blackwell, was on a ship headed through the northerly reaches of Baffin Bay, inside the rim of the Arctic Circle. He was a geologist working with the US military and was on an expedition to survey Greenland's ice sheet. The government wanted to know if it could build a top-secret nuclear missile installation there for rapid counterstrikes on the USSR in the event of major attack. They sent the *Hypatia*, an expedition ship with a crew of four scientists and two engineers, all of whom they'd contracted through America's most prestigious universities, and thirty-one Navy servicemen of various stripes. It was expected to be a seven-week mission.

What they found was not nearly what they came for. On the tenth day of the voyage, beneath the glow of a full moon, one of the sailors spotted a dark shape in the distance. It appeared to be another ship, anchored against an ice shelf. After obtaining clearance from high command, the crew decided to approach.

The mysterious ship was absolutely colossal; the *Hypatia* rose only to its hull, and could fit six of itself bow-to-stern alongside it. High above her as she passed, a Cyrillic sign loomed over the smaller vessel – no doubt the name of the strange craft. It took command only minutes to determine that this was no ordinary ship; it was a Soviet nuclear icebreaker. Even more, it was the only *Volgo*-class icebreaker ever built. Once a floating city that housed nearly four hundred men, the thing now sat as still as death, skewered against the ice and half-consumed by creeping frost. Its immensity cast an abyssal shadow on my grandfather and the other men as they gathered on deck in awe. The name translated to *The Spear of Kutuzov*.

After much deliberation, high command altered the mission objectives: my grandfather's crew was now responsible for investigating the abandoned ship and recovering any Soviet weapons and documents on board. The US government feared that the Soviets were planning to nuclearize Greenland first, and so it wanted to know the nature of their latest secrets. The enormity of the *Spear* indicated that it might be carrying nuclear missiles, so it became America's top military priority overnight.

Although unprepared for a task of this sort, Martin obeyed his orders and accompanied a party of sixteen other men onto the icebreaker. They scaled its hull in the dark using a harpoon gun as a rappelling device, and found themselves on the deck of a perfectly seaworthy vessel. Aside from thick layers of ice that had conquered most of its surface, the *Spear* looked to be rather new. The servicemen disassembled a door and made their way to the bridge, where they discovered the ship's logbook.

One of the sailors had basic Russian training, and

gleaned the following information from the logbook and other documents found there: At the time of the most recent entry, the *Spear* housed "318 souls," including one admiral, whose presence was highly unusual. The destination and recent coordinates of the ship were inconsistent with its current location, suggesting a top-secret itinerary. Few other details could be ascertained; many of the documents appeared phony. Scrawled near the bottom of the last page was the sentence "We let them in." It was dated September 6th, 1967; more than a year before Martin and his team had arrived.

The men began a search of the ship. On the deck and first level, there were no signs of her crew. The secret of their whereabouts was well kept, for behind each door and hatch lay only another silent passageway or empty cabin. The engineers checked the stability of the craft's electrical equipment and found it to be in working order. There were no signs of an attack or of any sort of toxic leak, so the team descended to the second level.

It was darker down here. Fewer of the lights worked, and many of them buzzed and crackled, as though the power grid was straining against failed circuitry. Furniture and personal effects were scattered throughout the passageways, suggesting either that the ship had been violently searched, or that the crew had very hastily fled. Martin staggered through the long corridors in search of answers, but each turn presented only more questions. At the end of a narrow passage he discovered the ladder room that led to the third level. It was completely barricaded with mattresses and chairs. Someone had even tried to jam a fire axe into the hatch wheel.

High above the deck, some of Martin's colleagues had located the captain's quarters. It was an elaborate cluster of well-appointed rooms, replete with life-size portraits of Stalin and other heroes of the Soviet Union. Behind an enormous desk hung a painting of a man in a decorated uniform, his features chiseled and expression stoic. His eyes bore downward into the sailors with a weathered bravery. Beneath the frame hung a plaque that read "Admiral Yuri Petrov."

The engineer and five sailors moved deeper into Petrov's quarters, where they found a door that was poorly concealed behind another painting. It took three men and a crowbar to open it, but when they did, a wall of revolting stench assailed them. The door had been barricaded on the other side with mountains of trash and miscellaneous equipment. Empty cans lay scattered about, the putrefied remnants of their contents dripping everywhere, and pots filled with human waste lined the far wall. In the center of the room rested a bed once fit for a king, but its sheets were caked and crusted with dried stains of unspeakable origin. A lone chandelier dangled above it, most of its bulbs now burnt out. It cast a dim and ominous light across the scene.

The men searched the room. They turned up several handguns whose bullets had all been spent, as well as a mysterious key. As they turned to leave, an emaciated hand reached out from beneath the bed and seized the engineer's ankle. The sailors grabbed onto the arm and ripped a man out from the darkness. He was filthy and shriveled, with an unkempt gray beard that snaked across his entire face. Long, brittle nails dangled off his fingers like icicles, and terrible sores lined the exposed parts of his flesh. It was Admiral Petrov. He groaned weakly and cried out in Russian, refusing to let go of anyone he could get his frail hands on. The only English phrase he could speak was, "No down there, no down there." He kept pointing to the floor. The men carried him back to the deck to prepare him for transfer.

It took several minutes for Martin and his crewmates to clear the third-floor hatch. When they finally pried it open, a gust of unusually warm air hissed through the open space. They descended the ladder into a velvety darkness, moving against the rush of otherworldly groans and thunderous clanking that boomed throughout the passageways. Their flashlights illuminated a labyrinth of cramped halls, each lined with rooms whose doors were sealed shut from within.

As Martin made his way down the black corridors, he noticed that the light bulbs on the ceiling had burst – or had been shattered. Along one of the walls, a batch of insulated wiring was cut, probably with an axe, and several cables had been ripped from their housing.

The group approached a hatch with a large porthole at the end of a long passageway. Through it, they could make out several tall forms standing in a large room. It looked to be the crew, gathered ominously in the dark. As Martin and the others moved inside, they shined their flashlights on the figures. There were dozens of them, maybe fifty, all well-dressed in clean uniforms. They dangled by their necks in silence; their faces bore a haunting calmness. Unlike the rest of the level, this room was cold, and frost coated most of the bodies.

Something moved behind them. A scraping, scuttling sound issued from nearby, followed by a loud crash and the clattering of metal against metal. Martin pushed through the maze of bodies. They swung to and fro, reminding him of cattle carcasses on meat hooks. He imagined some grim butcher lurking in the shadows, mindlessly carving and hanging his slaughters.

It was a man – a live one. He sat there with his back against a set of metal cabinets, surrounded by a mess of spilled utensils. He was a cook. This was a kitchen, once. Martin tried to shake off the thought that perhaps this man was the one who tended to all the swinging corpses.

A primal terror radiated from the cook's face. His blue

lips trembled, and between the chattering of his teeth he whispered the same Russian phrase over and over. As Martin reached out to calm him, the cook lunged for a nearby paring knife and rammed it into his own gut. He paused, momentarily silenced by the cold sting, and gazed into the faces of the men who'd come to help him. Then, he tore the knife out and stabbed it in again, five or six more times, until he slumped over dead. Blood washed out of his apron, but it froze before it reached the floor. It was only then, in the stillness, that Martin noticed a series of elaborate runes on the back of the cook's neck. They had been carved into the flesh, too complex and ordered to have been self-inflicted.

Martin and two sailors carried the cook up to the deck of the *Spear* while the others continued their investigation of the lower levels. Once topside, Martin convened with the engineers and their new prisoner. The admiral they escorted was now calm; his eyelids drooped nearly shut, and the frigid winds that battered the ship did not seem to bother him. As the two parties explained their strange encounters to one another, Admiral Petrov took notice of the brilliant moon at the edge of the horizon. He stared into it, spellbound in its icy glow, and did not look away until the cook's body was laid out before the commanding officer of the *Hypatia*. As the sailors examined the bloody runes, Admiral Petrov looked down upon his dead comrade. An instant and electrifying horror fell over him; he began shrieking and babbling at the top of his lungs. His entire body shook, and he thrashed against the two sailors restraining him. A struggle ensued, and Petrov broke free of his captors long enough to rush toward the port edge of the *Spear*. He stopped briefly to gaze over his shoulder at the moon one last time, then wordlessly hurled himself off the icebreaker into the hopeless dark.

The Americans used flashlights to peer over the edge of the ship, expecting to find the admiral's body.
Instead, they found hundreds of them.
Far, far below, splayed across the ice against which the ship leaned, was a mountain of corpses. They were long dead, and now the frost held them together in a solid mass of carnage. Whether they had been thrown off or jumped themselves was a mystery. In the distance, Petrov limped tenaciously toward the infinite expanse of Greenland's interior. It was a doomed quest; he would be dead within minutes.
During the struggle, the admiral's key had fallen out of its finder's pocket. Martin palmed it as the other men scrambled about the deck, shouting orders at each other. He slipped away from the melee and investigated the captain's quarters as his crewmates had earlier, but went so far as to toss aside the mountains of rancid garbage in search of a locker or safe. What he found was a bedside table that had toppled over long ago, and on its underside, a locked drawer. Martin removed his gloves and turned the table over.
The key slid in perfectly.
It took a bit of rattling, but the drawer screeched open, revealing a tattered journal. Its pages had yellowed and were beginning to curl, probably from the filthiness of Petrov's hands and the wretched staleness of the cabin's air. The contents were entirely in Russian, with no drawings or notable features, spare one. As the pages progressed, the writing deteriorated from elegant script to hurried scribblings.
Martin stuffed the book into his jacket and turned to exit the chamber. As he did, a faint banging sound echoed from somewhere in the room. He held still, listening as the sound repeated, and sank to his knees. With considerable effort he slid the bed a few feet, revealing a small trapdoor.

It was open. The admiral must have crawled out of it.

Peering down into it, Martin saw a dusty ladder that descended into the dark. Freezing air wafted up from it, carrying a strange scent that Martin did not recognize. Against his better judgment he clambered down, hands stinging from the bite of the ladder's cold rungs. This was a secret passage, perhaps an emergency hideaway for the admiral if the ship were ever boarded by an enemy. He counted his steps as he descended: a perfect one hundred.

The ladder finally ended in a narrow corridor. It was short; from the ladder to the opposite end it was only another twenty steps. No doors lined the sides. Only a single large hatch rested at the far end, with a small porthole fixed upon it. The entire corridor was completely dark, spare the pale beam of light that glowed through the porthole, guiding Martin toward it like a hypnotized moth. As he approached, he saw a large radiation hazard symbol painted on the door, and the number 5 beneath it.

The nuclear reactor, he thought. He moved his face close to the porthole. A bitter coldness emanated from it, freezing the tip of his nose and burning his eyes. It took a moment for his vision to adjust.

At first, there was only a white glow. It was so hazy that Martin couldn't tell if he was looking at frost on the other side of the glass, or a room full of fog. As his gaze moved across the vacant space, a form came into view. It was roughly the shape and size of a man, and appeared naked behind the fog. The skin looked dull and lifeless; it clung like crumpled paper around a bony torso. The arms, nearly human, dangled at his sides and bent at multiple joints. Its face was stretched taut by the cold, with lidless blue eyes that screamed from their shallow sockets, and sunken divots where the cheeks had once been. A maw of mismatched teeth that should have been hidden beneath lips lay bare, escaping in every direction from rotten gums.

The eyebrows, hair, and nose were absent.

As the man – or whatever it was – lurched forward, its eyes fell on Martin through the porthole, and immediately it dashed forward with inhuman speed. Its face stopped mere inches from Martin's, separated only by a few inches of glass. Martin was so shocked by the thing's horrific visage that he froze in place, unable to tear away his gaze. His quickening breath fogged the porthole, obscuring the view, but the thing's ghastly eyes still shone through and pierced into Martin. The dead skin around its face receded further and the pupils narrowed; a dark tongue flicked behind the teeth. The thing was *smiling*. And what a ghastly smile it was.

Martin had never felt so afraid in his life. As he peered back, he saw in those eyes a grim longing. They didn't examine or interrogate him. They weren't curious. They *knew* him. And they wanted something.

The poor geologist ripped himself away from the porthole and staggered backward in the gloom. He struggled up the ladder, trying desperately to catch his breath. It had been stolen from him, along with something deeper. Something was missing now. A heavy darkness was there in place of it.

The rest of the men had returned from the depths of the ship. They had found their way into the fourth level, where they discovered the remnants of a bloodbath. Human gore was streaked and splashed and slathered all across the rooms and corridors, but no bodies or bones were present. The grotesque stains all led to one place: the fifth and final floor, where the engine room and cargo hold lay. The way in was shut; the hatch seemed frozen to its metal frame. Through the portholes on either side of it, only the creeping frost could be seen. Whatever was down there would remain locked in.

The crew returned to the States empty-handed, spare the bizarre tales they reluctantly shared with their superiors. Martin was forbidden from ever discussing *The Spear of Kutuzov*, and was ordered to carry on as though the whole event had never transpired. He did, however, dream of it. He dreamed of being dragged across the deck by a pale figure, dragged down ladders and corridors until he saw the sixth floor hatch swinging wide open. He always woke up before its white glow swallowed him whole.

I've told this story as it was told to me by my father, and I have many more to tell. As my grandfather passed on his experiences, so too shall I. Perhaps there are more like me. Perhaps I am not alone. And perhaps my grandfather's curse will not bury me as it did him.

Clean
Colin J. Northwood

Dominic and Laura were silent as they drove up the country road to their new vacation home. Their marriage counselor had suggested that a quieter environment might help to reduce their stress, but neither of them was convinced. Their urban apartment was just a few hours' drive from here, but it may as well have been another planet.

Every few minutes, they'd pass by an old farmhouse or a few cows. Dominic gawked at these sights from the passenger seat of their luxury car, recalling a trip through the same area that his family had taken when he was a child.

Laura gripped her hands tightly around the wheel as if to strangle it. The smell of fertilizer was overpowering at times, and it made her dizzy. She reached over to the door and pushed the button to roll up the window, but it was already closed. This was going to be a long summer.

Their apartment back in New York was immaculate. Dominic had always been an irascible neat freak, but still had trouble coping with Laura's compulsive cleanliness. Fights would erupt daily about whether he had missed a spot when scrubbing the dishes or left one of his shoes sticking slightly out of its cubbyhole.

Their dog, Cooper, had been a particular point of contention. Cooper was well trained and well groomed, but couldn't help shedding his yellow fur on the blue carpet. Dominic had refused to give him up when they moved in together. Cooper would have more room to run around outside in this environment, as long as he kept his muddy pawprints off the floor.

Dominic tapped his fingers on the dashboard and thought about how best to reassure his wife. All he could muster was an unconvincing "The pictures looked nice."

"Please stop doing that," she responded. He always had to put his damn dirty fingers on everything. "You touched that gas pump and didn't wash your hands."

He knew better than to sigh.

With time, the flat landscape gave way to gentle hills, and the road began to wind in tangled knots around them. A turnoff led into a lightly wooded area where a village lay just out of sight of the highway. There was a single general store that served the most immediate needs of the locals. For anything else, it was twenty minutes up the highway.

Laura's blood boiled. "You didn't tell me we were going to live on an unpaved road."

Dominic didn't say a word. They had been through this kind of thing too many times. Cooper knew, too; he kept his nose between his paws on the back seat.

Laura pulled into a parking spot in front of the general store. "I'm *not* driving my car up there. The dirt will get all over my tires and we'll *never* get it off." She stepped outside and wondered how she could walk up the hill without getting dirt on her shoes. "I can't deal with this. I'm calling Dr. Rogers."

Dominic and Cooper just sat and watched as she paced furiously in front of the store, one hand holding the phone and the other on her forehead. They watched as her expression grew increasingly frantic. They watched as a truck came into sight from around a corner, tossing a cloud of dust into the air behind it, and they watched as it approached a nearby parking space.

Laura never saw it coming. As the truck parked, the light breeze carried the plume of dust with it. In an instant, she was a shrieking tornado. The phone did not survive.

Her husband frowned at the thin coat of dust settling on the windshield.

"This looks like shit. I can't live like this."

Dominic had to admit she was right. The house looked like it hadn't been dusted or vacuumed in weeks. "We'll clean it up."

"If I see one goddamn spider in this place, I'm driving back to New York, and I'm leaving you and your stupid dog here to rot."

Cooper was sniffing around the floor, leaving his human companions in dread of what he might find. Thankfully, he wasn't telling.

The house was two stories high, and built from gray wood. Both the architecture and the décor could be described as rustic by someone in a generous mood.

Laura had known all along that the house wouldn't be to her tastes, but this was just *beneath* her. "What kind of low-class people would live in a dump like this?" she wondered aloud.

"Remember what Dr. Rogers said. Let it go."

"Ugh. I'm going to look for the shower."

Dominic retrieved a linen cloth and some cleaning spray from his suitcase and began to wipe down the old hardwood chairs. When he was done, they exuded a luminous sheen, but the contrast only made it more apparent how dirty everything else was. *Everything.* "I can't believe this place, Coop. We've got some serious work to do."

Cooper couldn't believe it, either. The smells around here were like nothing he had ever experienced before. The upstairs area was newer, and Laura was relieved to find a modern shower there. Downstairs in the second bathroom, there was only a cast-iron bathtub.

Dominic examined the four-post bed that dominated the master bedroom. It *looked* clean, but you can't be too sure. It was still early enough in the day that there would be time to wash the sheets. He found the machines in the basement and started loading them up. A bark from upstairs let him know that it was time for Cooper to go outside and do his business.

The second bark surprised him, though.

"Just a minute, Coop. I'm coming." Dominic put another handful of laundry into the machine. Much to his irritation, Cooper barked again, then growled. "Cooper, stop it! Only once. You know that." When the barking didn't stop, Dominic considered that Cooper may have seen an animal outside. A smile crept across Dominic's face in spite of his intent to be stern. It had been years since Cooper – or anyone in their household, really – had shown such unrestrained enthusiasm.

Back on the ground floor, Cooper was at the back door, pacing with his nose to the ground and growling occasionally.

"Alright, Cooper. Come on." Dominic opened the door and walked out onto the back porch. "Over there." He pointed at a patch of grass a short distance away.

Cooper paid no attention, though. He kept his nose to the ground and sniffed all the way to the other side of the porch. There, beside an antique rocking chair that had seen better days, was a white circle painted on the old wood of the deck. Inside the circle, the wood was clearly rotting. Cooper growled at it.

Dominic laughed and patted Cooper's head. "I guess

25

you've never smelled rotting wood before, huh?" Upon a closer look, though, he saw that the wood wasn't just rotting; it was putrid. Had it not been part of a wooden deck, he might have thought it was rancid meat. The thought of this sickened him. He squinted his eyes and turned his head away. "Wow, Laura wasn't kidding. This place really does look like shit."

Cooper calmed down a bit, but was still curious. He walked laps around the painted circle, taking in the unfamiliar scent.

"Stay away from that, Coop. I'm gonna have to get that fixed up if we're gonna make it through the summer."

Those two are so much alike, Cooper thought.

Dominic paced angrily back and forth across the bedroom floor, shouting into his phone. "I don't know... No, it's not just Laura... No, I don't... Listen, it looks like fucking roadkill."

Laura stepped out of the bathroom and listened as she toweled her hair.

"Well I don't know how you could have missed it... No, I don't care, I just want it fixed... Yeah... Yeah, when can he get here?" Dominic grimaced. "Alright... Yeah, I will... Yeah... Bye."

Laura glared at him. "I'm afraid to ask."

"Don't go on the back porch."

"Believe me, the last thing I want to do is go outside right now." She marched back into the bathroom. "Oh, and tell Glenn to go fuck himself."

"He's sending a guy to do some repairs, but not until tomorrow."

"Perfect. Just perfect." She slammed the door, and the house rattled like a diving board.

After finishing the laundry, Dominic decided to take

another look at the back yard. None of it was paved, so Cooper would not be allowed to come directly inside without having his feet washed. Even so, there was plenty of space, so it would be good for a quick romp once in a while.

Cooper thought this looked much more fun than the park back in New York.

There were no fences, so the neighbors' houses were visible through the pine trees on either side. Dominic wondered how the locals knew where the boundaries of their property lay.

A strange feeling overtook Dominic as he considered how distant they were from any other people. He stood on the wooden steps. A dozen yards of space suddenly seemed very consequential.

If something happened here, no one would ever...

"Don't you get that dirt on your shoes," Laura shouted from the upstairs window. She waited for him to take a step back, then she disappeared back into the bedroom.

Resigned to his confinement, Dominic sat on the rocking chair to watch the shadows lengthen. He looked at his dog, then out at the trees, and his eyelids grew heavy.

"Hey! HEY! I'm talking to you!" Laura was at the window again. "Come inside. It's getting dark, and I'm hungry."

Dominic yawned and pulled himself out of his stupor. The sun hadn't even set yet. It couldn't have been more than twenty minutes. He stood up and stretched, noticing that Cooper had lain down at his feet. He also noticed...

"Goddammit, Coop. I told you to stay away from that."

The tip of Cooper's tail lay inside the white circle, and his tawny fur bore an oily black stain.

Another shout came from upstairs: "Did your fucking dog get into something again?"

27

"Yeah. Just a minute. I need to wash his tail."

Cooper bowed his head in contrition and waited for Dominic to return with a towel and a bucket of water. He was used to having his paws washed before coming inside from the park, but his tail was rarely a problem. He remembered what happened last time he jumped in the mud. Never again.

The stain proved to be resilient, and withstood Dominic's gentle scrubbing. A black spot formed on the towel, but Cooper's tail still wasn't clean. Dominic scowled at the cloth. "I just washed this, Cooper. Look at this. It's filthy."

He scrubbed harder, and Cooper protested with a whine. Fur began to come off in clumps. Still, the skin beneath was stained.

"Damn, Cooper. I'm sorry. But you really need to listen to me next time."

Laura peeked her head out the door and apprehended the situation with disgust. "You are not letting him back in like that."

"I know. Gimme just a minute, babe. This shit is really stubborn."

Suddenly, a ring of flesh came loose from Cooper's tail and fell to the ground, eliciting a yelp. Dominic sat in stunned silence, forgetting to breathe.

Laura shrieked. "Get it off the porch! Get that thing off the goddamn porch!"

Dominic snapped back to reality when he noticed the oblong pool of blood forming on the porch. "Shit. I need to take him to the vet."

"You're going to put *that* in my car?" Tears were beginning to well from her eyes. Even the raw, exposed bone of Cooper's tail was discolored.

"It's *our* car," he grumbled at her before leading Cooper around the house so as not to stain the hardwood floors.

"And I'll use a towel."

"The doctor says to keep him inside."
Cooper had returned after a few hours with a thick bundle of bandages around the tip of his tail. Dominic was crouching next to him and stroking his head.

"So you're going to let him shit in the house?" Laura's arms were crossed so tightly that Dominic wondered if she was hurting herself.

"I'll put some newspapers in the basement."

"That's disgusting." She aimed a reproachful gaze at Dominic and bit her tongue for the moment, remembering that Dr. Rogers had advised her to keep the worst of her anger to herself. Her nails dug into her skin, but she was careful not to draw blood. The last thing she needed right now was another mess to clean up.

"Babe, please..."

She groaned loudly and stomped halfway up the stairs before turning around to face him again. "Fine. But clean up that shit outside. Tonight."

"The guy's coming tomorrow."

"I know goddamn well when the guy's coming, and that's why you're doing it tonight. Don't you dare embarrass us by showing him that filth." She took another step up the stairs, then turned around again. "And wash your hands afterwards, for Christ's sake. You're a grown man, and you get dirt everywhere like a fucking child."

Cooper lay motionless on his bed of towels, drifting in and out of his medicated haze. Dominic envied him sometimes.

When the third towel was ruined beyond repair, Dominic finally gave up trying to remove the stain from the porch. He laughed for a moment at how difficult his assignment had proved to be, but stopped laughing abruptly when he anticipated Laura's reaction to his

29

failure, not to mention the three ruined towels. It was late at night now, so maybe he could sneak into bed without her noticing. Then again, maybe it was best to wait a while longer.

He wondered why someone would bother painting a white circle around the rot. Could it have been there before the damage occurred? Had someone used this spot to dispose of something dangerous? Maybe it had been a mistake to do this by hand; after all, it seemed likely that Cooper's tail had been injured by some kind of caustic discharge from the blighted wood.

Dominic smacked the ground in frustration, then leaned back against the house and sat down. After a good deal of effort, the stain seemed completely unscathed, as if more and more filth had been welling up from within it to replace any that he scrubbed away. Not only had he not finished the job, but it looked as if he hadn't even started. His head sank into his hands when he imagined again what Laura would say about this. He had better at least get started on that ugly white circle.

After a quick search of the basement, he found a can of paint thinner and some sandpaper. After his ordeal with the rotten wood, he had begun to wonder if the paint would be invincible too. Much to his relief, it reacted normally to his chemical weaponry, and was removed with relative ease.

As it was now nearly midnight, Dominic decided that this day had been long enough. He disposed of the paint scrapings and towels in a heavy duty trash bag and, in his exhaustion, retired to the house without noticing that the oily stain was spilling out onto the porch like an overfilled cauldron.

Laura awoke to find her room dimly lit, and was surprised to see that it was already 7:06 AM. *The weather must be really bad,* she reasoned. After all, the sun should have risen well over an hour ago at this time of year. She pulled the covers over her head and decided to make the most of her summer vacation by sleeping another hour. However, a faint noise kept intruding. It sounded like the crackling of a small bonfire, or perhaps a newspaper being gently crumpled.

"Knock it off. I'm trying to sleep," she said, before realizing that it wasn't coming from any particular direction.

Dominic wasn't ready to wake up just yet, but he heard the noise too. "Mmff...is it raining?"

It wasn't.

When Cooper started barking downstairs, Laura had had enough. She groaned and sat up to see that the outer wall of the bedroom had taken on the likeness of bruised flesh. The window through which the dim light was entering was no longer glass; instead, a sickly yellow translucent tissue, crisscrossed with pulsing veins, stretched uneasily across a misshapen portal and shivered as if in a bitter, freezing rain. The familiar wood of the walls was creaking as it receded at the boundary of the creeping rot. The room was being slowly enveloped.

Laura screamed and shook Dominic, who opened his eyes just in time to see a fist-sized glob of vile sludge oozing from the floor. It drifted slowly upward through the air before melting into the ceiling.

They jumped out of bed and ran to the door, which lay on the side of the room that hadn't yet been affected. They hurried out into the stairwell only to find that the entire back side of their house had been infected by the cancerous growth. Cooper was running in circles at the bottom of the stairs and barking madly. His entire tail was now covered with a noxious black crust.

All three ran out the front door, but not before Laura

stopped to put on her shoes.

The front of the house hadn't yet succumbed, and it was only after walking around the side that the infection was clearly visible. The back of the house had taken on an unearthly appearance, looking less like a building than the exposed organs of a dissected animal. Its wood pulsed and throbbed, appearing to be in pain. Rivulets of strange liquid flowed up the side and bled from the roof, as if a watercolor painting of a house were dripping into the sky.

The entire back porch, where once the rot had been contained within a small circle, had become a quivering, scab-covered orifice from which filth leaked out with a choking sound. The land nearby was coated with something that looked and smelled like a mixture of ash and vomit. A bird, flying over the afflicted area, screeched in agony and spiraled out of the sky. By the time it hit the ground, its form had been twisted beyond recognition. In the wake of its descent, it left a trail of smoke that lingered in defiance of the wind for a few seconds, then slammed violently to the ground.

Though they had both been frozen in shock at first, the couple took off running in response to the crashing sound of the smoke.

Dominic reached the front yard and turned around, heart pounding. "Holy shit. What are we gonna do?"

But it wasn't Laura who responded; rather, a whimper came from behind her. Cooper was struggling to keep up as the degeneration of his flesh was spreading into his hind legs.

Seeing his friend's struggle, Dominic started back toward the side of the house, but was halted by a shout. Laura could contain herself no longer. "What are you doing? We have to get out of here. *Now*. We do not have time for your goddamn dog." But Dominic gritted his teeth and resumed his rescue.

Cooper's legs were wobbling and his hind quarters were now completely engulfed. He had to be carried to the car, over Laura's objections. She gasped as his decaying skin made contact with the rear seat of her car, and shrieked when she saw the viscous residue clinging to Dominic's hand.

"Get that *thing* out of my car."

"I've had enough of your shit, Laura."

There was silence for a moment, as she absorbed the shock of his defiance. "*What* did you say to me?"

"You heard me. I've had enough of your shit. He's my dog, and we're taking him with us."

Laura smacked Dominic across the face. She reached back for a second strike, but stopped cold when he caught her forearm. A full-throated scream escaped when she saw that the grime from his hand had smeared onto her wrist. She ran around the car to the driver's seat, flailing and screeching all the way. Dominic barely had time to get inside before she backed out of the driveway, tires spinning.

A soft whine came from the back seat. Cooper's affliction was progressing rapidly, and his body had now been consumed up to his neck. His rotting flesh was twitching angrily. Dominic couldn't believe his eyes. "Hold on, buddy. We're gonna save you. It's gonna be okay."

Laura's anger had almost overtaken her panic as she neared the bottom of the hill and approached the village. She stepped on the gas and began to mentally compose the tirade she was going to deliver when they got back to New York, but her plans came to an abrupt halt when a sharp pain seized her wrist, flaring up from the spot where Dominic had touched her. She lost control of her hand first and then the wheel. The car careened off the road and smashed into a large pine tree, rendering all of its occupants unconscious.

Dominic awoke to a soreness in his head and a trickle of blood down his face. Beside him, Laura's unmoving frame was slumped over the airbag. He tried to check her pulse, but her entire wrist was now engulfed by the necrotic infection. He was relieved to find that he could feel her breath, but when he noticed that it was shallow and irregular, his relief gave way to sorrow.

The back seat was empty. The left window was shattered, and along its rim lay specks of blood and tufts of fur.

After a brief struggle, Dominic forced his door open and limped back out into the world. The dull ache in his head had left him so disoriented that he didn't immediately notice the road in plain sight. His ears rang and his eyes traced circles around the rocks on the ground. Slowly, he regained his composure and resolved to make the short hike back to civilization.

In that moment, from behind him, came an ominous but familiar growl.

It was Cooper – or, what was left of Cooper. His decaying flesh was now swollen and red, and seemed to be bubbling with a ferocity that his undulating skin could scarcely contain. When his bleeding eyes made contact with Dominic's, he let loose a soulless howl that thundered through all of Dominic's senses and banished the ringing from his ears. Perhaps most surprisingly, Dominic felt a strange resonance in his hand, where his earlier contact with Cooper had left behind a residue which was now eating through his skin like acid. The thin strands of tissue which remained seemed to vibrate in sympathy – instruments in an orchestra of pain with Cooper as its conductor.

Dominic instinctively recoiled in fear, betraying his attempts to exude calm for Cooper's sake. "Oh my God...Cooper...what's happening to you?" He took a step backward and watched as one of the last bits of yellow fur slid down his dog's exposed ribs and hit the ground with a sizzle.

Cooper's lowered his head and squinted his eyes, squeezing a fresh spurt of blood from each of them. He issued another growl, and this time it seemed to come from everywhere at once, echoing through the universe in search of a home it could never find.

When Dominic turned and ran, Cooper followed close behind. But not too close. First to this side, then to the other, then back to the first until it became clear what was happening. Even in a fog of panic and despair, Dominic realized that he was being herded back to the house.

In Laura's half-conscious daze, she dreamed of heaven. An immaculate heaven, with streets made of pearl and gold, lined with inexhaustible streams of pristine spring water. She dined on crumb-free banquets in the cool shade of artificial trees, served by faceless men who obliged her wishes before she dared to ask. Here, she lay down on a soft patch of grass, secure in knowing that it could never stain her in a place like this.

And so, she was surprised when she felt a bit of wetness on her right arm.

It was blood.

She dragged her eyelids open like heavy curtains, and found herself leaning on the airbag in her car. A thin red streak across the top ran down and to the right. Laura felt the soft touch of a drop on her arm, and was repulsed at the thought of a stain forming on her expensive leather seats. She sat up to take a look, and couldn't believe what she saw.

Her entire right hand and forearm had transformed into a knot of pulpy, swollen flesh wrapped in a cocoon of rotting skin. She flinched in shock, and a razor-sharp bone sliced through to the surface. Something that looked like oatmeal oozed from the wound.

She screamed and yanked her door open, then collapsed in a heap on the dirty ground outside when she found that her legs would not support her. She tried in to pull herself to her feet, but her efforts were in vain until a hand touched her on the shoulder and began to help her up.

When she turned, she saw the mangled remnants of Dominic's face, bleeding and blistering even as he smiled at her. He said something incomprehensible, then spat out a piece of his tongue and took her by her disfigured right hand.

Laura fought back with the last of her strength. She pulled away from him hard, and while she couldn't break his grip, she did break her own wrist. Thrashing with all her might, she nearly severed her hand before Dominic grabbed her by the neck. A thick yellow fluid oozed down onto her collar, and an unbearable stench filled her lungs.

Cooper unleashed an awful howl in the distance.

Dominic dragged Laura along the ground, muttering words no human had ever dared to speak. Though bruised and battered, she remained conscious. Pine needles and gravel shredded her knees on the long uphill trek back to the house.

She had lost the will to struggle now, wishing only for death, until she realized that something worse awaited her. Dominic was taking her to the back yard to complete her contamination.

He threw her to the ground, coating her in unspeakable filth. She writhed about violently, but to no avail; each time she rose to her feet, her legs gave out once again and she fell back down. In mere moments, most of her body had made contact with the polluted ground, and her frail human flesh was paying the price.

The change was taking hold now; her skin withered

and her organs began to corrode. She thought, for a moment, that she was dying. But although her body was rotting away, something new was arising within her. The uncanny harmonious quality of her pain was the first indication. Her brain tried to withhold permission, but its humbled state forced it to relent. And soon, Laura's eyes saw what her body was already feeling.

Heaven.

All her life, Laura had been seeking order in the chaos of the world. Now, she had finally found it. Her struggle was over. This place was just right. This place was home.

She looked over at Dominic's smiling face, and she smiled back at him in gratitude. Cooper ran to her side, and she wiped the last of his sickly Earthflesh away.

But after a few moments of bliss, Laura remembered that their perfect home was still surrounded by the same wretched world that had heartlessly kept her from her true purpose for so long. She glanced out at the blue sky and green trees with dismay.

Dominic understood immediately. "Can you believe this neighborhood, babe? It's disgusting."

Laura was never one to back down from a challenge. "Ugh, I know. It's hard to believe people can live this way. Looks like we've got some cleaning up to do."

Lily
Felix Blackwell

The storm was fading. Maddy stared out her bedroom window, waiting for another lightning strike. Her breath fogged the glass; she drew a sad face on it. It rained all the time here, not like back home in Tucson. In two weeks at this house, she'd seen the sun only twice.

Maddy's mom was in rehab again. It was the first time in five years, but this time it was bad. She was set to complete a sixty-day program, as part of a plea deal that saved her from prison. So here Maddy was, marooned on an old farm in rural Connecticut, with only her grandparents to keep her company.

She slipped on her shoes and grabbed the soccer ball. With no friends for a thousand miles and some of the crappiest cell reception in the state, Maddy maintained her sanity by practicing in the huge backyard.

"I'll be out back, Grandma!" she yelled, barreling down the stairs.

"It's muddy!" Grandma called from another room. "Don't track any in here or your grandfather will lay an egg."

Maddy planned to be back inside and cleaned up before Grandpa got home from work at five. He always found something to be mad about, so she had learned to sneak around in his absence. For all he knew, she was sequestered in her room, studying for Monday's tutoring appointment.

It was nice out. Yesterday's warmth clung in the late spring air; rainclouds floated away to reveal a low-hanging sun. Maddy dropped the ball onto the porch and booted it into the field. It sailed over the yard and bounced off the old barn. She chased after it, dodging imaginary players as she went. When she got back to Arizona, she'd be more than ready for the new season to begin.

About a half hour into her footwork drills, Maddy heard the back door swing open. She instinctively cringed, knowing that she was in trouble. Grandma never came out here, so it could only be one person.

"Madison," a gruff voice rang out.

"Yes, Grandpa," she replied flatly.

"Git inside," he said. "Don't need you muckin' up the place. Wait 'til the sun come out a few days."

Maddy picked up the ball and sulked back to the porch. She took off her shoes and dropped them and the ball near the door. Grandpa stood in the doorway; a scowl of disapproval hung on his weathered face. Maddy tried to squeeze by him as she entered the house. She kept her gaze on the ground.

"What I tell you 'bout that goddamn barn," he said over her as she passed. His breath stunk of chewing tobacco.

"I've never gone near it," Maddy protested.

"Alright."

Dinner was awkward, as usual. Grandpa drank more than he ate. He complained about the kids in town and the dip in sales at his furniture shop. Any time he wasn't at work, he was in the garage, sawing and sanding. He kept eyeing the hall, like his family was distracting him from a big project. Grandma didn't say much except her typical cheery interjections. She'd occasionally smile at Maddy during Grandpa's ramblings, as if to say, "Oh, don't mind him."

Maddy raced through her meal and retreated to her bedroom, where she listened to the old radio and worked on math homework. Occasionally, she'd glance out the window and down at the barn. It was an eerie thing at night, towering there in the dark. She wondered why Grandpa was so touchy about it.

It's probably where he keeps his porn, she thought.

The next morning, Maddy went straight back to practicing in the yard. She gambled that Grandpa might come home unexpectedly early again, so it was best not to wait until the afternoon to get started. She circled the barn so that it was between her and the porch, then practiced her defense there. She shuffled around the ball, guarding and manipulating it with different points on her shoes.

"Not in my house!" she yelled triumphantly, and kicked the ball against the side of the barn as hard as she could.

There was a noise.

A strange, muffled noise.

Maddy walked up to the wall and studied it. The wood was old and rotting; the paint had been stripped off in several places. The colossal building had withstood the onslaught of a hundred grueling winters.

But there was something inside.

Maddy's mom told her all about the horses she had as a kid. She told her about riding in the summer competitions, and how she once fell off and broke her wrist. Her mom told her about how Grandpa's farm fell on hard times, back when she was thirteen – Maddy's age – and how he had to sell the horses off to save the house. Mom never forgave Grandpa for it.

That was over thirty years ago. There hadn't been horses in this barn since. The building was totally sealed off with an old rust-caked padlock and chains. It looked like nobody had been inside for almost as long, not even Grandpa himself.

Maddy's curiosity compelled her to knock on the wall. After a long pause, a faint knock responded from the other side.

Oh my God, she thought. *Someone's in there.*

She circled the barn, examining the rotten wood. She noticed two small windows up above, near the roof. One had wiggled its way open over the years of neglect.

Maybe it's a raccoon?

Maddy knocked louder.

"Hello?" she called out. "Is someone in there?"

The knock responded louder, followed by what sounded like the cry of a small animal. Maddy circled the barn once more, searching for a way in. It took a bit of work, but she was able to boost herself up on the soccer ball just high enough to peer through the window.

The barn was dark and spacious; she couldn't see to the far wall. Little blades of light pierced through cracks in the roof here and there. They fell on old boxes, broken furniture, an abandoned workbench. Maddy checked for spider webs and wiggled through the open window. She tumbled down onto the dirt below.

The air was dank and frigid. The girl scanned the room and rubbed warmth back into her arms. There was nothing here – no raccoons, no people, no traces of life.

"Where are you?" she whispered.

"Help me," a dry voice whispered back.

A tingling wave of fear washed over Maddy's back. The sound came from somewhere near the workbench. She moved closer and studied the miscellaneous supplies bunched around it.

"Yes, here," the voice whispered. It sounded muffled and distant.

Maddy could barely make out a suspicious pile of trash bags behind the table. She kicked a box out of the way and examined the bags.

"You found me."

Maddy reached out and pulled bags off of the pile. They were light, probably filled with leaves and grass trimmings from the old mower nearby. She jumped back as the last bag fell away.

There was a trunk. It was a big, black vanity trunk that probably belonged to Grandma, once upon a time. The old thing was tattered and scuffed; it looked like it had been sitting here for decades. Several thick chains were wrapped around it, joined together at a huge padlock on the front. Two cinder blocks rested atop the chest, unmoved for ages.

Creepy, Maddy thought. She hugged herself in the cold.

"Who are you?" she asked.

"Lily." With the trash bags removed, the voice was clearer.

"What are you doing in there?"

The sound of nails dragging on a hard surface resounded from within the trunk.

"It's so cold," Lily cried. Her voice was tiny, and there was something unusual about it. The intonation was all wrong. "I can't feel my legs."

Maddy fingered at the padlock. It was rusted to oblivion. No key would open it.

"I'll...I'll go get help," she said. She couldn't explain why, but Lily scared her. "I'll get my grandma. She's home."

"No!" Lily yelled. Her voice went raspy. "No no, you can't tell anyone I'm here. Please."

"Why not?" Maddy asked.

There was a long pause.

"You're a good girl, Madison," Lily said. "I know you'll help me."

Maddy took a step back.

"How...how do you know my name?"

The room got colder. Maddy's teeth chattered; she tried to hide the fear in her voice.

"I hear them talking to you," Lily replied. "I hear you playing."

Maddy studied the chest carefully.

"Do you know my grandparents?" she asked. "Do you know where you are?"

A deep, rumbling gurgle escaped from the trunk.

"Tell me," Lily said. "I don't remember. It's been so long. So cold."

"You're in a barn," Maddy replied, "in my grandparents' backyard. Alfred Cole is my grandpa. It's his farm."

"*Alfred...*" Lily repeated. She made another deep, grumbling noise. The trunk began to shake violently. The sound of nails scratching wood grew louder and frantic. "Let me out!" she bellowed in a hideous voice. "Let me out now!"

Maddy dashed back to the other side of the barn. She vaulted off of a nearby box and caught the window sill with her fingers. She hoisted herself up with all her strength and flailed through the narrow opening. She dropped into the grass outside and lay there, blinded by the sunlight, relieved to be out of the dark.

Whatever that thing is, she thought, *it can stay in there.*

Later that evening, the old red truck rolled up the driveway. Grandpa staggered out of it and fumbled with a table he'd brought home – probably a piece he couldn't sell. He was too drunk to manage it, so he left it on the ground and came into the house. Maddy watched him from the hall window and shuddered at the thought of having to interact with him.

Dinner was an exercise in avoiding eye contact.

Grandma and Maddy stared down at their food, gritting their teeth through Grandpa's bluster, until he got bored and wandered into the garage. Maddy hugged Grandma and hurried back up to her room.

The girl tried to distract herself with math problems, but she could still hear Grandpa occasionally coming into the house to rummage around or to shout about something. She tried to drown him out with the old radio on her desk, but he made too much racket.

As the hours passed, Grandpa only got worse. He stomped up and down the stairs and argued with poor Grandma. She followed him around, pleading with him to calm down.

And then it happened.

Grandpa raised his voice once more, and a loud slapping sound rang out. Grandma's screams of pain followed. The clamor shocked Maddy and broke her heart. She felt the sting of the hit on her own face, and shed tears as she listened to her grandmother's sobs. There were soft footsteps up the stairs. A door closed, and then it was over.

Grandpa returned to the garage. Maddy wanted to check on Grandma, but she was frozen to her chair, too afraid to make a sound.

"Maaaaaaaddyyyyyyyyy..." a muffled voice drifted in through the open window. The crickets fell silent.

Maddy looked out the window to the barn. Its dim form perforated the blackness. She stared at it, almost hypnotized. The world around her fell away. She didn't hear the clumsy footsteps coming up the stairs.

"Madison," Grandpa's voice boomed. He was right outside the bedroom.

Maddy jolted out of her stupor. The door creaked open. She risked a glance.

Grandpa stood there, his crystal blue eyes piercing through her. He lurched in and closed the door behind him.

Maddy's heart raced. Grandpa shuffled toward her. He loomed over her and examined her homework. The reek of booze and cigar smoke hit Maddy like a brick wall.

"Writin' poetry, eh?" he asked, feigning interest.

It's math, she thought. *He can't even see straight.*

"Hope I didn't scare you," Grandpa said, resting his hands on her shoulders. They were dry and calloused and heavy. "Grandma and I had an argument, thass'all." He burped. His stomach burbled.

"Okay," Maddy said, cringing under her Grandfather's touch. He ran his fingers down her arms. His hands felt like leather belts against her skin. The sound of that awful slap reverberated through Maddy's mind.

Grandpa stumbled backward and sat on the bed.

"Come sit next to your old grandpa," he said, eyes drooping. "You're becoming a very beautiful young lady, do you know that?"

Every hair on Maddy's neck stood on end. She couldn't swallow the giant knot in her throat.

"I have to go to the bathroom," she said, slipping past him.

Grandpa reached out a lazy hand and grabbed Maddy's wrist as she went past.

"Wait a minute," he said.

Maddy instinctively slapped his hand away and went for the door.

"You little bitch!" he shouted. He tried to stand up from the bed but fell back onto it. "Get back here!"

Maddy whipped the door open and flew down the hall. She raced down the stairs and hid in the dark kitchen, trying to figure out what to do.

Grandma won't be able to stop him, she thought. She rushed over to the old rotary phone on the wall and tried to dial 911, but Grandpa was already making his way down the stairs.

45

"Madison!" he bellowed.

Maddy grabbed the old flashlight in the drawer near the sink. She snuck out the back door and crouched down on the porch, hoping Grandpa wouldn't spot her. He ambled around the bottom floor, flicking lights on and off, calling out to her. He grew more and more angry as the seconds ticked by.

"Maaaaaaaddyyyyyy..." the voice called out from the barn. "Hide in here..."

The girl didn't pause to think. She darted across the yard and clambered into the open window of the barn, trying not to make any noise.

"Madison!" Grandpa shouted in the kitchen.

The barn air was freezing cold. Maddy clutched herself, fighting back tears, but they came anyway.

"Why are you crying?" Lily asked from inside her box prison.

"Get back here!" Grandpa screamed from the porch. "You better not be near that goddamn barn!"

Maddy wiped her cheeks with her sleeves. "He's crazy," she sputtered, "he hit my grandma and—"

"I'll lock you out here all night!" Grandpa shouted. Dogs started barking in the distance.

A tapping sound emanated from the trunk.

"I never liked him much," Lily said, her voice barely above a whisper. She emitted a sinister chuckle. "Don't cry, Maddy. I'll protect you."

"Why are you in here? You never told me."

Lily didn't respond for a long moment. Then finally, she offered,

"...Because I was a little bitch, too."

Grandpa's footsteps resounded just outside the barn. He stomped in a circle around the building, looking for Maddy. He pulled at the door.

"You better not be in there!" he yelled.

Enough, Maddy thought. She approached the trunk and took a deep breath.

"Okay, Lily."

She pushed the cinder blocks away. They toppled to the wooden floor with loud thuds. The chains were harder to remove; she pulled and wiggled and slid them off one by one. Then she stepped back. Grandpa fumbled with the door behind her.

Maddy wasn't exactly sure what she saw come out of that trunk. It happened so quickly that by the time she could muster a gasp, it was over. First, there were fingers – long, bony fire-poker fingers that scraped along the rim of the trunk. Then there were limbs, maybe even more than four, that stretched and bent and twisted in every direction. Maddy saw hair, black and stringy, uncut for decades. It slithered across a head as white and dry as paper. With a gruesome lurch, the form was out of the trunk, towering over her.

Maddy kept her eyes on the floor, too terrified to look up. She tried her best to become invisible. She imagined, almost felt, those wretched hands upon her. The stench of death and sweat nearly choked her.

"*Maaaaddyyyyyy...*" it called.

The girl sniffled.

"Yes," she replied in a helpless voice.

"Go away from here, child," the thing gurgled, "and never come back."

It dashed past her, joints crackling and popping from years of imprisonment. Its oily hair whipped about in the corner of Maddy's vision. The barn door swung open and crashed against the wooden wall. Grandpa gasped in terror.

Don't look, Maddy told herself. She snuck back out the window and ran across the yard. All the while, Grandpa screamed and cried in agony. He begged and pleaded as

Maddy walked up the porch, entered the house, and locked the door. He coughed and whimpered as she turned on the radio. Eventually, there was nothing left to hear but old jazz.

In the coming days, the police came and went. Neither Maddy nor Grandma had seen a thing; they swore up and down that Grandpa had gotten drunk and stormed out of the house, never to return. It appeared that someone had unlocked the barn and taken something out of an old chest, then wandered off into the endless Connecticut woods.

Life went on. Maddy returned to Arizona, where her mom had made a healthy recovery. The months and years drifted by, until one summer night, they received a phone call. Grandma had passed.

Maddy and her mother attended the funeral. As mourning neighbors and church folk shuffled out of the house, Maddy went out to the back yard, where she had played soccer all those years ago. It was unkempt and overgrown. The barn was dilapidated beyond repair; its roof sagged and parts of the walls lay in ruin. No one had been back here in a decade.

Curious, the young woman approached the barn, and poked her head inside one of the many holes.

There, in the darkness, was the trunk.

Chains had been hastily wrapped around its bulk, and cinder blocks sat atop it.

"Is...is someone there?" a voice croaked from within.

Maddy tried to scream, but no sound came out. Her veins filled with ice. She nearly fell over in shock. The voice was gruff and unmistakable; it belonged to her grandfather.

"G...Grandpa?" she stammered.

"Madison?" he called. Gurgling sounds punctuated his words. "That you? Oh God, it's been so long...it's so cold. Please, please let me out." Scratching and tapping sounds pitter-pattered against the chest.

Maddy's hands shook. She struggled to catch her breath. She backed away, dizzy with fear, and made her way back to the house.

"Maddy!" the voice called out, dropping in pitch. "Maddy...Let me out, Maddy..."

The young woman stumbled back inside and slammed the door behind her. She plugged her ears with her fingers, but she could still hear the awful noise drifting in the air.

"Maaaaaddyyyyyyyyyyy..."

Spare Parts
Colin J. Northwood

"Someday, you're going to put us all out of business," said Dr. Yang with an uneasy grin. He glanced out the window and across the river to see the last drops of sunlight trickling over the horizon. His shift was almost over. This phone call would have to be his last.

The door opened slightly and Dr. Bartlett peeked inside. "James, do you have a minute?" A quick glance and a single raised finger were the only answers he received. He hadn't noticed the phone at first, but when he did he knew immediately what this was about. His questions about the night shift could wait. He took a seat.

"Don't be so modest," Yang continued. "It's already got an encyclopedic knowledge of human anatomy and a steadier hand than any surgeon alive today. Just imagine what you'll be making ten years from now." As the conversation went on, Bartlett detected a rare glimpse of excitement in Yang's expression. He answered a few questions from the manufacturer, then hung up with a smile.

"Are we getting one?" Bartlett asked.

"I think we're getting one."

The following weekend, the truck arrived. Out came a wooden crate the size of a refrigerator. A forklift brought it into one of the operating rooms. It took the better part of an hour to unbox and reveal the machine. It consisted of a barrel-sized main computer on wheeled treads, and four spider-like arms that could reach the ceiling if extended vertically. On each arm was a small camera and a pair of mechanical grips resembling pliers. Several other tools, such as saws and drills, could unfold from within the arms. The ultra-modern device seemed out of place in the hospital's old wood-and-brick structure.

Dr. Bartlett had spent months following the development of the prototype, so his hospital was among the first to acquire a finished copy. He had been in touch with the engineers and had contributed to the conceptual design of the artificial intelligence, although not to its programming. While not quite adequate for independently performing the most intricate operations, it was quite adept at recognizing and repairing damaged human tissue. It had been tested on cadavers and the latest versions had performed flawlessly. It was capable of rapid and precise movements that no human could replicate, and it could quickly detect internal injuries. Future models were planned that would be capable of bloodwork and DNA testing on site.

Dr. Yang noticed a logo on the machine's rear panel. A cartoon bear on a silvery label sat contentedly above a line of blue text reading "URSA: Ucritech Robotic Surgical Assistant." He was slightly annoyed at the attempt to humanize the appearance of such a device. It was not only futile, but unnecessary; this thing was going to save lives.

Bartlett, however, took quickly to the ursine branding and, much to Yang's chagrin, had all the office staff calling it "the bear" within the first week. Eventually, Yang gave in. Perhaps it wasn't such a bad idea to make automated surgery seem less intimidating.

The team immediately incorporated "the bear" into its

emergency response routine. When a wounded patient would arrive, the surgeons would boot it up. When the surgery was over, it would shut down automatically and return to its station to recharge and check for software updates.

Over the following weeks, URSA proved its worth. Initially, the hospital's board of trustees had balked at the expense, but it soon became clear that the surgical team had become much more efficient thanks to its new addition. For some operations it was simply an added convenience but for others it was essential. Eventually, even the skeptics admitted to Yang and Bartlett that their doubts had been unfounded.

URSA was available at all times of day, and its powerful battery allowed it to work long hours. It was able to quickly respond to emergencies and persevere tirelessly through protracted operations. One night, it provided critical assistance in the treatment of six people involved in a four-car pile-up, saving all of them. After that, URSA had gained the full confidence of the entire staff, and was even allowed to perform some simple operations by itself. Only on the most complex operations did it require guidance from the human surgeons.

Six months after URSA's arrival, a major train crash occurred just outside the city. There were dozens of deaths and hundreds of injuries. The doctors and their mechanical assistant worked tirelessly to accommodate the injured. URSA was as efficient as ever, quickly repairing broken bones all day and night. It never tired, but the human doctors did.

The following day, rescue workers were still pulling bodies, alive and dead, from the wreckage. More and more of the injured kept pouring through the doors, and eventually it became clear that only URSA was keeping up with its workload. After their second night with no sleep, the human doctors knew they could not continue at this pace; if they stayed awake any longer, they would do more harm than good. Even URSA had to stop and recharge after a full day, but it resumed work soon after.

Though it resided on the rim of a large city, this was a small hospital, and the staff was simply not adequate for a disaster of this scale. The other hospitals in the area helped out by taking on a greater share of the routine workload, but they weren't as close to the site of the crash. And they didn't have URSA.

On the second night, it was decided that Dr. Bartlett would have to stay up alone for a few hours with only the assistance of URSA and two nurses while the remaining staff got some rest. Dr. Yang stayed on site and slept in his office.

Two hours into Bartlett's shift, a major earthquake hit the city, and the old hospital was damaged badly. Bartlett was knocked unconscious in a room full of the most grievously injured patients, all of whom were already incapacitated. The two nurses were outside the room when this happened and found themselves unable to get back inside due to rubble blocking the door. They shouted for Dr. Bartlett, but could hear only the whirring of URSA as it worked on and on and on.

Without the assistance of a human guide, URSA did the only thing it knew how to do: find and repair damaged tissue. It was unable to revive Bartlett, and without the guidance of a human surgeon it was not competent to save the lives of the patients. Yet, it did not entirely fail at its mission.

Humans tend to think of bodies as singular organisms and of death as a singular event – a point of no return. URSA, somewhere in its silicon brain, had a more accurate understanding. Humans are colonies of cells, which live and die together only because their symbiosis allows them the luxury of depending on the wholeness of the system. The rate at which this arrangement fails is just slightly low enough to allow for survival. Humans think of machines as conglomerations of spare parts. URSA knew that the same is true of humans.

And so, without supervision and surrounded by damaged human tissue, URSA trudged heroically onward. When it found itself unable to save an entire patient, it did not give up; when there were no more lives to be saved, there was still life to save. It had performed organ transplants before, and it salvaged as many parts as it could.

Using microscopic sutures, it stitched skin to muscle, muscle to sinew, and sinew to bone. It stitched nerves onto limbs, limbs onto bodies, and bodies onto Bartlett. It carried out its task with loving care, imbuing its new creations with sustenance and applying the latest techniques to suppress the immune responses that lead to rejection of transplants.

A new awareness of unbearable agony took hold in a spindle of nerves. Reaching out across the strange mesh of its neighbors, it explored its own body. It could find no memories to help it steer the unwieldy mass it now occupied.

The pain was constant and sharp. Every moment was torturous. The creature flailed and struggled to interpret this flood of exquisite sensation. Rancid smells filled its noses and blinding light assailed its many eyes.

Gradually, it found itself to have a multi-fold radial symmetry like a starfish. It consisted of a roughly circular main body equipped with many human legs and filled crudely with human organs – many more than were necessary for survival. On its underside was a monstrous orifice, lined with a patchwork of mucus membranes. Pustulent odors oozed from below and wafted into sensitive tissues above. Protruding from the upper surface of the body were six stalks, each molded from a few vertebrae and tipped with three eyes.

The creature would have wished itself dead had it retained the ability to think like a human. Instead, its simulacrum of a nervous system, which contained very little brain tissue, struggled to cope with its anguish and to understand its environment in a rudimentary way.

Its fight against the pain was futile, but its sensory apparatus was not. Though it could not comprehend what it saw, its eyestalks were eventually able to gather that it rested on a floor slick with blood in the corner of a room full of objects that its eyes could recognize but its simple mind could not.

Finding itself cornered, it attempted to move. It kicked its legs wildly and was greeted with a new shock of pain even more intense than the first. It could not find its balance, but there was no room for it to fall between its crowded mass of legs.

Nearby, sitting still along the wall, was URSA. Having completed its work to the best of its ability, it was now recharging. The faint green pinpoint of light from the charging station seemed to shine only on the clean portions of the floor, tiptoeing around the blood.

In another direction, the eyestalks perceived movement. In the opposite corner of the room were the bodies of several humans. Towering above them and sorting through their remaining parts was another creature, three times larger than the one that beheld it. One end of the beast was a bulbous mass of flesh, built to sustain the organs of twenty-some people. This was supported by many limbs, some of which were clearly arms, some of which were mangled beyond recognition, and some of which were unrecognizable products of URSA's creativity in combining parts.

The remainder of this second creature consisted of an enormous horizontal pouch whose surface was covered with an arabesque flowering of ribs. This allowed it enough flexibility to serve as a makeshift mouth, larger even than the rest of its body. Somewhere in its formless abdomen, there must have been some brain tissue, as this creature had figured out its own mobility. When its arms felt vibrations in the ground, it turned to face its newly awoken sibling. It began to crawl and slither its way across the room to administer a proper greeting.

Upon reaching the younger creature, the great beast found the smell of living flesh irresistible. Its starved internal organs issued a command, and the maw stretched open with a sound like the cracking of knuckles. Within, where one would expect to find teeth in a naturally birthed creature, were many mismatched arms grabbing at the darkness. With a gagging motion, the arms parted and revealed, far in the back of the creature's throat, a human skull wagging about on a swollen, fleshy neck. Affixed to the top of the skull was a layer of retinal tissue, its curvature granting a wider field of vision than the shape of the mouth would allow.

When it saw the flailing of its sibling, its fluids began to gurgle. Several of its arms reached out from within the maw and grabbed onto two of the legs. For one soothing moment, the unwitting prey relaxed as its skin responded to a familiar comfort: the touch of human skin. The kicking ceased and the eyestalks stood still. But hunger is an impatient master, and the tight grip of the arms began to widen. Fresh stitches were no match for the strength of the creature, and it yanked until a chasm ripped open between two of the legs. The eyestalks spun violently as blood gushed from the yawning wound, but the legs were held in a firm grip and there was nothing to be done. Two more pairs of hands reached out and cupped themselves to catch the blood. They tossed it deep into the darkness as the beast reveled in the first taste of its meal.

Dr. Yang awoke to a muffled scream that pierced an uncanny silence. Ordinarily, the sounds of the busy hospital were audible even in his insulated office, but now there was nothing. Seeing his desktop in disarray, he wondered how he could have slept through the disturbance that must have caused the chaos. He stretched his sore limbs and wandered into the hall to find that the ceiling lights were not working. A few rooms with open doors allowed shafts of sterile white light to penetrate the hall, but all else was dark and quiet. There was no sign of the nursing staff, nor the other doctors, nor the source of the scream.

As he proceeded down the hall, Yang observed that some of the patients were still lying in their beds, helpless and unconscious. All those who were mobile were gone. How could this have happened? In the event of an evacuation, an alarm was supposed to ring. Had he slept through that too?

He briefly checked on the remaining patients. All were still alive, and the machinery that sustained them had remained intact. Relief washed over him, but he still didn't understand why the hospital seemed to have been deserted. In search of answers, he went downstairs toward the emergency room to find Dr. Bartlett, or anyone else who could tell him what the hell was happening.

Upon reaching the first floor, he heard a sound like a fish flopping in the mud. He expected to hear someone react to this, but no one did. He followed the noise down the hall. Flies buzzed aimlessly around piles of debris, desecrating the hospital's once-sanitary environment. The severe structural damage to the first floor indicated that something was very wrong.

Yang found the door of the emergency room littered with rubble, but a passage appeared to have been cleared through the middle of it. The clamor continued from inside. He braced himself for the unexpected, but even his two decades as a doctor could not prepare him for what he found.

Inside the emergency room was a great mass of bruised flesh standing on many limbs in a pile of bloody bones. From behind it, it was obvious that a body was being ripped apart. The creature was entranced with its task and paid no attention to Yang as he entered. An arm emerged from behind the swollen abdomen holding a human spine, tossed it aside, then returned into an unseen orifice. Yang was frozen in dread from the moment he first laid eyes on the creature, but even the shock of its monstrous form was surpassed by the horror of his next observation.

Among the features of the beast's skin, Yang recognized the face of Dr. Bartlett. It was stitched into the surface between an elderly woman's breast and an exposed lung that was still breathing steadily. As the creature continued its feeding frenzy, Bartlett's face was in a serene repose. His eyes and mouth were closed and his skin was purple. Unable to process what was happening, Yang absently wondered how Bartlett could stand the rancid smell of decay.

Just then, the creature stopped. Though no sensory organs were evident, it took on the bearing of an animal trying to detect a distant sound. Dr. Yang stood as still as death, refusing to run for fear that his footsteps would give away his presence. After a moment, the creature settled down and let out a belch. Yang thought he could hear the muffled clapping of hands from inside the creature's body, but wasn't sure if his addled mind had imagined it.

As the creature relaxed further, Bartlett's eyelids opened, but his eyes were gone. Instead, a thick reddish sludge began to ooze from the sockets. His lips parted a few seconds later, and soon this substance was emerging from Bartlett's mouth as well, along with a few other newly exposed orifices scattered about the surface of the creature's abdomen.

This horrid spectacle was more than Yang could bear. He was unable to stifle himself any further, and he began to gag and cough. With this, the creature took notice of his presence. It squeezed out the last of its excreta and began swiveling to face him.

Yang's survival instincts overcame his frozen panic, and his feet began to obey his commands. As he backed into the doorway, the gigantic maw opened and a dozen wet hands reached out for a ghastly embrace. The fresh, slick blood on the arms contrasted with the drying red crust that lined the edges of the maw like lipstick. A few of the hands still held ragged yarns of flesh they had ripped from the bones of their last victim. Then, in sickly synchrony, the hands parted, allowing Yang and the beast to behold one another. The creature's skull-eye twitched excitedly as it began to lumber forward.

Scrambling into the hall, Yang summoned a surge of energy and clambered over the rubble. He took a deep breath and began to sprint toward the front door. He ran past empty desks, open doors, and pockmarked walls until he rounded the corner. The crashing of debris rang out behind him as the monster shoved obstacles aside. Yang wished he had done a little more cardio in recent years.

But there was the front door, visible as he rounded the corner. Yang wasn't sure he'd be safe outside, but he couldn't risk staying in here with that *thing*. The wet hands slapping the floor behind him drummed out a steady and eerily soothing rhythm, but he could allow himself no relief. Not yet. Not until he made it out that door.

And so he charged on until he burst through the front entrance into the night. A glance behind him confirmed that he had indeed outpaced the creature, which had just now rounded the corner. Maybe he would be safe outside after all.

Dr. Yang caught his breath for a moment and spun around, surveying his surroundings. He was in the parking lot behind the hospital, overlooking the riverbank. There was no one else in sight; even the security post had been abandoned. A single ambulance remained in the lot, watching over a few empty cars. Yang's tired mind imagined a dog herding sheep.

The damage to the hospital was extensive. It had been built from wood and brick several decades ago, and had never experienced a quake like this one. But still it stood. Most of the lights were still on, too. Yang looked up at the second floor and spotted his office.

Down by the riverbank, the crickets chirped their sonata under a haze of moonlight. People were born at this hospital, suffered here, and died here. The crickets sang on, unmoved. For them, today was no different. The world still turned, the trees still grew, and the river still flowed. The serenity of it all was a siren's song to Dr. Yang's weary heart. The familiar starry sky lulled him and his pulse slowed.

He stifled a mad cackle and wiped the sweat from his brow. The monster had not followed him outdoors. His shaky hands groped his pockets, turning up his keys but no phone. Maybe it was in the office. He realized he would have to find someone else to call for help, and began jogging toward his parking space. He'd have to lie about what happened; no one would believe this.

But then, just as he was approaching his car – *CRASH!* A window on the second floor of the hospital shattered and a chair tumbled out.

The patients were still inside.

Yang grappled with his fear for a moment. He thought about the ordeal he had escaped. He thought about Bartlett's face. He thought about the Hippocratic Oath and the serene embrace of the cold night air on his skin as he hesitated. He remembered seeing his dog run over by a car when he was eight years old, and watching helplessly as she groaned her last breath.

Not this time.

He turned back toward the old hospital and headed inside.

Yang burst through the front door in a rage. The racket upstairs echoed through the halls, but by now it was clear that there was no struggle. No matter, Yang decided. There was going to be a struggle soon enough. He dashed past the front desk, down the hall, and back around the corner – just as quickly as the first time, to convince himself of the courage he knew he was going to need.

Over the rubble. Past the emergency room. Into the stairwell.

Here, Yang found what he was seeking. On the wall was a dusty glass case. Inside it, resting against a fire hose, was an old red ax.

In case of fire, break glass, the front of the case advised.

Close enough.

With a surge of adrenaline, Yang drew back his fist and took a mighty swing at the glass, shattering it to a dozen pieces.

The commotion upstairs was intensifying. Yang didn't know if the beast could hear the glass breaking, but he was pretty sure it was too engrossed in its feeding frenzy to pay attention. He had to strike soon, while it was distracted. He grabbed the ax and continued up the stairs, barely noticing the shallow cut etched into his hand by a stray shard of glass.

No time for pain. Not right now. Up the stairs and out the door.

There was no doubt about where the creature had gone. Even in the hall's dim light, it was easy to see the trail of wet handprints leading directly to the end of the hall, where a pair of double doors were still swinging from a recent disturbance. This was a room where a woman in a coma had been convalescing since the day of the train accident. Two windows, smeared with blood, allowed the light from inside to penetrate the hallway, and red shadows danced on the wall like a fire.

Yang quivered with fear, but did not slow down. He burst through the doors and into the room, where the creature was feeding on the woman's remains. He had hoped to approach it from behind. No such luck; its maw faced directly toward the door, with its hands gripping the dismembered corpse. Her severed head lay in the corner, looking down as if in shame.

Noticing Yang's entrance, the creature spread its arms apart to take a look. The ravenous hands would not release their prize, and simply ripped the woman's torso in half. There, behind it, was the single eye, swaying gently back and forth. There was a pause as the doctor and the beast regarded one another – two aliens from the same Earth.

Yang knew he had to strike now. He raised the ax above his head. Then –

WHACK!

He brought the ax down with all his might. His strike landed with a satisfying crunch, crippling one of the arms.

The beast thrashed in pain, tossing the woman's body to both sides. The arms recoiled as it realized its predicament.

WHACK!

Again, Yang hacked at the creature. This time, he left a

gash on the side of the maw.

But now, the creature was enraged and began to charge. Yang pulled the ax back, preparing for a third swing, but was caught off guard by the suddenness of the beast's movement. This time, when he brought the ax forward, the arms were ready for him. They lunged at him with unnatural speed and two of them grabbed his forearm.

Within seconds, four more arms had grabbed the ax and were trying to yank it out of his hands. Yang resisted with all his might, but there were too many arms. As they squeezed his wrist, he finally noticed the stream of blood that had been running from the gash on his hand. When two more hands arrived to pry his fingers apart, he could no longer maintain his grip. He released the ax and yanked his hand away, nearly escaping, but by now another hand had snatched his ankle. When another seized his neck, the fight was all but over.

Yang thought he felt a shiver of pain run through the creature's body. The eye glared at him with something that didn't look like hunger. He spat defiantly as the fingers tightened around his neck. A warm feeling washed over him for a few seconds, and then his consciousness was gone.

At first, there was only a blur, and then a dim green light.

Dr. Yang hadn't expected to remain alive after his encounter with the creature. Now he was confused and disoriented. He tried to move, but his limbs didn't seem to respond.

The green light was blinking.

Yang was lying on a cold, hard floor. Everything felt wet. He struggled to focus his eyes. He coughed, but could hear nothing.

Gradually, the world came back into focus. There, standing above him, was URSA, its blinking green light indicating that it was almost done recharging. The meter read ninety-seven percent, and the blood-smeared bear logo gave off a cheerful smile. It seemed like a miracle. Just when he most needed medical help, here was URSA to provide it.

Yang gasped with relief, not understanding how he could have lived or why the creature had declined to kill and consume him.

But then he felt a gentle drip on his head and slowly looked upward. There, right next to URSA, was the creature, perfectly still. Blood trickled from the weeping wound on the monster's side, joining a gentle cascade down the rim of the maw. An occasional drop landed softly on Yang's forehead.

With a panic, he wondered what was going on. Had the creature brought them both for repairs? Did it understand what URSA could do?

Ninety-eight percent.

Looking to his other side, Yang saw that a few arms were reaching toward his torso. One arm dangled limply, bleeding; here, Yang recognized his own handiwork.

And then, following the arms, he looked at the rest of his body. There was so much blood that he could not see his skin. The arms, which he had expected to see holding him down, were instead holding on to some limp objects above him. He surmised that the thing must have removed his bloody clothing, in order to allow URSA access to his body.

Ninety-nine percent.

For a few confused seconds, Yang relaxed a bit, still wondering why the creature had wanted to save him. But then he looked more closely, and his medical expertise kicked in.

Those weren't his clothes.

The creature was holding large sections of his skin, which it appeared to have ripped directly from his torso. In a panic, he tried to get up and run, but his body remained completely still. He realized why the creature wasn't bothering to restrain him: he was paralyzed from the neck down. He tried to scream, but his voice was gone.

One more drip on his forehead, and then...one hundred percent. URSA whirred and started to boot up. The creature squirmed excitedly, pulling Yang aside. As the spidery, metallic arms came to life, the beast exposed its wounds and presented URSA with a gift of freshly plucked skin.

A disaster relief crew arrived at the hospital the following morning, prepared for the worst. They were relieved to find that many of the patients on the second floor were still alive; these survivors were quickly transferred to other hospitals in the nearby city.

None of the hospital's staff were found alive, and no one knew what had become of most of the patients who had been recently admitted to the emergency room. A few were identified from their partial remains, along with one of the nurses. Dr. James Yang was found with his skin flayed, his neck broken, and an arm missing. It was a seemingly implausible set of injuries for an earthquake victim, but no other explanation was forthcoming. Dr. Sydney Bartlett was never found at all.

URSA was gone, presumably looted overnight. Even the charging station had been removed.

Many bloody handprints were found inside the hospital, but the trail outside, leading down to the river, had been washed away at dawn by a heavy rain.

The Cold People
Felix Blackwell

The rain came down so hard it appeared not to move at all. Instead it painted the world a soupy gray that darkened everything it touched, including the winding little road that led up to Daniel's house.

It was autumn of the year 2000: long before humanity had been conquered by its smartphone overlords, a time when Incubus dominated every rock station on air. I was fourteen years old, and had just entered that sacred interlude between dueling action figures and pining for my classmates of the fairer sex. Beside me sat my mom. She kept one hand on the steering wheel and fumbled through a CD booklet with the other.

"Mrs. Blum says you boys are looking after Alex tonight."

Damn.

Daniel and I had only known each for other six months, but were fast becoming something like brothers. We had both come from faraway middle schools, and thus had bonded over our status as loner freshmen in a new high school. I was on my way to sleep over at his new house for the weekend.

The rain made the houses look older than they were. My mom had driven me to Dove Canyon, a little town with big homes nestled in the empty foothills of South Orange County. To this day I can't remember what Daniel's father did for a living, but I do remember that he was always away on business. To make up for his absence, he lavished expensive things on his family, so I was always envious of Daniel's video game systems and surfboards.

When we rolled up to the place, I couldn't believe its size. Three copies of my house could have fit inside with ease, and there appeared to be backyard big enough to fit a pool. The rear of the house overlooked a huge, sweeping valley.

"Looks like Dan's father does alright," my mom said.

Daniel's mother came out and hurried us in from the rain, squeezing my shoulder as we ducked into the front door.

"I'm so glad you're here!" she chirped. Her tiny frame was clad in a tight spandex outfit, and she clutched a tennis racket under her arm.

Tennis court. No pool, I guessed. My mom politely introduced herself, and Mrs. Blum immediately insisted that we call her Carrie.

Daniel and Alex came bounding down the stairs as our moms chatted. Dan was the tallest freshman in school, and he always wore green Celtics jerseys, so we called him the Jolly Green Giant. Just like his brother, Alex was a tow-headed, blue-eyed Viking child, but was far less shy. He never stopped talking, screaming, laughing, moving. It exhausted me to be in the same room with him, so it wasn't hard to guess why Dan was always so quiet and lethargic.

"Hey guys," I said, dropping my backpack against the shoe rack. I noticed a plastic box affixed to the wall above it. It looked like a speaker.

"Hey dude," Dan said, barely above a murmur.

"Hi Felix!" Alex shrieked. He leaped off the fifth stair and landed on the tile floor at the bottom. We had met once before; the little twerp had tagged along once when Dan and I went to the skate park.

"Dammit Alex," Carrie said, scowling at her son. She resumed her conversation with my mom but kept an eye on him.

"What's this?" I asked, pointing at the box on the wall. It reminded me of the security system in our house, but didn't have a screen. Only a little button.

"That's the intercom," Dan said, pointing up the stairs. "They're all over the house. It's so my mom doesn't have to come up to tell us dinner's ready."

Carrie laughed. "I should disconnect that thing and whip these back into shape," she said, slapping one of her thighs. My mom smiled.

Alex sprinted out of the hall and into another room.

"I'll show you, Felix!" he called.

A moment later, the intercom button lit up.

"Fuuuuuck yooouuuuuuuuuuuu!" it cried in Alex's voice. The curse echoed through every speaker in the house and assaulted my ears from all directions.

"God dammit, Alex!" Carrie screamed at the top of her lungs. Obnoxious laughter poured through the intercom. My mom started cracking up.

After a few minutes, I said goodbye to my mom and watched her race out into the rain.

"Okay boys," Carrie said, ushering us into the kitchen. "Money's on the counter. Order a pizza. Don't go outside, don't bother the neighbors, don't have visitors. Your dad and I will be home late. Our car phone number is on the fridge, and Ted's number is on there too. He's the guy throwing the party."

We bolted upstairs and fired up Daniel's new Playstation 2, which he'd gotten a month before anyone else through his dad's business connections. I couldn't help but notice how spectacular his house was; the staircase was as wide as my garage, and the top floor was one giant living room with four big bedrooms attached to it via decorated halls. We sat in front of an enormous TV surrounded by shelves of hundreds of games and movies. Alex lay prone on the floor, organizing big stacks of Pokémon cards.

"Wish *we* had an upstairs living room," I said.

"We call it a bonus room," Dan replied.

"I call it a boner room," Alex added.

"Frickin' rich people," I said, picking a loose card from between the cushions and flinging it at Alex. He was seven years old and had ten times as many cool toys as I had at that age.

The intercom crackled to life.

"Okay, we're leaving, guys. Be good. Alex, be good."

"Bye mom!" Alex shouted down the stairs in an earsplitting cry.

Far off in the house, I heard the front door open and close. The sound of Dan's parents' car faded into the distance. Through the window by the TV, I could see the hazy sun dipping behind the hills. More rainclouds were gathering over it, casting the bonus room in gloomy shadow.

The intercom made a soft, fuzzy noise. It sounded like Carrie whispering through static.

Tssssss "We lo-"pshhhhhh

I strained to hear. Dan was fixated on the snowboarding game we were playing, and Alex was enraptured by his cards.

Kshhhhhh tk tk tk "...you-"

I set my controller down and slowly walked over to the intercom. The light was blinking intermittently. I figured it had some sort of electrical interference.

Carrie's voice came through again, but it was distorted and scratchy:

"We love you, Alex." Tsssssssssss

The intercom popped and the light went dead. Alex looked over at the speaker, then studied me.

"What did you say?" he asked.

Feeling a little creeped out, I asked him if his mom was still home. He hopped up and peered out the window at the driveway, then shook his head.

"Their car is gone."

I assumed Carrie's voice had somehow been preserved momentarily in the wires, as if her last transmission had been stalled and delivered late. Maybe the storm was messing with the electricity.

"Nevermind," I said, dropping back down onto the couch and picking up the controller.

At around 7 PM, we ordered a pizza. The sunlight had completely died away, and most of the bottom floor was pitch black. I made my way downstairs to grab a few CD's out of my backpack, and immediately felt unsettled by the enormity of the house and the darkness that closed in on me from all sides. Dan and Alex were still upstairs, glued to the couch as South Park blared on the TV. As I reached for my backpack, the intercom once again lit up.

Ksshhhhhhhhhh

"-ex...Al-" pshhhhh

"-et us" tsssssssss

Goosebumps erupted all over my arms. I pushed the page button a few times, then spoke into the receiver:

"Hey, are you guys hearing that?"

My announcement was lost in the din of Cartman's laughter, and no one responded. As I walked back up the stairs, I thought I heard the word *"in..."* seep from the intercom, but when I looked, the button was dark.

About thirty minutes later, the doorbell rang. Alex bolted down the stairs and threw the door open, shouting

something in glee. Dan and I rounded the corner to find the pizza guy standing in the entryway, dripping from the rain. We traded a handful of bills for two boxes of pizza, then watched the guy run back to his car. Alex just stood there with a dumbfounded look on his face. He didn't move or blink the entire time, he just stared at the teenage delivery boy throughout the exchange. Dan carried the pizzas to the kitchen and I followed him, leaving Alex in the dark hallway. The little creep suddenly burst out laughing. He howled like he'd just met Cartman in real life.
"You coming?" I asked.
Alex just looked over at me, and said while laughing, "That guy."
"The hell's wrong with you?" Dan called from behind me.
Alex ignored him and exploded into more hysterics. He ran past us, ignoring the food, and headed back upstairs. As he moved away from the front door, I noticed that his head had been right by the intercom. And the light was on.
Dan and I wolfed down a whole pizza. We sat at the kitchen bar, talking about people from school and watching the rain slam against the glass door that led to the backyard. Alex was somewhere upstairs, up there in the dark, doing God knows what. The gigantic house felt more claustrophobic as the night wore on; it seemed like the shadows were slowly taking over, like water rising in a ship.
Laughter suddenly pierced the silence upstairs, and interrupted my conversation with Daniel.
"I know, I know," Alex said, his voice faint and far off.
"Who the fuck you talkin' to?" Dan yelled. He got no response.
We marched up the stairs to find Alex on the couch, staring up at the ceiling. His feet dangled off the armrest and bobbed back and forth as he laughed.

"What's the deal?" Dan asked.

Alex calmed himself enough to make out words.

"Pizza boy gonna die," he said. "Pizza boy gonna die." He issued another howl of laughter, then suddenly fell quiet. His gaze snapped toward the intercom on the far wall. Dan and I looked at each other, both of us unsure as to what was going on. Alex stretched and yawned.

At around 10 PM, Dan told his brother to go to bed, and surprisingly, Alex didn't argue. The little bastard trudged off down the dark hall and disappeared into his room. He never ate a single bite of pizza. Dan and I remained in the bonus room, watching old horror flicks and shoveling handfuls of peanut M&M's into our mouths. Dan said his mom had a weak spot for them and usually bought the industrial-sized bags, so the house was always well stocked.

At some point, Dan broke out a handle of vodka from his father's stash. For the first and last time in my life, I drank, and did not enjoy myself one bit. That awful cocktail of scary movies and too much chocolate and hard liquor set my stomach at the edge of my mouth, so I went into Dan's bedroom to unroll my sleeping bag and lie down. My head spun and an evil tide of pizza and booze swirled in my gut. I prayed that I would just fall asleep and be done with this strange night.

I lay there for a half hour in the dark, but no matter how hard I tried, I couldn't force the voices in the intercom out of my memory. All manner of terrifying creatures took form in my imagination, giving shape to the strange sounds I replayed over and over in my head.

"We love you, Alex."

My eyes kept falling on Dan's closet. There was nothing strange about it, but the creature I had dreamed up needed a place to live, and the door near my feet seemed like the worst place for it. I imagined that door creaking open, and a black, slimy claw reaching out and grabbing my foot and pulling me in. For several minutes this morbid thought danced in my head alongside other scenarios, until finally I jumped to my feet and threw the door open with a surge of bravery.

It was pitch black inside. I half-expected something to reach out of the shadows and grab me, but nothing happened. I pulled the string that dangled from the ceiling. The dim light above lit up a fancy walk-in closet filled with clothes, a snowboard, a box, and a stuffed shark with a smiley face.

"That's Alex's," Dan said behind me, staggering through the doorway. I jumped at the sound of his voice. "He got it when we visited SeaWorld. Tell that little prick to stay out of my closet."

I hesitantly grabbed the stuffed animal and inspected it, then made my way out of the room as Dan climbed into his bed. The world spun around me as I moved. Darkness washed over the halls like oil, and the moonlight seeped and swirled in from the windows as I passed. Alex's door was cracked open, and I stumbled inside without knocking.

"Alex?" I whispered.

"Yeah," he replied. There was no sleepiness in his voice. The nightlight in the corner revealed the outline of a bunk bed, and a boy sitting on the top bunk.

"Uh, Dan wanted me to give this to you." I handed the shark to him.

"Mom?" he asked.

I leaned against the bed.

"She won't be home until really late tonight," I said.

"No," Alex replied, "I just saw her."

The way he said it set my arm hairs on end.

"You...saw her?"

He shifted under his covers.

"Yeah, she was right there." Alex pointed to the doorway behind me. I looked over my shoulder, almost expecting to see someone there. "I asked her for some water."

"What did she say?" I asked, glancing around the room to make sure no one was with us.

"Nothing," he replied. "She walked up to the bed and stood right where you are now. She just looked at me. All I could see was her eyes."

The nausea swept over me once again. Goosebumps rippled across my skin, and everything felt cold. I told Alex that he should probably camp out in Dan's room with us, and he agreed. We quietly set up a sleeping bag for him across from my own. Dan snored and babbled all the while.

I was almost asleep when the doorbell rang. The sound jerked me from a half-conscious reverie. Alex had heard it too. He shook Dan awake.

"What? What?" Dan grumbled.

"The doorbell," Alex whispered. "Someone's outside."

Dan reached over and grabbed his watch from the desk. Its little glow lit up his face.

"It's after midnight," he said. "You think mom and dad locked themselves out?"

Alex shrugged.

"They have a cell phone," I said. "They'd have called."

Dan and I instructed his little brother to stay put, and made our way downstairs. I glanced through the peephole and saw two men in uniforms. Dan opened the door.

"Sorry to disturb you folks," one of the men said. "We're with Canyon Security."

"Uh, hi," Dan said, blinking his haggard eyes.

"Are your parents home?" the other guard asked.

"They're at some party," I interjected, trying to save Dan the effort. I wasn't much better off. "They should be home in a few hours."

Raindrops began to sprinkle around the men as we talked. The air was so cold that their breath looked like thick smoke.

"Mrs. Beckman next door called us. Says she saw a woman walking around in her yard, looking through the glass. You boys see anything like that tonight?"

Dan and I exchanged glances and shook our heads. My mind went to Alex's weird story, but I didn't say anything.

"Mind if we take a look out back?" one of them asked.

"Uh, sure," Dan said.

As the guards started off toward the side gate, deafening screeches erupted from inside the house. The screams were distant and inhuman, filtered through a mess of popping static. We whirled around to see the intercom's light blaring red. The damned things – all of them – were spewing that infernal noise, as though they'd been simultaneously tuned to the frequency of Hell. I covered my ears, but as I did, the explosive cries of a child echoed from upstairs.

"Alex!" Dan shouted. He bolted down the entry hall and rounded the corner to the stairs. I went hot on his tracks, and the guards followed me. A chorus of the dying sang all around us, moaning and shrieking and begging through the walls. Terror ran up and down my spine, freezing every inch of my skin as it went. As we rounded the corner into Daniel's room, I saw Alex cowering under his sleeping bag. Seeing that he was unhurt, one of the guards ran back downstairs, and a moment later, the intercoms fell silent. My ears rang out in the stillness; big drunken bells bashed and gonged over and over in my skull. My heart flitted like a tiny hummingbird behind my ribs.

"What the hell was that?" Daniel said to the remaining security guard. The man looked terrified, and that deeply unsettled me.

"I...never heard nothin' like that before," he said, inspecting the intercom in Dan's room. His voice shook. We all returned to the first floor, where the other guard met us.

"I disabled the whole system," he said, scratching his bearded chin. "We should call the homeowners, Neil."

His partner nodded.

"You boys alright?" Neil asked, placing a fatherly hand on Alex's shoulder. The kid had no expression. He stared at the ground, probably scared out of his wits.

"I'll call them," Dan said. "I've got the number where they're at."

"Don't you worry, now," Neil said. "Could be that your unit's just pickin' up signals from nearby houses. These things get interference all the time. Wires get all crossed up in storms, you know. Maybe they're watching a movie next door."

We stood there with blank expressions, obviously unsatisfied.

"Have your folks give us a call at this number," he continued, handing a card to Dan. "We'll drive by again later."

The guards left the house and circled the outside perimeter. They must not have found anything because they drove off quickly.

Daniel couldn't reach his parents at the two numbers they left us, so we all went back to bed still shaken up. I felt sick, and the jackhammer in my skull would not abate. I lay there in the dark, trying to ignore my nausea, and trying not to speculate on what exactly was talking through those speakers. The rain grew stronger, and battered the house rhythmically. After focusing on it for a long time, it lulled me to sleep.

Images of dead things in the walls haunted my dreams. Decayed, white, humanoid *things* clawing and scraping at the plaster, groaning at our scents. Little cracks and holes appeared all over the wall beside my sleeping bag. Long, pale fingers burrowed out first, then hands, then arms. They reached for me – dozens of them – from all sides of the room and the ceiling. A whisper pulled me out of the nightmare.

 I gazed around the room. The walls were now pristine; no holes or hands desecrated them. Behind me, a shadowy figure stood by the door. I turned over and squinted through the gloom.

 It was Alex. He stood there at the intercom, ear pressed against it. The red light faintly glowed. A voice came through again – a woman's. It whispered something I couldn't make out.

 "I can't," he whispered. "My brother doesn't want me to go downstairs."

 Gentle static seeped out of the panel. The same voice murmured again; she sounded like an old vinyl recording from the 40's.

 "Felix...he's my brother's friend," he replied.

 "Alex!" I hissed. He jumped. "What the *hell* are you doing?"

 We both looked over at Dan. He was still out cold. I jumped out of my sleeping bag and marched over to the kid. The button lit up and the woman's voice came through.

 "Help mommy, Ale-" sssssssss

 "That's not your mom," I said, pulling Alex away from the speaker.

 "I know," he said.

 I squinted, trying to make out his expression in the dark. Was he smiling?

 "What do you mean, you know? Who is that?"

 We both looked at the intercom.

 "It's the cold people," he said, barely above a whisper.

 "The what?" I leaned closer to him.

"The cold people," he said. He reached out and ran his fingers across the foam grid of the speaker. "They're outside. They want in so they can get warm."

Every hair on my body bristled.

"Why did you tell them about me?" I asked. "Why'd you tell them my name?"

Dan groaned behind us. Alex took his eyes off the intercom and looked at me for a long time, studying my face.

"They keep asking," he said.

I'd had enough. This freak show had finally gotten to me, and my last resort was to call my parents. I hadn't failed a sleepover in years, but I was now beside myself with fear. I moved past Alex and headed for the door.

The bonus room was pitch dark. Images of "the cold people" bombarded my mind. My eyes darted around in a futile effort to spot one of them in the shadows. Before I could reach the stairs, the whole room was suddenly bathed in an eerie red glow. The intercom crackled to life, and heavy breathing rushed out of it and flooded the house.

I stormed up to the light, smashing my foot against a vase table in the process. The breathing cut out just before I smacked the page button.

"Who the fuck are you?!" I shouted into the speaker. "What do you want?"

A deep buzzing noise came out of it, followed by a voice that was so garbled and choppy that I couldn't make out a single word. I hurried to the stairs, more distraught than I'd ever been. Just before I set foot on the wood floor at the bottom of the stairs, I saw a woman at the end of the hall. She was there for only a second, and turned the corner toward the kitchen. It was too dark to make out more than her shape.

"Carrie?" I called out in a mousy voice. I wanted so desperately to believe that Daniel's parents had come home, but I knew deep down that they hadn't. Whoever was in this house with us, they did not belong.

I shambled forward in the choking dark, arms out in front of me, guided by the little bits of light that fell through the windows on the vaulted ceiling.

"Who's there?" I whispered, unsure of whether I wanted an answer.

The phone was just ahead, somewhere in the kitchen. I took a deep breath and rounded the corner, following the path of the mysterious woman.

The kitchen was big. A huge marble island sat at its center, pizza boxes still strewn upon it. The far wall was pocked with huge windows that overlooked the tennis court, and beyond that, the valley below. The moon poured in through the glass, bathing the room in faint silver. Rainclouds wandered across the sky.

The woman was standing there, in the only corner untouched by the light. She was not much more than a shadow, impossibly dark and featureless, but I could *feel* her gaze searing into me. She looked me over, tilting her head slowly as she did, then began to move. She walked past the big table and toward the sliding glass door that led outside. When the woman stepped into the moonlight, she began to fade into the air around her, and the moment she reached the door, she completely vanished.

I just stood there, anchored to the floor by leaden legs. My body shook so hard it could not be commanded to move or be still. I tried to scream, but the last ounce of breath had been wrung out of my chest. The phone sat on the table in front of me, either a foot or a thousand miles away. I'd never reach it.

And then they came. Four figures, veiled by the night, approached the sliding glass door from outside. At their center, a fifth emerged from seemingly nowhere – a woman. The one who had just been inside. Yet she looked different; they all looked different from the phantom I had seen moments ago. The moonlight did not pass through their bodies, but rather fell upon them from behind, and traced their outlines. These were real, corporeal bodies, not ghosts, staring in at me. The woman approached the glass and pressed herself against it, hands cupped around her eyes as she peered inward at me. I could not make out her face, nor any features, but her breath left an unnatural frost on the glass that grew thicker with time.

A cloud drifted in front of the moon, darkening the patio and kitchen. The beings did not notice, but instead remained utterly fixated on me. I sunk down into a terrified crouch and cowered there on the cold floor, too petrified to move or make a sound. All I could do was stare back, stare into those lonely pits of darkness where their faces should have been.

Terror is a curious thing. In short bursts it can give strength, speed, or heightened awareness. It can elicit a scream or stop a man dead in his tracks. But when applied over many hours, it can break down the mind and render the body catatonic. It weakens the spirit and puts every flaw on stark display, so as to salt the wounds it inflicts at its onset. So there I sat, neither awake nor asleep. Pure and exquisite terror, unlike anything I'd ever known, paralyzed my body and hypnotized my mind. Hours passed. I stared at them staring back at me, and watched them dissect and devour me with their lifeless gazes. Clouds slogged across the vacant deep, and little else broke the deathly stillness between us. On occasion, the woman knocked her bony knuckles against the glass, always in threes.

My terror rotted me from the inside. It hollowed me out. Left me less than I was before. Took something from me. I could feel it changing me on a very base level – the slow realization that these things had found what they were looking for, and were determined to take the rest of what their horror had left behind. Their eyes did not behold me with new fascination; instead they regarded me with grim relief. They had searched many faces for mine, and at long last their hunt was over. They *knew* me, and had dark plans for me. All of this could be read across their faces, which burned into me with baleful satisfaction. It was a pitiful thing for a thirteen-year-old to understand that he was doomed, but I did not cry that night. In all the hours that I sat and watched my tormentors looking down at me, I did not shed a tear. I just let them take with their stares whatever they could.

When the sun finally crept up over the valley, I caught a better glimpse of my new acquaintances. The yellow light struck them harshly, revealing *things* that very much looked like people – eyes, noses, hair. But each of these familiar features bore the mark of corruption. The eyes had sunken deep and died there, yellowed with decay; the noses were hardened and rotten. The hair draped like cobwebs over sallow skin, and the mouths…the mouths curled up in permanent, menacing smiles. Never have I seen such unbridled joy in a smile, such singular delight framed in a countenance of death.

Only a moment after their forms were revealed, the creatures faded to nothingness. The sun burned them away like morning fog, but their minacious grins and wild, wide eyes made promises of their return. I knew with absolute conviction that they would find me again someday, and something deep inside me died at that revelation.

My mother picked me up shortly after breakfast, but I never said a word about the events of that night to anyone. I never went to Daniel's house again, and for several years, I lay in bed awake, wondering when the cold people would return.

Cubes
Felix Blackwell

There was something sketchy about the guy who gave us the bag. His teeth were too yellow, too crooked for my liking. He was too skinny. And he was way too happy to be making thirty measly bucks for a few little pills. Danny didn't seem to mind, though, and made the swap as I nervously glanced around. We watched the guy stroll out of my apartment complex and take off running when he thought he was out of sight.

"So many creeps in this town," I said, cracking open a glass bottle of root beer.

Danny reclined on the couch and put his feet up. I cringed.

"Housemate coming back tonight?" he asked.

"Tomorrow," I replied, handing him a bottle. "But it'd be just my luck if he came back early, wouldn't it."

Danny laughed and knocked back some of the drink. "God damn," he said, smacking his lips.

"I know, right?" I said, sending a text to my girlfriend. "Puts IBC in the shade."

"*Looziana cayne sugah,*" he said in a thick drawl, reading from the label.

I fumbled around in the kitchen looking for a snack, while intermittently responding to Faye's messages. They say you should eat something light, just before. I followed the online guide carefully in preparation for this little experiment.

Danny was an experienced psychonaut, but I had only recently become interested in exploring other worlds through hallucinogens. I was turned on to the idea by a near-spiritual experience on an evening walk with my headphones and a bit of pot a friend had given me. It was my first time, and truly an awakening for me; I was so moved by the music and the reveries it painted across my mind that in the coming weeks, I found myself wanting to return to that emotional space. So here we were, in my college apartment, with six hits of ecstasy and a couple of gourmet sodas.

"Well," Danny said, standing up and setting the bottle on the coffee table, "I gotta get home before this kicks in."

I shut the fridge and looked at him.

"What? You're going? You want me to do this alone?"

Danny laughed. "Uh, yeah, I mean, I figured you'd be cool with it? This isn't really the kind of stuff you drop with your bros, you know."

"But you took yours already?" I asked, frustrated.

"Yeah. I left yours right here," he replied, pointing to the table. "Just chill, man. Throw on some tunes and ride with it. You'll be fine."

I bade Danny farewell and stared at the little bag. Most people get good and bad "feelings" about things. In that moment I wished I'd had an intuition, a gut to follow. But I felt absolutely nothing. The only feeling I had was the fear that I'd throw up on my housemate's carpet and not get my deposit back.

About forty-five minutes after downing the pills, I began to have regrets. The little ones came first: the mourning of a wasted Saturday night, the loss of fifteen dollars, the disgust with myself for swallowing pills some meth head probably made in his bathtub. But shortly after, other feelings bubbled up inside me. A coldness slithered over my skin, as though the blood was receding from my fingers, up my arms, into my torso. This was followed by mild nausea, tightness of the chest, and other minor symptoms of anxiety I'd read about online. I swallowed back my fears and tried to remain optimistic. The sunlight crept across the room and vanished shortly after; the crickets began their sonatas.

Tremendous waves of warmth and cold strobed through my body. They came and went so intensely that I had to pull my headphones out of my ears and pace around the living room. Sweat dripped from my pores and seemed to freeze the moment it contacted the air. It felt like I was coming down with a bad flu. My phone buzzed on the coffee table. It was Danny. For just a brief moment, I thought to myself, *I don't know a Danny.*

"Felix," he said, panting heavily. "Felix, Fe..."

"What's up, man?" I asked, instantly aware of the dread in his voice.

Danny burst into tears. He sobbed into the phone, mumbling gibberish beneath his breath. In the background, I could hear his girlfriend panicking.

"What is it? What's wrong?" My heart jackhammered in my ears.

He began howling with laughter, punctuated occasionally tearful whimpers and wails.

"It's..." he struggled to breathe. "It's—"

"What did you do?!" his girlfriend screamed.

"It's not E!" he screamed into the phone, crying hysterically. "It's not ecstasy!"

My heart seemed to stop beating altogether.

"I took a pill," Danny said to his girlfriend. "Throw these away. Throw away."

"Danny!" I shouted, trying to get his attention. "What

do you mean you took *a* pill? We bought *six*, Danny."

He laughed and cried and hyperventilated.

"I think I'm losing my mind," he whispered. "I can see into hell. It isn't like they say."

"Danny, how many pills did you take?" I demanded. "This is important. Pay attention."

His girlfriend screamed something in the background.

"Yes, yes, one dose," he said. "One dose. Took the pill. One dose."

Visions of death invaded my mind.

"Danny," I said, trying to maintain composure, "Listen to me. I took *all three*. I thought that was the dose."

He began screaming. They were screams of pure terror. The screams of a dying man.

"Put it down!" his girlfriend yelled. The phone cut out.

I stood there in the silence of my empty living room, staring down at the phone. Cold sweat waterfalled down my back. My skin crawled. I was on a rocket ship that was just taking off, and the G-force of panic multiplied with each passing minute. In my loosening grip on reality, I reasoned that sitting in the armchair in absolute silence would keep me safe and understimulated. My sole objective now was to deprive the drug of fuel that it could use to drag me into a waking six-hour nightmare.

I turned off the TV, set down the iPod, and threw the block of kitchen knives into a cabinet. I poured a glass of water with a shaking hand and stumbled back to the sofa. The moment I sat down, utter silence overtook my senses, and I became hyper-aware of the physical sensations in my body. My stomach growled. It promised me untold havoc the next morning, and gurgled angrily at the poison I had sent to it. It burbled in patterns. It was trying to communicate with me. I tried to make out the words.

"It's not E!" Danny's voice rang in my memory. My stomach matched the syllables. The very thought

85

catapulted me into a new state of terror, reaffirming how utterly doomed I was. My blood thickened to sludge and strained through my veins, slowing my movements and breathing.

I tried to turn my attention away from my failing body and outward into the room. The cream white ceiling rippled like the surface of a pond, then went taut and rigid. It repeated this over and over until thick, white gobs of it began dripping down onto the carpet. I held my hands out and caught some, then rubbed it between my fingers. It dried quickly and caked my palms in brittle plaster, then disappeared.

My ability to control my own thoughts waxed and waned. One moment I was capable of surmising that I had ingested LSD, the next I was totally unaware that I was on drugs at all. Meaningful consciousness flickered on and off in my brain like a crackling bulb. Before long I realized that the entire living room had dried out; it no longer possessed the likeness of melting wax, but instead appeared dehydrated, like the façade of a Roman tower. My body had fossilized into sandstone and fused with the chair, and only my eyes were wet enough to move. They slid around in my skull and examined the stacks of DVD's, the coffee table, the television. All of it cracked and crumbled and toppled down under the weight of long-forgotten eons. I became a dying statue among the ancient ruins, and each labored breath sent dust spewing into the air before me.

Something colorful appeared on my lap. It wiggled and blossomed into a floating sequence of various geometric shapes. It glowed myriad colors and chirped beautiful songs like a bird from a distant land. I reached out and scooped it up with shaking hands. Across its many surfaces flashed unintelligible runes. A thousand-eyed head formed at the center, which then condensed into the familiar face of a human being. The runes spun in place until they were legible. They became "Danny."

"I. Don't. Know. A. Danny," I said, dropping the object back onto my lap. I looked to the window and noticed the blackness radiating from it. A terrible realization dawned on me: the world outside had fallen away, and the little room I sat in was everything that existed. I peered into the vacant face of the Deep, trying desperately to prove myself wrong. But only darkness peered back. It was not the darkness of empty space, but rather the surface of a textured nothingness; the universe simply did not extend past the glass. There was no outside.

The room went hot and claustrophobic at this revelation. I touched the window and felt its bitter cold, which brought me some measure of comfort. I breathed across its surface and traced little runes on it with my fingers. My hand droned along with purpose, and although I had no idea what I was writing, it calmed me to do it. When I ran out of space I moved to another, larger window nearby. The carpet clung to my feet and sloshed back to the ground as I walked.

In this window, I could see my own reflection. My ghostly doppelganger peered back at me, mimicking all of my movements with a slight delay. He looked aged, more sinister. Colder. A white veil obscured the details of his face. At first I thought it was fog on the window, but after sliding my hands across it, it felt like spider's silk.

"Cob...webs..." I mouthed, flicking my tongue all around as I did. "Cobcobcobcobwebwebwebweb." As I spoke, I watched hundreds of tiny gray spiders march their way across my reflection's face, obscuring it further with more webbing. I reached up to my own and gently dragged my fingers over my skin. In the window, I could see the cobwebs falling away, but the spiders returned. I brushed faster, chuckling in amusement as the spiders tried to race me. I took to catching the spiders and peeled them off one

87

by one.

At long last, my reflection was clearly visible. The cobwebs had fallen away to reveal a disturbing sight: a pallid, pasty face of death glared back at me. Its dry eyes were sunken and shone with the color of rotten pus, and its nose was bloodless and shriveled. I beheld it with horror, and it returned my gaze with intense fascination. My heart flopped around and spasmed in my chest. I could not tear my eyes away from the wretched sight.

We stared into each other for a thousand years. The room aged all around me and shifted to purples and grays and blacks. It spoiled and decayed and died away in my peripheries, then budded and bloomed once more. I felt compelled to reach out again and draw more runes on the glass, but as I did, my reflection's fingers copied me and smeared the window with blood. The vibrant red mortified me, and I tried to scream. Alien sounds poured out of me while my reflection simply smiled and watched. Behind him, several shadowy outlines formed, each roughly in the shape of a person. Their faces were too dim to make out, as they stood much further away, but even through the fog and blood I could see that they were smiling.

My screams shook me out of the trance that trapped me in front of the window. I crumpled back into the chair, burying my face in my hands. The air vanished from the room, and I was left gasping for breath between cries of terror. A dozen thick black lines slowly grew out of the floor, moving horizontally and vertically until the room was divided into a grid of squares. They shifted mechanically like a Rubik's Cube, until the multiple surfaces of reality reconfigured into another view. When they settled into place, I watched as cars rushed past me in every direction. Their headlights lit up the heavy rain that blasted the ground all around me. I perceived them at only a few frames per second, and thus they looked more like they were teleporting than driving. The roars of their horns and engines deafened me. The rain deafened me. My screams deafened me.

Then, the black lines returned. The world again broke apart into squares, then cubes, and they realigned to an infinite hallway. Wild creatures in blue rags danced all around me, touching my face and hair, pulling at my shirt. They spoke in unintelligible tongues and forced me back down into the chair when I tried to escape. Although I was seated, my chair slid down the hallway and rounded several corners. Larger creatures in white occasionally peered down at me as we went.

"...severe lacerations," I thought I heard a voice say. Fragments of things I could understand echoed around me.

"In shock," said another.

"Weapon...blood test..."

"What did...swallow, Mr. Blackwell?"

"Felix..."

I spent two days in that hospital. Faye was beside me when I woke up. She wept as they changed my bandages, begging me to tell her why I did it. The nurse drew more blood now and then, and always shook her head at the charts afterward. I had no recollection of what had happened until Faye informed me that Danny was in jail for attempting to kill his girlfriend's dog. Bits and pieces of that night began returning to me, but my memory was still dim and scattered. Then Faye opened her cell phone and showed a photo to me that she had taken the night I ended up in the emergency room.

It was a picture of a window. Smeared across it in dried, flaky blood, it read:

Let us in.

The words were written on the glass from the outside.

The Bleeding Window
Colin J. Northwood

We shouldn't have split up. We came running when we heard Father calling for help, but it was too late.

Tol Centa, the old shaman, was the first to arrive, but he did not have a weapon and was also attacked. By the time Dejani and I arrived with our spears, the beast had knocked the old man into a jagged rock and impaled his left hand.

I had never seen such a creature before. In a grotesque inversion of nature, its organs were on the outside, dangling from its body like the fruits of some hellish tree. When we shouted our chants, it churned and convulsed until it was swallowing its own skin. Our spears pierced its body, but it simply shrieked and swallowed the wounds as well.

A dizzying succession of organs appeared on its body, seemingly from nowhere at all, only to be swallowed and replaced like all the others. One moment it glared at me with a hundred mournful eyes, and the next moment it had no eyes at all. More and more body parts came and went, faster and faster, less and less recognizable.

As we chanted on and on, stabbing it from every side, its newly gigantic mouth became a twisting vortex. No longer able to stand, it writhed on the ground and let loose a scream so violent that I feared it might shatter the sky. None of us dared to approach it any longer; but still, we chanted. It moved with an unholy speed, as if time itself were in a panic.

When it turned toward me for one last time, I saw in its shifting form something that I instantly knew from the legends of our tribe: the Land of the Dead. It was an endless labyrinth of burning flesh, where we are propelled ever forward by the swelling of blisters; and where we gasp for air constantly, only to choke on toxic smoke.

I saw Father's spirit enter that place, and I saw the door close behind him. The creature was gone, having taken what it came for.

In that moment, the vision was mine alone. The others had seen Father mauled by a she-bear.

Our expedition was not in vain. The land here was lush. The rest of our tribe would be relieved that our days of famine were over. Winter was beginning, so our discovery was crucial.

Father's remains were not in suitable condition for a proper burial. We had to leave his body behind, but I vowed to come back for his bones.

Tol Centa's hand had been impaled clean through, but the wound was not fatal. Despite the pain, he promised that he could still lead the memorial ceremony. We returned to our camp, built a fire, and began our prayers for Father's soul:

May the tenderness of your welts cushion you from the beatings you receive on your journey, and may your blackened lungs go numb to spare you from the pain. May the Three Thousand Evils show you no mercy, so that your destruction will not linger incomplete. Father, please forgive me.

I looked across the fire at Tol Centa. His eyes remained closed as he held up his hands and hummed the final refrain of the funeral dirge. And so, I saw it first.

Through the hole in the old man's hand, I could see a dark landscape strewn with snow. It was still daylight where we stood; the Eye of the Master had just begun its descent toward the horizon. But through the shaman's hand I saw the night sky. The pristine snow and gleaming stars might have been beautiful had the previous winter not killed so many of our kind; but in the very emptiness of the scene I regarded the menacing face of death. A ghostly green flame floated in the sky, and strange figures crept about on the horizon.

Tol Centa felt the sting of ice in his wound and turned his palm to face his eyes. His expression of stern bewilderment confirmed for me that this was no dream.

Dejani watched in wonder, and I in terror, as Tol Centa stood entranced. Icy wind flowed from the palm of the old man's hand; blood dripped from the back and sizzled as it landed in the fire. None of us dared move.

And so it was that we stood paralyzed while a single thin claw emerged from the wound and impaled the old man through his right eye. It stirred the contents of his head at a leisurely pace as if digging for something unseen, then retreated back from whence it came.

Dejani and I regained our composure and ran to Tol Centa's side, but it was too late. A soup of blood and brain dribbled down his face, and he mustered only a single grunt before falling to his knees, never to stand again.

I know not the essence of the magics that I've witnessed, nor the machinations that take place in the spirit world. I know only that in those dark and icy lands lies something wicked. The old man had been slain by a claw, but not with the savagery of a wild animal. The killing was done with grace, elegance, and an unmistakable murderous intent. I saw in the movements of that claw, and felt in those icy winds, a malice too pure to belong to any mortal creature. I will tell my people of this evil, and search my dreams for omens of its coming.

Going Down
Felix Blackwell

Preston Lyle closed the manila folder and pushed himself away from his desk. The chair rolled backward a foot or so and stopped. He spun around to face the big window. A sickly orange Philadelphia sky loomed beyond it. Minutes before, the sun had dipped behind the ring of distant skyscrapers. It was 7:20 PM.

Preston peeled off his glasses and wiped a forearm across his oily face. He grabbed his briefcase and loosened his tie, then hobbled down the hall toward the elevators. Empty cubicles lined his peripheries. If someone had been sitting in one of them, he'd not have noticed; his eyes were glued to the cell phone in his hand.

Finished both portfolios today, he typed with a chubby thumb. *Sending them to you and Bryan first thing in the AM.*

Excellent, his partner replied. *You carried this one, Pres. Owe you a steak.*

Preston smacked the Down button on one of the elevators. As he waited, he glanced down the hall he'd walked through. The sky was changing to a deep purple. When he first began working at Wessman & Schultz, Preston spent an inordinate amount of time gazing out his office window, admiring the city. As the years passed, he barely noticed it anymore. For some reason, today the view beckoned to him. The compulsion to look was almost foreign. It sort of felt like he'd never see it again.

A soft *ding* pulled him from his reverie. The elevator doors slid open with a gentle hum and Preston stepped inside.

The phone buzzed in his hand. While checking it, he poked the Level 1 button by mistake, then corrected himself and hit P1.

It was a text from his wife, Beth.

Are you still at work?

On my way home, he typed. *Ever been to Milan?*

The phone rang.

"Hi sweetie," he answered.

"You didn't," Beth said. Preston could almost *hear* her grinning.

"I did. Booked 'em today. Figured it was about time. Closed a major project today."

Beth squealed in excitement.

"Get home quick," she said. "Let's go out to celebrate."

Preston obliged and hung up the phone. He glanced up at the digital readout above the button panel.

21...20...19...

He compulsively scrolled through the emails on his phone. There was a message from Alison Briggs in management. He stuck the phone back in his pocket.

"Not tonight, y'old hag," he muttered.

13...12...11...

He tried to clear work from his mind, but ended up going through mental lists of things he had to finish the next day. The job was never far from his thoughts. It was medication to him; the busyness of it all helped him avoid the things in life he couldn't control, the memories he tried to bury.

Preston found himself instinctively reaching back into his pocket for the phone. The elevator lurched.

95

3...2...1...

The doors slid open. The ground floor of Wessman & Schultz was empty, spare a lone security guard reading his paper. A set of huge glass windows near the entrance framed a scene of twilight streets. People in suits walked by, laughing and chatting. Cars passed now and then. Preston stared out for a while, longing to be outside, then tapped the Close Door button repeatedly. He wanted to get home as fast as possible.

The doors slid shut and the elevator lurched again. As it descended, its mechanical hum made Preston feel anxious.

Too much coffee today, he thought.

The readout glowed its soft blue light.

1...P1...P2...

Preston's brow furled. He pressed P1 repeatedly, but the elevator did not stop.

"What the hell," he complained. "Parking, you stupid shit. *Parking.*"

The elevator didn't respond to his command. He tried pressing several other buttons, but none of them lit up.

B1...B2...

"Great. This is great." He smacked P1 over and over with his fist to no avail. He loathed the idea of walking up several flights of stairs to get back to the underground car park.

C1...C2...C3...

Preston stared in disbelief at the display above the button panel. He had no idea there were this many floors beneath the parking structure. He didn't even know what C stood for.

A shrieking sound of metal on metal deafened Preston. He clutched his ears, then nervously paced around the little room. The elevator seemed to speed up as it descended; it almost felt like it was in freefall. The metallic sounds alternated between high-pitched whines and deep, shuddering groans. Floors flew by.

C18...C19...C20...

A waterfall of sweat poured off of Preston's head, smearing down his face and glasses. He stumbled to the emergency panel and opened it, revealing a button marked "STOP" and a red phone. He slapped the button but it didn't give; upon further inspection it was stuck. When he picked up the phone, it rang and rang endlessly, but no one ever answered.

C36...C37...C38...

The air went out of the room. Preston's old claustrophobia crept back into his conscious thoughts. He smoldered under his heavy suit. He couldn't breathe. He fumbled for his cell phone, but forgot which pocket it was in. When he finally found it, he dialed Beth. The call refused to connect. Preston was alone.

C43...C44...C45...

"Somebody help me!" he screamed at the top of his lungs. "Stop this thing!"

As if in response to his cries, the elevator came crashing to a halt. The jolt almost knocked Preston to his knees, but he caught himself against the button panel. The readout flashed in bright red letters inches from his face:

C46. C46. C46. C46. C46.

The doors struggled to open, but finally did so with a loud rumble. A single drop of water collected on the carriage's metal ceiling and dripped onto his neck. He didn't notice.

Preston practically threw himself out of that godforsaken elevator. A wall of musty air assailed his nostrils. He strained to catch his breath. Before him lay a long, dark hallway, dimly lit with yellow tube lights every few yards. The hall was strangely, incomprehensibly, terrifyingly long. It vanished into a distant, dark point. He could hear water dripping somewhere far ahead.

Preston found his phone in his hand again. He couldn't remember reaching for it. No service. He whirled around as the elevator doors slammed shut behind him. He heard the carriage heading back to the upper floors.

"Wait!" he shouted, bashing his palm against the metal. There was no button panel on this floor. He could not recall the elevator.

Shaking and sniffling, Preston shuffled down the hallway, wondering where on earth he was. His footsteps echoed all around him, the sound of Italian leather scraping on concrete. The ground and walls were unmarked gray surfaces.

He walked for what seemed like a mile. After a long time, he reached the distant point. It was a single door in the otherwise barren hallway. Preston pushed the door open. Beyond it lay a wooden staircase that descended down, down, further into the dark. There were no lights here. The dripping noises grew more intense, but he still couldn't see any water.

"Hello?" he called out. His voice bounced off the unseen bottom and returned to him warped and faded. "Anybody here? I have no idea where I am."

Again, the cell phone appeared in his hand. Preston used it to illuminate the stairs as he made his way down. He clutched the railing with his other hand; its metal surface was warm to the touch. The stairs, like the hallway before them, seemed to go on forever. He made his way down, counting the steps as he went.

72, 73, 74, 75...

With each step, Preston felt the growing urge to turn around and run back to the elevator. It felt like he was heading the wrong direction, like he was going to a bad place. The sense of doom grew with each footfall.

After one hundred one stairs, the wooden thuds

beneath Preston's feet turned back to concrete scrapes. There at the bottom, the light from his phone revealed a metal door. Rust had nearly conquered it; the handle looked unturned for centuries. With a bit of strain, he forced it open.

It was another dimly lit hallway, similar to the one before the staircase - only, this one made a left turn. A frantic fear now gripped Preston. He walked faster. There were little metal pieces strewn everywhere, as if some appliance had been disassembled and tossed onto the ground. As Preston rounded the corner, a strange sight came into view.

An ancient, rusted bicycle leaned against the wall in front of him. It was badly damaged; one of the tires was missing and the entire frame was bent. For a moment, Preston imagined some sort of animal crawling around down here, powerful enough to crush a bike and eat its rider whole. The chubby man squeezed past the bike, careful not to touch it. His designer suit dragged against the concrete wall behind him as he snuck by. His foot came down on a puddle of water.

Still glancing at the bike over his shoulder, Preston tripped over another piece of it and nearly fell. He looked down at the ground and saw that it was no longer concrete. Heavy asphalt lay beneath him. It looked like a road. Pools of water collected everywhere. Baffled, he spun around and checked in both directions. Black pavement covered every inch he'd walked on, and spread out before him toward another door.

This door was made of old, rotten wood. Dust collected across its surface, spare one area at the center, where some sort of sign or plaque had once rested. Its outline was in the shape of a shield. Preston looked back at the bike once more; the lights flickered as he did. The scene felt distantly familiar. He carefully opened the door and stepped through.

    Preston wasn't sure if he was in a hall anymore. He wasn't even sure he was inside a building. The asphalt path he walked on stretched out before him into the yawning black. Only the light from his cell phone guided him now. It was so dark he couldn't see the walls; he wasn't sure there were any at all. The air smelled like rain, and the sound of rushing water met his ears from far off. He took a step forward, and something clanked under his foot.

    It was some kind of metal sign. Preston bent over and scooped it up. It was soaking wet. Its familiar shape fit the outline on the door he'd just come through. He studied its blank surface, then turned it over.

    "California Highway 46."

    Preston gasped and instinctively dropped the sign. It clattered to the floor, but the noise did not echo. A breeze kicked up.

    Heart thundering, Preston turned around and went back for the door. Its lock clicked audibly as he did. The sound sent him into a panic.

    "Let me out!" he screamed. "I didn't want this!" His voice was drowned out by the rising sound of water. He bashed his fists against the door, but it didn't give at all. It felt like a brick wall now. The handle broke off when he grabbed it; it had been glued on.

    "No, please," he panted, trying to avert an anxiety attack. He didn't have his medication. It was back at his desk, far, far up above somewhere. In another world. "Please God. Please no."

    Preston stood there in the dark, cell phone clasped in one shaking hand, the other brushing cold sweat from his face. Repressed memories rushed to the surface of his mind – things he'd trained himself for years to forget. The watery cacophony died away, leaving him in silence. He plodded onward, sucking in huge breaths in an attempt to maintain composure. The highway marker clattered under his foot once more. He didn't look down.

Preston's round face went flush. His glasses fogged with perspiration. His heart boomed inside his chest. He imagined himself walking a plank. The scraping sound of his good shoes on asphalt gave way to stickier, wetter noises. The sickly smell of metal overwhelmed him as he pressed on.

The dying phone's light reflected off the wet ground. It looked like black liquid, but when Preston lifted his foot and ran a finger across the bottom of the shoe, he saw dark red. A path of it stretched on another few steps and stopped at a large circle in the asphalt. When his eyes found that circle, Preston's muscles loosened. Warmth rushed through his gunky veins. A relief washed over him – not one of redemption, but one of certain doom. For Preston, it was less terrifying *knowing* what was about to happen. Before this moment, he only worried about what *might*.

The man walked past the circle. He shuffled through the dark with purpose, knowing exactly where to go. Up ahead there was an SUV; its cabin light glowed and the driver's side door hung open. He slid his hand beneath the seat and retrieved the crowbar. He didn't need to look. Then he returned to the circle and pried it open. He tossed the manhole cover aside and listened as the blood dripped down into the hole. The reek of long-forgotten death made him swoon.

He'd seen it all before. Each morning he blinked those dreams back into the depths of his mind. This place was a bit different, but Preston knew exactly where he was. He knew what he had to do to wake up again. He pulled in a half breath and surrendered himself to the darkness of the hole. His wet shoes smacked against the ladder bars, and his hands picked up the blood they left behind.

Soon he reached the bottom. Preston laughed

morbidly, and begged God one last time. But he knew that even God could not hear him where he was: a long elevator ride from the surface, and a short walk to hell. Water splashed and sloshed all around him. The air was musty and freezing cold; it made the sweat on his body sting.

The cell phone appeared in Preston's hand again. He dialed 911, but did not dare to hope the call would connect. Of course, there was no service. Not down here.

But then, the phone lit up brightly, and a name flashed across the screen.

Beth.

A flicker of hope sparked inside him. With a shaking hand, he answered.

"...Hello?" he said.

"Hey you!" a familiar voice chirped.

"Sweetheart?" Preston asked in disbelief.

"How are the boys?" she asked. "Sorry to bother you. I just wanted to let you know that I'm still out with my mom."

There was something strange about Beth's voice. Beneath the static and poor reception, her speech was different. It was brighter, younger.

"Uh...the boys?" Preston asked.

Beth laughed.

"Uh, yeah, you said it was Robb's birthday. Didn't you get drinks?"

The will to lie bubbled up inside of Preston. It was such a primal feeling that he barely noticed it as his lips moved.

"Robb's fine. I'm on my way home now."

"Okay great," Beth replied merrily. "You'll probably beat me home. Are you alright? You sound upset."

"I'm fine," Preston sighed.

"You okay to drive?"

"I...I hit a deer," he blurted out. "Didn't even see the fucking thing 'til it was too late."

In that moment, Preston had no control over his words. His subconscious simply vomited them up.

"Oh my God," Beth said. Preston heard her say something to her mother. She gasped. "Honey? Are you hurt? Do you need me to call an ambulance?"

"No! No," he replied. "No, I'm fine, don't worry. Don't call anybody. I'll be home soon. Everything's fine. I'm fine."

The call abruptly cut out. Preston pulled the phone away from his ear and examined it; *no service* flashed across the screen. He fought back a sudden urge to cry. For all these years he'd carried on in silence, wearing a thin smile over his terrible desperation.

A hair-raising sound erupted from behind him. It was the sound of someone taking a deep breath. Someone who hadn't breathed in ages. Every inch of Preston's skin crawled when he heard that noise.

He turned around and shined the phone's light out in front of him. Filthy water rushed past his ankles and flowed through a giant metal grate. Its smell was overpowered by the stink of rotting meat. Above him, something metal scraped and dragged, then clunked into place. The manhole cover had been replaced. The way out was shut.

A dozen feet away, illuminated in faint blue light, a torso rose from the water. It looked like a young woman – or what used to be one. She groaned and sputtered and threw up black water. Her face was dark and mangled; the cheek bones were crushed and jutting beneath her bloated skin. The head sat wrong on the shoulders, indicating a broken neck. The form rose to its feet and lurched toward Preston.

"Jesus...Jesus Christ, help me!" he screamed. He backed into a wet cement wall and pressed himself against it, as if trying to disappear into one of the little cracks. He shrieked uncontrollably as the woman came within arm's length.

"Please don't hurt me!" he begged. He held the phone

out in front of him defensively. Its light revealed a face like rotten porridge, with two cloudy eyes set deep beneath the surface. They peered into Preston's. They gazed past them, right down into his soul. The woman reached a flayed arm out and traced the lapel of the man's suit. She ran a brittle finger across his lips.

"What is your name?" she gurgled. Stinking water dribbled down her lips as she spoke.

"P- P- Pr-" he tried to speak. His teeth chattered and chopped up the words.

"What is your name?" the woman asked again, drawing even closer. Her face stopped inches from his.

"Preston," he managed to get out. "M- my name is Preston."

"Aaah," she breathed. "I never knew."

The man stood rigid and kept his eyes closed.

"What is my name?" she asked.

Preston whimpered and opened his eyes.

"...Katie," he said, after a long pause. "Katie Alvarez."

The woman inhaled sharply.

"Now I remember," she said. Her daisy-slaying breath did to Preston's nose what her appearance did to his eyes. She smiled, revealing a set of broken teeth, and laughed a nightmarish laugh. Water droplets splashed and sprayed all over Preston's face.

"Please," he whispered.

Katie's hands ran all over his face as if to help her remember him. Her fingers felt like slimy eels as they glided across his skin.

"How long?" she whispered back. Her eyes widened. She wrapped those fingers around his throat.

"Th- thirteen," Preston choked. "Thirteen years."

"Mmmm," she replied, digging her nails into his neck. She jumped backward, dragging Preston with her, and threw him down with unholy strength. The chubby man collided with the water and the mossy cement beneath it.

"Why did you come back?" she demanded, striding toward him. Her wet hair slapped her bare skin as she moved. Some of it fell into the water.

"I'm so sorry, Katie," Preston said, shielding himself with his arms.

"Thirteen years!" she screamed. Her voice boomed across the dark sewer and portended a horrific vengeance. "Thirteen years!"

"Please don't!" Preston sobbed. He fell silent as Katie lifted him out of the water and slammed him against a wall. She pressed her face against his; it sapped what little warmth was left in his cheeks.

"I want to hear it," she commanded. Preston desperately wanted to lie to her, and to himself, but the force in her voice pulled the words right out of his mouth.

"Okay," he breathed, shaking violently. "Okay. Okay. I was coming home. It was late. It was the last year of my Master's program. One of my friends had a birthday. I was visiting him way out in Paso Robles. We drank. I'm so sorry, Katie. I'm so sorry." Preston began to cry.

"Tell me," she pressed.

"I...I didn't see your bike until it was too late. I swear I didn't do it on purpose. It was raining so hard that night. So hard I couldn't see. I'd been drinking...I was going fast. Too fast."

Katie growled. Her lidless eyes bore into Preston. They yearned for his blood.

"I didn't know what to do. It happened right off the exit. I thought about calling the police, but it was too late. The second it happened, you were gone."

"And then what?" she asked, baring her shattered teeth.

"I got your bike off the road. Kicked all the little pieces into the tall grass. The rain took care of the blood." Preston dreaded the words spilling out of his mouth, but he couldn't hold them back. "Th- there was a sewer line. So I got my crowbar. I put you down there, Katie. I put you down there in the dark. I didn't know what else to do. I'm so sorry."

Katie did not respond. She stood there, holding her victim, frozen in thought.

"Every time I saw you on the news I wanted to die," he added. "The feeling never left me. They stopped searching after a while, but I thought about you every day. Every time I shut my eyes. Every time I dream. I wish I could take it all back."

Katie set Preston down gently and took a step back. She examined her hands, her arms, the bones that protruded from them.

"You broke me," she said, rage and anguish intersecting on her voice.

Preston sobbed. Her words sliced into him like claws.

"And you put me here," she continued. The woman dry-heaved suddenly, then spewed black water all over herself. She wiped an arm across her lips. The skin sloughed off like wet dough.

Katie's pathetic state, her misery, broke Preston's heart. His disgust with himself overtook his terror of her. He cried harder.

"And while you were off living your life," she said, "getting promotions and nice suits, I was down here in the cold. Where my mother would never find me. For a long time it was all black. I felt nothing. Like a deep sleep. But then, I began to dream. You lay in your bed and dreamed of me, Preston, while I lay here in the water. I dreamed of you. I never saw your face, but somehow I knew you all along. And though the water washed away my body over time, and scattered my bones over all those dark miles, I keep coming back to this place. Over and over."

Preston's cries fell to silence. He wished for the relief of death. He sank down into the water and sat against the sticky sewer wall.

"I can't leave," Katie said. "I have nowhere to go, and so I keep waking up right here. Maybe it happens each time you dream of me, and what you did. For so long I dreamed you'd come back and carry me out of here, up into the sunlight. But you never came back."

"Katie," Preston breathed.

"No," she interrupted. She waded toward him through the water.

Preston still held the wet cell phone in his hand. Its light flickered.

"I can take you out of here now," he said, desperation welling in his voice. "I'll show you the sun. I'll tell everyone what I did."

"It's too late," she replied. "It's my turn to show you something. I want to show you what thirteen years in the dark feels like."

Preston burst into tears and begged for his life.

"Don't cry," she whispered. "I won't do what you did to me. I won't abandon you." Katie sat down on Preston's lap and put her arms around him. She leaned her wet and rigid body against his, and nuzzled her rotting face into his neck. The cell phone flickered once more, then went off. A veil of inconceivable darkness fell, and Preston's cries of anguish were muffled by the sound of running water.

Edwin
Felix Blackwell

5 November, 1987-

There's a little boy living in my house. He's been here for sixty years.

His name is Edwin. I'm writing this to nobody in particular; I just hope that after I'm gone, whoever comes to the house is gentle with him. He needs a loving family, and I won't be able to provide for him forever.

I inherited this house from my father, Gary "Orion" Orenthal, a decorated Army sergeant who lost both his legs following the botched removal of Kraut shrapnel. At least that's the official story. He died shortly after, and this house and a bit of money were the only things he left to my mother and me. She succumbed to a rare skin disease when I was twenty, so now I'm all alone.

Well, not entirely alone. I've got Edwin, and he's got me. We grew up - or, I grew up - in this house, side by side. For the past thirty-five years we've laughed and played and told ghost stories, we've explored the woods that cut this house off from the world. We've even tried to go fishing a few times at the little lake just east of our home, but he's afraid of water so that never works out.

Edwin looks like any other six-year-old boy. He's got

platinum blonde, almost white hair, and is just as clumsy and curious. There are a few things about him that always struck me as odd, though. Edwin's skin is pretty pale, sometimes it even gets pink and patchy, so he's always got it covered with this ancient-looking schoolboy uniform. I have no idea what era that outfit is from, but it's got to be as old as this house.

Edwin gets upset. Like any child, he's prone to tantrums, especially when he's hungry. So I try to keep him fed and entertained. I simply can't deal with the screeching and the stomping and the growling. If I come home late from work (I own a small grocery store in town) and haven't fed him, Edwin will take to pitching ungodly fits and skulking around in the shadows, clawing on the walls, making messes of my father's antiques. And if he goes too long without food, his eyes get dark and sunken, his skin gets feverish and blotchy, and his teeth – well, I don't really know how to explain it – his teeth get longer and crooked. I worry about Edwin's limbs as well; they take to bending in strange ways, reminding me of a gnarled winter tree. I've tried to get him to a doctor, but he refuses to leave the property, and gets violent if forced. I once brought the town doctor over for a checkup (he's never had one), and he screamed so loud I had to ask the doctor to leave. I thought the kid would give himself an aneurysm.

Fortunately, Edwin doesn't have to eat often. About once a month is all he needs, depending on what I feed him. You have to understand, he doesn't like anything from the grocery store, he doesn't like anything I can cook; the regular food you give to kids makes him violently ill. I tried to give him Spaghetti-O's when we were kids, and he threw the bowl at me, leaving burns all over my neck and hands. No, what Edwin needs is a bit stranger than that. He's fond of hair and skin, and will take what he can get. When I was twelve, after my mom told him to leave for good, he skinned our dog Gunner and ate until the color came back to his face. Edwin tried to explain it to me; he says he was just born this way, and it isn't something he necessarily likes, but as long as he's being fed, he doesn't have to hurt anyone. He didn't want to hurt my father and my mother, and he doesn't want to hurt me.

We have an understanding now. And although that understanding has largely left me bald, my scalp scarred, and my arms permanently consigned to long sleeves, Edwin doesn't throw tantrums, and he doesn't sleep in the bed next to me anymore. We keep a regular feeding schedule, and everybody's happy. I never have to see what he becomes when he's "feeling sick," as he calls it, and I don't have to worry about my safety when I can't find him in the house at night.

But recently, things have sort of fallen apart around here. Edwin and I haven't been getting along. His fits are worse, his attitude has changed, and he just isn't the same kid I grew up with. He barely laughs anymore, and his eyes are always a tad sunken. His blonde little head is silver-graying just a bit, and he's deviating from the schedule. I can't ask him to go (who would take care of him anyways?), and I can't myself leave. I'm pretty much stuck here. He's constantly accusing me of not loving him anymore, and it breaks my heart.

I've given a lot to Edwin over the past year. Our friendship has left me with seven fingers, one ear, and most of my toes, and now he's really starting to get on my nerves. He wants more, more, more, all the time. This morning before heading to work, he asked me for my leg.

"Only up to the knee," he said, "I promise. And we can wait 'til the weekend so you have time to rest for work. *Pleeeeaase?*"

He gets me with those charming little eyes. I've been thinking about it all day, and I've decided that this is my opportunity to really prove to him that I care. Edwin can have both my legs, as a show of my appreciation for him...but if he asks me for anything else this month, I'm going to be really sore with him.

-Thomas O.

Nothing Goes to Waste
Colin J. Northwood

They say the most common fear is public speaking, but it's just about the only thing that doesn't scare me. I'm afraid of spiders, snakes, food poisoning, earthquakes, and places that are too high or too enclosed. But I can give a speech.

So I get to deliver the eulogy.

Sometimes I blame the old man for my phobias. He thought it was funny to scare me as a child. In his mind, it must have been innocent. Just a father playing with his son. I guess it makes sense; he grew up in a different time.

I exposed my arm, twisted my valve, and put four drops onto the shower's control panel. It used to be only three drops, but there's a drought.

I opened the window before stepping into the shower. Enclosed spaces.

As the warm water flowed over me, it rinsed away the sweat from my last anxiety attack. Usually I can make it through the night with only mild jitters, but I guess my father's death was beginning to sink in. I recited my speech to myself while scrubbing.

My father had seen the old world crumble all around him, and had never quite adapted to the new one. In his final years, he had quietly confided to me that the blood economy had always made him uneasy. The old man didn't want to risk his reputation, so I was the only one who knew about his misgivings. Someone a little younger than me might have been ashamed to hear him say something so crazy, but I found it endearing. After all, doubts like his were still commonly spoken in public just a few decades ago. His confession was a sign of the trust we built as he became dependent on me. But that wasn't the side of him that I had to show in the eulogy. He was a war hero.

The shower ran dry after a few minutes, but I was clean enough. I decided not to reactivate.

As I got dressed, I thought about the kind of funeral I would have wanted for him. Just me, my wife, my sister, and her husband. The people who knew him best. We could all come together to share memories and comfort each other. I think Mom would have wanted it that way, too. But not Dad. Dad was too proud for that. He was a pillar of the community, so it had to be a big public affair. I had to present him as a soldier, and talk about how valiant his deeds were long before we were born.

I would most likely not be able to hide my shame while extolling his bravery to the crowd. Even in his old age, Dad hadn't given up glaring at me whenever I used the poison detector. "That's a waste of blood," he would often say, and was unmoved when I'd respond that it was only one drop per use. "It adds up. It may be one drop per use, but you've been doing this three times a day for *years*. Think of all the blood you could have saved."

"Yeah, I know," I would sometimes say just to shut him up, but I had no intention of stopping. All that blood wasn't going to do me any good if I wasn't alive to spend it.

When I was a kid, he used to tell me about the way machines worked before the war. Fuel from under the ground. Electricity from holes in the wall. I hadn't been to school yet, so it sounded crazy to me at the time. It probably didn't help that most of his stories really were his own fanciful inventions.

That's the Dad I wanted to remember. Not the hero from before I was born. Not the shell of his former self that he became in his later years. The Dad who told us stories when we were kids.

I tied my shoes, double-checked that my valve was tightly sealed, and headed down the hall to have breakfast. With no poison in it, thanks to one more drop of blood. Screw you, Dad.

My sister and I spent our childhood on an isolated farm and had little contact with city folk. Dad had insisted on that; he wasn't happy with the direction the world was taking. In private moments, he'd sometimes talk to Mom about how the blood economy was like something out of a horror story, but I didn't know that at the time. I guess horror stories were pretty different when he was a kid.

In fact, I'm certain that all kinds of stories were different in his time, because Roxie and I were raised on them. She was six years younger than me, so neither of us had ever known the world before the war, but we still felt like outsiders.

When I was small, I was afraid of the dark. Every time I mentioned it to Mom, she admonished me to grow up. "Big boys aren't scared of the dark." When the two of them were together, Dad would nod along. But he was a little more sympathetic to me, and had his own way of dealing with things.

Dad would always put me to bed with a story. Sometimes he would read to me from old books – the kind with real paper. But I liked his improvised stories better.

My favorites were from an ongoing series about an adventurous rogue named Victor. Dad used to tell me that I was named after him, before I figured out that he wasn't a real person. Victor would travel all around the world searching for treasure. Of course, he inevitably found himself in danger along the way.

I remember when Victor was lost in the desert, and when he traveled to the moon. I remember when he had to escape the traps in a hidden labyrinth. But most of all, I remember when he was stranded on an arctic island, because that was when the met his greatest nemesis: The Dusk Serpent.

The Dusk Serpent was a sentient shadow who pursued Victor around the globe. He would often disguise himself as the shadow of a person or a tree, but his natural shape was that of a monstrous snake. Dad voiced him with a menacing hiss.

These stories were the key ingredient in my father's plan to combat my fear of the dark. Dad explained to me that shadows can only exist in the light, so Victor would have to escape by hiding in the dark where his foe could never follow him. Dad's scheme was not only cunning, but effective. I stopped asking him to leave the lights on after the Dusk Serpent's first appearance.

That's when the nightmares began. No sooner would I drift into dream than I'd find myself trapped in a narrow, endless hallway under blazing bright lights that hung just out of my reach. I would proceed cautiously at first, examining the walls and trying to see if anything lay in the distance. I would occasionally catch a glimpse of something out of the corner of my eye, but I couldn't get a good look, and I'd end up dismissing it as a figment of my imagination.

But slowly, it would inch nearer, and take a little less care to dodge my glances, until I was sure *something* was there. Closer and closer it would draw until finally I would hear that terrible *hiss*, and then I would know it was too late.

When I would take off running down the hallway, I would hear that breathy laughter just behind me. I didn't dare to look. Even dashing as fast as my little legs could carry me, I could never get away. I knew he was toying with me. If only I could make it to the dark, I'd be safe. But the hallway stretched on and on, and the glare of the lights was merciless.

Eventually, he would tire of his game and take a swipe that knocked me off my feet. I always knew it was coming, but I was helpless against it. I fell flat on my face with a brutal impact that I could physically feel even after the dream ended. But it wasn't quite over yet.

I would try so hard to keep my eyes closed as the shadowy coils tightened around me, lifted me, and held me upside down in the air. When I felt his sickening cold breath on me, I turned my head away and squinted even harder, but I was helpless under his control.

"*Dear child...*" he would whisper. The same words every time. "*Can you hear me?*"

The coils tightened and my breath escaped my chest.

"*Listen to me,*" he would hiss. "*Open your eyes.*"

I was too terrified to disobey, but every time I looked at him I regretted it immediately. Beholding those empty eyes was like gazing into the depths of hell. Somehow those featureless black orbs exuded a malice unlike any I've seen before or since. This was not the bumbling villain of Dad's stories. This was a hateful, pitiless thing whose malign expression promised me a fate more terrible than even its hideous voice could threaten. When he unhinged his jaw and stretched it to a horrible size, I somehow knew that what awaited me was worse than being devoured.

And that's when I would wake up, safe in the darkness of my room.

Caroline's valve was loose, and a ruby archipelago was forming at the side of her chair. She had breakfast ready for me before I even asked. That wasn't like her. Usually I felt a little guilty for testing her food, and for making her pretend not to acknowledge it as a sign of mistrust, but not today. Still, she didn't flinch when I scanned the plate.

"Roxie called. She'll be here in two hours." Her voice was unusually calm.

My breakfast was safe. I put the detector away. "Thanks."

Caroline stabbed her eggs absentmindedly. Without Dad, she would be the only one around to keep my eccentricities in check. She had been remarkably patient with me throughout our marriage, but she had never been my sole caretaker before. Maybe age and stress would finally start to take their toll on her. First Dad, now this. Why do these things always happen to me?

I dug into my food. "You better get dressed," I said. Normally Caroline would scold me for talking with my mouth full, but this time she just kept staring at her plate. Courtesy for the grieving, I supposed.

She put down her fork, but didn't look up. Another drop of blood fell from her valve and hit the floor. "I talked to Noreen this morning. Do you remember Noreen?"

"Yeah, of course." I lied. Her friends are all the same.

"She says Ted is really broken up. I told her they could come to the funeral if they want."

"Alright." I took a gulp of my juice.

"Victor..."

"Yeah?"

She didn't answer. Her food was getting cold, even as I finished mine.

I stood up and headed for the door. "Get dressed, honey. We have a lot to do today. Oh, and your valve is leaking."

She didn't bother to adjust it.

One night, when I was eleven years old, I awoke to the sound of Roxie screaming. At first I thought she must be

117

having a nightmare. Dad must have told her a scary story tonight, I figured. But this time it was different, because pretty soon Dad started yelling too.

 He burst into my room and picked me up before I had time to process what was going on. Even when I saw smoke in the hall, I was still too dazed to understand.

 Dad put me down outside next to Roxie and told me to keep her safe. Then he ran back inside the house to look for Mom. It wasn't until I saw the orange light on Roxie's face that I realized what was happening.

 I don't know how the fire started, or why Mom didn't wake up when we were all screaming. Dad pulled her out, but it was too late. There's no hiding in the dark from life's real dangers.

 I wish I hadn't seen her. Her hair was mostly gone and her face was swollen beyond recognition. Her skin was so charred that she looked more like an overcooked steak than a person.

 But worst of all, those eyes – burnt and blackened – seemed to look at me with that same malicious gaze I knew so well from my dreams.

 When we moved to the city, Dad's stories stopped, but my nightmares stayed with me. Living on those well-lit streets, the comfort I had found in the darkest country nights became a distant memory. Every moment I was haunted by flashbacks of those brilliant flames destroying the blanket of night over our home. Only in such bright light could so dark a shadow have fallen. Every time I saw mom in my dreams, those blackened eyes seemed to pierce right through me just as they did when I was a boy, and I was terrified of what they might find beneath my skin.

 As time went on, things only seemed to get worse. Nothing made sense anymore. The world around me reeled violently, and its dreadful winds gnawed away at my sanity. My health deteriorated, and I was losing the will to endure.

Until I met Caroline.

From that day forward, my burdens were hers to bear.

I don't know why she loved me. Maybe I was just her pet project. Someone for her to manage and to curate. Someone to make her look respectable. Someone who needed her. Someone who would never run away. Maybe she didn't love me at all. When I was young, I thought it mattered. But now we've built a life that suits us both. Two rickety spires made steady by mutual support. A durable balance that satisfies me more than love ever could.

I stood at an old wooden podium, ready to deliver my speech to a handful of friends and a hundred strangers. I connected my valve to the microphone and inserted a single drop of blood to activate it. The bright lights of the cathedral made me uncomfortable, so I looked down and pretended to read my speech from the empty surface in front of me.

"Before the war, we withheld from one another our most basic material needs. Nothing could be had except in exchange for tokens. Metal trinkets, stamped certificates, and the tallies of designated scorekeepers.

"Among the people of that time were some who hoarded these tokens. Who built empires of decadence and scarcity upon the backs of the masses. So great was the greed of the few, and so complete was the servility of the many, that countless millions starved in the streets when the scorekeepers withheld their favors.

"This was the world where my father grew up. This was the world he called home. And this tyranny was what he fought against in the war.

"So for all of you who never thanked him while he was alive, now is the time. And for those of you who did thank him, now is the time to do it again."

Applause thundered throughout the hall.

"Remember my father's generation, and remember those who fought and died for what we have today. Remember that we are the lucky ones. We may not have tokens, but we all have blood."

I felt guilty about receiving a standing ovation for this. Dad fought in the war, but the world we have today isn't what he wanted. Alas, this was the way it had to be. As the adage goes, funerals are for the survivors, not for the deceased.

My mind wandered haphazardly, even as the magistrate made the first cut into my father's throat. I absentmindedly watched his blood drain down the altar and into the goblets. I held Roxie's hand tightly while she cried and mouthed the familiar prayer.

Sanguis vita est. He will live on in all of us.

The magistrate handed his blade to me. I thrust its hook-like tip into my father's belly and made four oblique incisions that allowed me to peel away his abdominal wall. I reached inside and held aloft a handful of his viscera, revealing the morsels that would be his final gifts to us all.

Father's flesh had been marinated to perfection in the cathedral's cellar, and his blood was perfectly infused with the flavor of the wine that I had requested. His heart and tongue were served exclusively to our immediate family, while the humbler meats had to be used as garnish since there were so many guests. Everyone said it added a tender touch to the meal. Roxie scowled at me when I pulled out the poison detector. I guess a part of him really did live on in her.

I had to make a special request for Dad's bones to be buried. It may be barbaric, but that was the custom of my father's time, and I felt obliged to honor it – at Caroline's urging. I think Mom would have wanted it that way, too.

She herself hadn't had the honor of a traditional burial. In a cruel irony, and against my father's wishes, she had been cremated.

When I had eaten my fill, I looked up at a woman I didn't know and saw her holding a spoon up to an infant in her lap. She was trying to feed a little of my father's brain to her child, who was not in the mood to cooperate. A smile crept across my face.

It was in this moment that my courageous veneer began to show its cracks. I remembered being a small child myself, and sitting in my own mother's lap. I remembered refusing to eat the brain of her beloved sister, and the scolding I received from her that night. I remembered wanting to run away from home and live a life of adventure like my namesake from Dad's stories.

And I remembered the terror that stopped me: the bright lights, the narrow halls, the inescapable coils, and two eyes blacker than the night sky.

The room was spinning, and the lights above took on a blinding intensity. The walls were collapsing in. I stood up to run, but I felt the breath being choked out of me. Everything around me was white now. The brighter the light, the darker the shadow.

I fell to the floor, but the floor wouldn't hold me. I was upside down again, and being crushed by familiar coils. I always knew I would be caught in the end, but I still couldn't bring myself to look. I knew what awaited me if I did.

"*Dear child...*" came a voice from the abyss. "*Can you hear me?*"

I squinted hard and thought about a distant dream. That one where I was in the cathedral at my father's funeral. Where I was surrounded by others who respected me. Where my fears were sustainable, and the architecture of my mind was equipped to weather any storm. That place had always been my safe haven. And so, as the air was crushed out of my lungs, I found my resolve. Even in the face of certain death, I knew I had to hold out.

"Listen to me. Open your eyes."

But I didn't open them. I went back to my dream. The magistrate was standing over me, and Caroline took me by the hand to help me up. It was time to go home.

Motherbird
Felix Blackwell

Westmaple is a dark place in late October. The warm summer days finally give way to shorter, cooler ones, and the sun starts to hide behind the big redwoods much earlier. Their shadows cover everything, shrouding the world in a premature dusk by three in the afternoon. Just after the night settles in, owls fill the woods with their solemn hymns.

By this time in 2015, I was a student in my second year of graduate school, and had just moved into faculty housing with a professor I knew. The neighborhood was a quiet shelter from the din of campus housing; only young faculty members and their children lived here, and there was barely a noise to be heard. The houses were old and bunched up like cottages, nestled at the edge of a deep valley and surrounded by a thick belt of oaks and maples. Only one road led out of the neighborhood and through the open pastures up to the university. I walked up that road every day and back down every night.

I noticed something was wrong at precisely that moment between the last gasps of the leaves and the winter winds that shake the trees bare. By now I'd seen a dozen or more young children in the area, and even recognized some of them. But upon passing the old playground one afternoon on my way to school, I realized I'd never heard a single laugh, a squeal, a disagreement, or any of the familiar sounds of rambunctious kids. The playground itself was smack dab in the middle of three clusters of homes, protected on all sides by the watchful eyes of parents from their dusty windows. It was close enough to my house that I should have been able to hear kids playing on it.

Alas, despite having seen children there before, I could not for the life of me recall them ever actually *playing*. They didn't run around or exude any of the spastic energy their obnoxious species is known for. The kids in this neighborhood were more like lawn gnomes. I dismissed this strange observation as quickly as it drifted into my thoughts, and did not consider it again until one night when I went to close the blinds before bed. My window faces the street and the thicket of trees behind it. Also visible is a cement footpath that ducks behind a house and leads to the playground. Standing there on the path, about a dozen yards from my home, was a little boy. He was probably six or seven, and had no shirt on. He just stood there, without an ounce of emotion in him, looking off into the distance.

I looked across my room at the clock. It was after 10 PM. Instead of opening the window and shouting for the kid to go home, I just stared, curious about what he was up to. He remained still, occasionally scratching his belly. After a few minutes he spat on the ground and wandered up the path, presumably back to his house.

There were a few other strange occurrences that week. When I walked to class the next morning, I saw a little girl – even younger than the boy outside my window – sitting listlessly on the swings in the park. I waved as I passed, but she just looked at me with an empty gaze. Her eyes were unfocused. Hours later on the way home, I heard children mumbling to each other in the bushes, and almost stepped on one of them lying prone in the grass. He was fast asleep.

That night when I looked out the window, I saw that same little boy from before. This time he was standing in front of my car, staring intently up at the night sky. Feeling a little creeped out by all the odd encounters with the kids of this neighborhood, I decided to go outside to ask him what exactly he was doing. However, by the time I got my jacket on and went out the door, the kid was long gone. I heard a child crying from far away, but it was too faint to tell which direction it came from.

A few days passed, and I started to notice sticky black puddles all along the sidewalks. When my shoe first plopped into one of them, I figured it was asphalt, spilled by the road workers who occasionally stopped by to fill potholes. But then I saw it on the outer wall of the housing office, and on the door of a residence.

In about a week, my interest in the weird behavior of the local kids was replaced by thoughts of grant writing, endless grading, and final projects. As the semester drags on, this flood of obligations can swallow a grad student whole, and in a while, there are no intellectual resources left to commit to the real world. I didn't even notice the children anymore until one of them walked straight into me while I was unloading groceries from the trunk of my car.

It was sunset. She bumped into my leg and uttered something I didn't hear, then shuffled away like she was sleepwalking. I set the bag down and followed her at a distance, trying to figure out just what the hell was wrong with her. If she were a teenager I'd have assumed she was on drugs, but this little girl wasn't a day over seven. She grumbled as she staggered along, intermittently stopping to look up in the air all around her.

"Are you okay?" I called out from behind her.

"Mh, didn't see," she replied, more to herself than to me. She didn't stop to look at me.

"Uh, where do you live, sweetie?" I asked, trying my best to sound fatherly. I had no idea how to talk to kids.

"Up in the trees," she said, "up in the trees."

"You live up in the trees?"

"Mh," she said, "Mh, don't look." The girl studied her fingers and wiggled them. She walked up to one of the houses, pushed the door open, and disappeared into the dark.

I thought about marching up there and lecturing her parents, but that was just a dream. Confrontations were not the province of graduate tenants in this neighborhood; technically I wasn't even allowed to be renting a room from the professor I lived with. So I went home.

On the short walk back to my car, I heard children talking in the distance. Their speech was low and monotonous, like they were engaged in a boring quarterly meeting. I made a few rushed trips inside with the groceries and then tried to locate the source of their chatter, but they hushed as I patrolled the street.

"Go home!" I shouted in no particular direction. "All of you!"

I couldn't believe how terrible the collective parenting was in faculty housing.

Things got much weirder that night. I woke up in the dark to the sounds of children crying. Through the barely open window I could make out five distinct voices. Three of them sobbed, while the other two issued commands like "be quiet!" and "no, this way." I jumped out of bed and threw the curtain open.

The kids were emerging from the forest across the street and coming back to the housing complex. My gaze snapped to the clock and then back to the kids. It was after 1:00 AM.

"What the fuck is going on here?" I said aloud.

I followed the kids with my eyes as they made their way across the little meadow. When they hit the street, some of them returned to their homes, as if nothing out of the ordinary had ever happened. Two boys remained in the parking lot on my side of the street for a minute, whispering to each other. The bigger one hugged the smaller, and then they parted ways.

I made it my business to cross paths with some adults on my way to school the next day. There was a woman smoking a cigarette on her patio as I passed by, so I asked if she had seen anything strange in the neighborhood lately. She gave me a terse "No" and stubbed her cigarette out, then walked back inside. The lock audibly clicked after she slammed the door. A man and woman were loading their little girls into a minivan nearby; I recognized one of the kids as the girl who claimed to live "up in the trees." I approached to have a word with the family, but as I did, the girl saw me and made a *shhh* gesture with her finger.

This threw me off, and I stood there, almost forgetting what I'd walked over for. The father slid the panel door closed and turned around, spotting me. He looked me up and down, then squared his shoulders at me in an assertive stance.

"Help you?" he asked, eyeing me suspiciously.

I was caught off guard by his defensiveness, but then realized that I probably looked like a creep watching him and his children.

"Sir," I said, trying to present myself in a friendly way, "I saw your daughter wandering around by herself yesterday evening. She looked like maybe she was sick—"

"She's fine," he interrupted, and got into the car. That was the second time this morning someone had slammed a door at my presence.

I continued along toward campus, passing through the

playground as I usually do. Two kids sat idle on the swings, watching me as I moved. Today, there were oily, black pools everywhere: in the sawdust, on the picnic table, on the pavement. Long streams of it ran down the entire slide. I couldn't figure out what the hell it was, so I crouched down and poked a bit of it with my finger. It smelled foul.

"You guys know what this is?" I called out, pointing at the ground.

They just stared vacantly. Further up the path, a little blonde girl stood, sipping from a cup. As I passed by, she bent over and vomited pitch-black sludge down her blue dress and all over her little shoes. My stomach leaped into my throat and my breakfast almost washed back out of me in a gesture of biological sympathy. The girl then looked up at me, eyes unfocused, and wordlessly offered her sippy cup to me.

"Uh...no thanks," I said, putting my hands up. The hair on the back of my neck stood on end. I got the hell out of there as fast as I could. At the end of the path, I stopped a jogger and told him there were some sick kids back at the playground. It was his problem now.

I spent the day dashing to and from meetings with my advisor, my Qualifying Examinations committee, and my undergraduate students. I skipped dinner and instead tried to take a bite out of the mountain of ungraded essays in my office. I caught the last bus home at midnight. To my relief, there were no creepy children sleepwalking around the playground or staring at me from the bushes. The neighborhood was quiet, and only the gentle refrains of owls and crickets broke the stillness.

As I approached my house, I saw the little girl from earlier. She darted between cars in the nearby parking lot. She was heading for the meadow across the street – and probably the forest beyond it. I quietly jogged over in pursuit, and noticed two boys walking slowly across the field up ahead. The whole space was bathed in the moon's glow, but the light did not penetrate the woods. The kids disappeared into the darkness almost without a sound. Three more came from the north side of the meadow, walking along the tree line, looking for the path their friends had taken. They were carrying objects I couldn't quite make out.

I wanted to get to the bottom of this. I grabbed the flashlight I keep in my car and headed into the meadow. The faintest sounds of talking and twigs snapping trickled from the woods, so I found the kids easily enough. About thirty steps in, I turned on the flashlight and shouted, "What the hell are you all doing out here?!"

My light fell on a group of seven or eight children, all bunched around the base of a huge tree. When they saw me, they scattered like minnows, bolting in every direction and screaming as they did. I tried to chase one of them but I lost him in the mayhem. Instead of following them home, I investigated the tree where they'd met, and found that its base was littered with toys. Water guns, dolls, action figures, and even a tricycle were strewn around it like some macabre Christmas scene. Everything was stained with that horrible black slime; some of it was still dripping down the trunk.

A nauseating fear crept over me then. My skin crawled. The sky spun behind the net of tangled branches above me. Although I could not understand it, something was incredibly wrong with this place, and I could feel its malice looming over me in all directions as though the trees were alive.

The sobbing of a child interrupted my train of thought.

"Cassie?" a boy cried out. His voice was weak and afraid. "Nathan?" He cried pitifully.

I shined the light all around me, but its pale circle barely reached the nearest trees.

"Where are you?" I called out.

The boy didn't reply. He sounded very young, probably five or six. He was much deeper in the forest.

I followed the sound of his muffled crying. It took me farther east, around big trees and down a little hill. Then I found him, sitting in a clearing underneath the moonlight. I rushed over.

"Hey buddy," I said, crouching next to him. "Are you okay? What are you doing here?"

He looked up at me with a withdrawn sorrow. In his arms he clutched a stuffed animal. It was a rabbit in overalls, wearing a big smile on its face.

"I can't find my friends," he said, hugging the doll tighter.

"They left," I said. "But I can get you out of here. Come with me."

I took the kid by the hand and led him back through the woods the way I came. Even with the flashlight, it was unnervingly dark. Our footsteps crunched so loud on the forest floor I thought we'd wake the dead. *Feared*, actually.

"What's your name?" I asked, ducking under a claw-like branch.

"Robbie," he replied, looking up at the tops of the trees.

"What are you kids doing out here? Some kind of satanic ritual?" I forced a laugh, but the boy didn't return one. He held the rabbit to his chest and looked all around us, uninterested in my question.

"Robbie, how'd you get lost?" I pressed.

"I got scared," he said, squeezing my hand. He looked right at me for a moment.

"What scared you?"

The boy looked up into the trees again. He was searching for something. I stopped walking and scanned the flashlight across the canopy above us. There were many dark places that the light could not reach.

"Come on," I said, patting his back and urging him forward. A wet, sticky liquid greeted my hand. I shined the light against my palm, and saw that it glistened with a substance that looked exactly like oil. It smelled like death.

"What the hell is this stuff, dude?" I asked. "Did somebody barf on you?"

He lurched forward and coughed up a bunch of phlegm.

"I feel sick," he said, looking down at his feet.

After a few minutes we came upon the meadow. I tried to tell Robbie that I wanted to talk to his parents, but he dashed off toward the houses before I could finish my sentence. Instead of chasing after him, I surrendered to my lethargy and trudged home, even more baffled than before. This neighborhood was going to be the death of me.

When I opened my front door to go on a jog the next evening, I slipped on a Frisbee that was sitting on the welcome mat. My foot slid out in front of me and I dropped into the most graceless split ever performed; my hips made the sounds of crackling firewood, and every muscle in my legs vibrated like a plucked banjo string. I barely managed to get back up, and when I did, I spotted a little note on the ground beneath the toy. It read:

pleas give to the tree for me
i am to sick
robbie

I didn't know how to react to this. An image of the tree from the night before flashed into my mind, toys placed oddly around it as offerings. It was likely that Robbie had come down with whatever weird stomach bug all the other kids seemed to have. I had no intention of fulfilling his request, so I took the Frisbee inside to return it to him in a few days. I went on my jog, slightly hindered by my unexpected foray into ballet on the welcome mat, and then went downtown to a friend's birthday party.

It was late when I got home. My buddies dropped me off around 1:00 AM, and I staggered blurry-eyed toward the door to my home. Out of the corner of my eye, I saw movement in the meadow on the other side of the road. Something flopped over into the grass. As my friends pulled away, the car's headlights lit up two children near the trees. One was trying to lift the other off the ground. Anger and confusion welled inside of me. I rushed over, wanting to scream at them, but then I saw how sick they were.

They were a boy and a girl. The girl had that unmistakable fluid all down the front of her pajamas, and the boy had it all over his hands.

"What happened?" I asked, trying not to scare them.

The kids didn't respond. They just limped off toward the neighborhood, leaving me in the meadow. They'd come out of the woods, so I surmised that more of them were still inside. I crept across the boundary and into the dark.

I didn't have my flashlight with me, but the cries of children guided me through the gloom. Eventually I could faintly discern the huge tree. Kids sobbed and whined all around it. It was too dark to see much more than shapes, but I guessed that maybe seven more kids were out here.

I popped on my cell phone's flashlight. My own horrified gasp temporarily deafened me. The scene unfolded so rapidly that my brain didn't have time to process it.

There were children everywhere. Some lay on the ground clutching their stomachs and moaning; others sat silently, looking down at their hands. Their faces donned twisted expressions of terror and agony. Black slime caked each of their little mouths.

At the center of their congregation was the big tree, toys still scattered around it, covered in even more of the liquid than before. Something dangled from a heavy bough. I noticed two little legs first. A boy was suspended about five feet off the ground. He kicked and thrashed and reached upward but didn't make a sound. Holding him by the neck was a huge creature, wreathed in a veil of shadows, hanging upside down by some appendage high above. I could not make out the details of its body, but it appeared branch-like, as if a part of the tree itself had awakened from its slumber, and its movements made the crackling sound of bone against wood. The creature held the boy's face with spindly hands and yawned wide its terrible mouth, pouring a stream of that dark bile down into his throat like a mother bird feeding its babies. The boy choked and sputtered and went limp. The light from my phone glinted off the creature's eyes and it snapped its gaze toward me, then dropped the child and scurried back up into the darkness of the treetops.

The purest horror I'd ever felt washed over me. Every inch of my skin rippled into goosebumps, and my spine softened to rubber. Every word I tried to speak escaped my lips as an inarticulate scream. A cold little hand slid into mine, and my arm went taut as I was pulled in the opposite direction. One of the children was trying to lead me out of the forest. The others limped along behind us. They said things to me, but I couldn't stop shrieking long enough to hear them.

At the tree line, the boy stopped in his tracks and let go of my hand. I knelt down, eye-level with him. No words came out of my mouth.

"It knows who you are now," he said, fear in his eyes. "It wants you too." Then, he turned and walked away, back toward the pale yellow lights of the housing complex.

It took a moment for me to collect myself, but I finally rose to my feet. There in front of me, about ten yards away, was a little girl. She was all alone. She stood there in the meadow in a white nightgown, completely motionless, gazing up at the moon. Her back was turned to me. As I moved closer, I saw that one of her arms was a long, dark appendage that hung all the way to the ground; it was as if someone had sawed off her arm, and in its place, jammed a piece of gnarled driftwood. My breath caught in my chest. I moved past her quietly, then dashed off to my house. She never noticed me. She just kept staring up at the moon, completely hypnotized by it.

That same week, I moved out of faculty housing. I had no more questions about what was going on in that place; I just wanted out. Forever. I now live in graduate student housing. The room is a bit smaller, and the rent is a bit higher, but this neighborhood is on the other side of campus – miles away from the old one. Best of all, in this community there are no children allowed.

Chocolate is Rocket Fuel for Nightmares
Felix Blackwell

My fiancée, Faye, has an undiagnosed sleep disorder. When we first started dating, she recounted several of her most unusual dreams to me, and a few of her memories of sleepwalking. One of the stories always stuck with me. When she was a child, she climbed out of bed and crawled across the floor, growling like a rabid dog, and hid in the darkness while her older brother watched late night TV. She watched him for several minutes, fixated on his throat, then suddenly came to. She could not explain why she'd felt compelled to do that. As an aspiring horror author who was writing a book about nightmares, Faye's sleep disturbances were fascinating to me.

It did not occur to me that she suffered from night terrors until I began spending several nights in a row at her house. Night terrors are different from nightmares; they are prolonged, intense hallucinations that persist even after the person's eyes are open. The fantasy does not end upon awakening – instead it pours into reality. These phenomena occur at a different level of sleep from the one that produces regular dreams, and to find a person with pronounced night terrors is actually quite rare. Faye's are, to put it lightly, unsettling.

Each night is a new adventure when my fiancée and I go to bed. Typically the strange behavior occurs when she's under extreme stress from her job, or when she's jet lagged. Sometimes it happens when we're staying in a new place, like at a relative's house or in a hotel. Any sudden changes to her life can trigger one of these incidents, but chocolate seems to compound the issue dramatically.

The first time I experienced her peculiar quirk for myself was on Halloween in our senior year of college. We munched on some leftover candy from a party we had thrown, then went to bed. In the middle of the night, Faye sat up slowly, ran her fingers across my cheek, and said, "I want to wear this." She started laughing, then slumped over snoring.

Sometimes Faye's sleep disturbances were funny. Late one night, a year after graduation, we were in bed. She was passed out as usual, and I was next to her, writing on my laptop. Suddenly, her hand shot straight up into the air. She snapped her fingers over and over.

"Babe?" I asked, "what are you doing?"

She shushed me and motioned down toward the floor.

"There's a snake under there," she whispered. "Huge. All coiled up in the bedframe." She snapped her fingers a bit more and then covered her mouth. I laughed it off and gently rubbed her back until she returned to sleep. It works every time.

There were a few other occasions that really scared me. For two weeks straight, Faye would wake up and ask me if I could hear a child singing in the dark. I always told her no, but she persisted in her belief that there was a little kid somewhere in our house, singing about teddy bears. Another time she woke up screaming, pointing at the bookshelf across the room. She swore there was a shadowy entity in a tuxedo standing behind it, running a clawed hand along the wood.

But Faye's night terrors started to become far more acute about a month after she and I moved in together. And, of course, chocolate was the catalyst.

It was October. My birthday is on the 30th, so most people have come to associate it with Halloween. Because of this, I always receive a windfall of chocolate chip cookies and candy as gifts, and the stockpile usually lasts several weeks. Faye and I would munch on the mountains of home-baked cookies and candy bars with reckless abandon, totally disregarding its propensity to make her into a midnight psychopath.

After a few nights of gorging, Faye began to talk in her sleep. This wasn't unusual; she did it from time to time, but normally it's just babble about work or giggling. However, on this night, she said something about a man.

"Go away," she mumbled, slowly moving her head back and forth on the pillow.

I was awake, as usual, writing beside her on my laptop. I nonchalantly reached over and stroked her hair until she fell into a deeper slumber. But about an hour later, just after I had dozed off, she called out into the dark.

"Leave us alone."

As far as my fiancée's night terrors go, there are a few omens that a serious episode is approaching. One of them is clearly enunciated words. If she's talking like she's awake, it's bad. If she's actively addressing someone, it's worse. And if, God forbid, she gets upset, there's going to be a hurricane.

I snuggled up against her and said, "Everything's alright, sweetie. Go back to bed."

She exhaled sharply, eyes still closed, and responded, "I don't like him."

The next morning, as we ate breakfast, I asked my fiancée if she remembered what she had dreamed about. She couldn't recall, so I dismissed the event and didn't bring it up again. It's better not to prod Faye about her sleep disturbances in detail, because she occasionally gets embarrassed. It also runs the risk of causing more of them. So I went about the day without saying anything else, and hid the cookies in the back of the pantry. I had to deliver a lecture early the next morning, so I needed a good night's rest.

That evening we went to bed early. Faye watched a rom-com on her computer while I graded a few papers, and by the time I came back from brushing my teeth, she was fast asleep. As I leaned over her to turn off the light, I saw a Snickers wrapper on the floor below it.

"Dammit, Faye," I said, rolling my eyes. I turned over and went to sleep.

It was about 2:00 AM when I woke up to her talking.

"Why?" she said, after a string of words I was too groggy to make out.

I rolled over to see her sitting straight up, strawberry locks cascading down her bare back. She stared past the foot of the bed.

"Faye—"

"Shh!" she hissed. "Can you hear it?"

"Faye," I said, "honey, go to sleep. I really need to get some rest." I gazed up into her eyes and saw that they were closed. She looked down at me, right at my face, and said,

"Go tell the man in the bathroom..." she paused, "...he needs to leave."

The hair stood up on my arms. Faye always said stuff like this, but it still creeped me out. I looked across the darkness to our bathroom. The light was on inside, barely lighting up the edges of the door. Faye was an expert sleepwalker, so I reasoned that she had gotten up to use the bathroom, forgot to turn off the light, and then dreamed that someone was in there.

I gently laid her back down, then shambled to the bathroom. The light stung my eyes as I pushed the door open. Of course there was no one inside. I flicked the light off and stood there in the dark for a moment, rubbing my tired eyes, then went back to bed.

"Is he gone?" she muttered, falling back to sleep.

"Yeah, babe. Took care of him."

I dragged myself through the next day. I'd struggled to fall back asleep after the bathroom ordeal, so when I got home I expressed to Faye that I was upset with her for eating candy in bed. She had just returned from the gym, and her petite figure was wrapped in curve-hugging spandex.

"Do I look like I need to watch what I eat?" she laughed, leaning against the kitchen counter and stirring a protein shake.

"That's not what I mean and you know it," I said. "You've been keeping me awake. I'm just asking you to cut the chocolate for a few days."

Faye walked over to me and threw her arms around me. Even when she was a sweaty mess, she smelled good.

"I will, Poptart," she said with a big smile. "As soon as we run out."

Things got a lot worse that night. I hid the candy with the cookies and searched our bedroom for a hidden stash. I found nothing.

"I haven't had anything," she said flatly. She crawled under the sheets and buried her head in the pillows. I shut off the lights, closed the door, and joined her. As I climbed into bed I glanced out the window. It was starting to rain.

I don't know how long I slept.

At some point I jerked from a dead slumber to hear

Faye shouting in the dark,
"Stay out of there!"
She was sitting halfway out of bed, feet on the floor, staring at the door that leads into the hallway. My protective instinct surged, so I got out of bed and investigated the hall.
Nothing.
Faye murmured behind me.
"What?" I asked.
"Tell the man in the hall...he needs...to leave."
"Okay," I said, closing the door and walking back to the bed. I was exhausted and getting sick of this, but I always tried to be patient with her.
"Get out!" she screamed at the top of her lungs.
I shook her awake.
"Faye!" I whispered. "Keep it down! You're going to wake up the damn neighbors!"
She came to, and looked around with tired eyes.
"What's wrong?" she asked, confusion in her voice.
"No. More. Chocolate," I replied. I got into bed and yanked the sheets up over my head, then fell back to sleep. The last thing I heard was,
"I'm not a fucking child, Felix. Don't treat me like one."

Faye was already gone when I woke up. She typically hit the gym on her way home from work, so I wouldn't see her until later in the evening. It was my day off, so I stayed in bed and napped on and off, and intermittently caught up on my grading. When she finally got home, we had dinner together. She accepted my apology for parenting her, and acknowledged that she had been inconsiderate about my lack of sleep. We decided to watch a movie. I intentionally chose a slow and boring drama so as not to get her riled up before bed. Had she realized why I picked it, she'd probably have made me sleep on the couch.

When 10 PM rolled around, she passed out right away, but I didn't even feel tired. Instead, I stayed up writing, but this time I did it downstairs on the couch so as not to provoke any dreams. Any noise made while Faye was asleep could potentially lead to a night terror. Rain splashing against the window could conjure up a creature tapping on the glass. A movie playing on my computer could manifest people inside the room. I had to become a ninja each time she went to bed.

I sat there on the couch, wrapped up in a blanket, sipping on honey tea and revising a draft of a horror story. The little lamp next to me was just bright enough to cast eerie shadows all over the far end of the house. At about midnight, I heard a noise upstairs. It sounded like muffled footsteps. Someone was walking across the long throw rug in the hall. I quietly headed up there, intending to stop Faye from sleepwalking right off the staircase. But when I got to the top of the stairs, no one was there. The door to our bedroom was closed. I crept toward it and peeked inside.

The bed was empty.

"Faye?" I called out, flipping on the light.

She was standing by the bathroom door, lifting up one of the large framed photos that hung on the wall. It was a picture of a stream. Another frame laid on the floor nearby.

"There are windows behind these," she said, voice trembling with fear. "That's how he got in."

I rushed over, worried that the frame would fall on her head and shatter. I gently pulled her away from it, then led her back to the bed and tucked her in.

"There's no one here, sweetheart," I said, rubbing her back in a vain attempt to get her to go back to sleep. "It's just me."

"Not here," she replied, face half-buried in the pillow. "He went downstairs."

Just as she finished her sentence, there came a thump

from far off in the house, as if someone had bumped into a wall in the dark. I turned and looked over my shoulder at the door – it was closed. I thought I'd left it open when I came in. I left the room and closed the door softly behind me, then turned on the hallway light and stood at the top of the stairs, listening. Rain battered the house, and nothing else made a sound.

Maybe a tree branch fell on the house? I thought. After all, the storm was getting worse.

The lights were off downstairs, including the lamp I'd kept on while writing. Only my laptop glowed on the sofa now.

"Is someone here?" I called out, trying to keep my voice down. Only the rain replied. I made my way through the entire bottom floor, flipping on each light and looking around. As I entered the kitchen, I found an empty thermos with chocolate stains inside. It was Faye's protein shake thermos.

"For God's sake," mumbled. I turned off the kitchen light and grabbed my laptop, then went upstairs to bed. I felt like an idiot for playing into my fiancée's dreams.

Sleep came quickly, but nightmares came with it. The same one, over and over. There was a man in our house, standing at the bottom of the stairs, wreathed in shadow. He didn't feel like a person, but more like a husk. A thing imitating a human. He was no doubt the consequence of my listening to Faye's sleep-talk over the past few nights, but he scared me to death, and the dreams woke me up all night long.

I was an exhausted wreck the following morning. I called out sick from work and once again stayed in bed, intermittently seeing the shadowy figure in my dreams. Faye called to check on me twice, and told me that she would come home early to make me soup and grilled cheese – my favorite "at home sick" meal. Secretly, I wished

142

she'd stay at work late. In fact I wished I could spend the night somewhere away from her.

That night, Faye was kind enough to offer to sleep on the couch. I reluctantly obliged, knowing that I'd be in serious trouble if I missed another day of work. We took extra blankets out of the closet and got her all set up, then she came upstairs to tuck me in.

"I'm sorry about all this," she said, kissing my forehead as I lay in bed. "I don't understand why I'm like this. You should find a less creepy girl." She smiled, then I smiled.

"It's not all bad," I replied, pointing at the framed artwork for my first book. "You're pretty good inspiration."

"If you hear me talking tonight, just ignore me. I usually wake myself up if I move around too much anyway."

"Faye," I said, putting my hand over hers. "Maybe we could talk to someone about this? Maybe there's medication or something that could help."

Her eyes narrowed in protest, but instead of arguing, she nodded.

"Okay, Poptart." Her smile came back and she left the room, closing the door behind her. The rain pounded rhythmically against the window, lulling me to sleep. It hadn't stopped all week. It took only a few minutes for me to drift off.

The shadowy man appeared again in my dreams. This time he stood at the top of the stairs, looking down the hall at our bedroom door. He called out my name. I jolted awake, nearly leaping straight up into the air. I opened my eyes to see the ceiling, dimly glowing in the moonlight. The raindrops running down the window cast their silhouettes upon the surface, making it wriggle and writhe.

I took a deep breath, trying to calm myself.

The second I looked down, my heart twisted into a knot in my chest. A lightning bolt of fear zapped through every nerve in my body. He was there, at the edge of my

143

bed, holding tightly onto my foot through the blankets. I screamed in terror and pulled my legs up to my body, cowering in a ball against the headboard.

"Who are you?" I yelped. I reached over and yanked the pull chain on the lamp beside me. Light flooded the room, revealing Faye, standing there with her eyes rolled back in her head. She was sleepwalking.

"Faye!" I shouted. "You scared the f—"

She silenced me with her hand, then put her finger to her lips.

As she did, the unmistakable sound of someone moving around downstairs met my ears. The door was open, so I could hear it clearly: a long scraping sound, like a hand dragging on a wall. A thud. A chair sliding on the tile floor.

"He's here," Faye whispered.

I got out of bed and stood there next to her, straining to hear more.

A door creaked open.

Another thud.

Slow, uneven footsteps on the carpet.

"Who is he, Faye?" I whispered. She didn't respond.

"Faye...where is he?"

She turned her head slightly. Only the whites of her eyes showed. She slowly pointed downward.

"In the basement."

I leaped out of bed and stormed down the hallway in my boxers, ready to maul anybody I found in my house. As I jogged down the stairs, something caught my eye. Someone was sitting at the dinner table. Sitting in the dark. The icy feeling of death gripped my hands, compelling them to shake violently as I reached for the light switch at the bottom of the staircase. The chandelier flashed on above the table, revealing four empty chairs – one of them slightly out of place.

"Who's in here?" I shouted.

The sound of bones crackling beneath skin echoed through the dining room. It came from the short hall that led to the basement. The image of a man shuffling around my house, popping his knuckles and neck, arose in my mind. Maybe he was some drug fiend looking for pills. I grabbed a knife and the ancient flashlight from the kitchen, then made my way to the basement door.

It was open slightly. Faye and I always kept it closed to block the cold drafts that might otherwise pour in from the uninsulated basement. I poked my head inside and peered down the stairs.

There, at the bottom, was a face, looking back up at me. It was so wreathed in darkness it appeared disembodied. I couldn't make out any of its features – only an outline – but it seemed to be looking at me. I shook so hard that the batteries in the flashlight audibly clattered. Without taking my eyes off of the face, I reached over and pulled the light string, but it would not turn on. The stale air went even colder.

The face retreated into the darkness, and again, the sickly sound of bones popping echoed all around me. I turned on the flashlight and directed its beam down the wooden stairs. Its pathetic glow barely reached the bottom; I probably hadn't changed the batteries in a decade. The tiny circle of light illuminated only a few boxes and a broken vacuum.

I slowly walked down the stairs. They moaned under my feet, joining the symphony of disturbing noises that emanated from the dark. I reached the cold cement and rounded the corner, scouring the walls with my flashlight.

A box fell to the floor. I whipped the light toward the sound, and there he was. A man, facing away from me, hunched over and sliding his hands across the concrete wall. He was feeling his way around. As the light moved over him, that terrible dread from my nightmare once again took hold. I was overcome with the sense that this was not a person at all. His skin was gray and pallid, and his bones poked against it as if trying to escape. He looked like a skeleton draped in rotten ham. Big, festering sores pocked his back and arms. He was naked.

"Who..." the words bubbled up from my throat and dribbled off my lips, "who are you? What do you want?"

The man turned his ear toward me, listening for my voice.

"I'm lost," he whimpered. His voice was impossibly raspy. There was not a drop of spit in his mouth. "Help me."

He turned his bald head in my direction. The skin on his face was taut and dry, clinging to a pair of sharp cheekbones. Where his eyes should have been, black divots remained.

A frantic scream came rushing out of my mouth. I stumbled backward, falling onto a pile of boxes, and dropped the flashlight. It rolled away. The room went pitch black.

"I'm in the dark," he said, shuffling toward me. I could hear him bumping into all the clutter. "I'm lost!" he cried, rage building in his voice. "Give them back!"

"Leave us alone!" I shouted back. I tried desperately to hoist myself off of the boxes, but the man fell on top of me and grabbed me by the throat with hands as cold as death. His face pressed against mine, and his waxy lips brushed my ear.

"Give them back," he whispered.

In a burst of panic-induced strength, I threw him off of me and scrambled up the stairs. As I reached the top, I yanked the pull string one more time, and blinding light flooded the basement. I waited there, listening, but no more sounds of movement came from below. Against every instinct in my body, I descended a few steps and peeked into the room again. The man was gone.

I raced out of the basement and slammed the door shut. Terror compelled me as I made my way upstairs; every shadow in the house seemed to come alive around me. The horrible man could be standing in any of them, waiting to reach out and pull me in. The light was off in our bedroom, and when I pushed the door open, I was shocked to find Faye sleeping soundly in a pool of pale moonlight. The storm had lulled, leaving the house eerily silent. The blankets on her chest rose and fell rhythmically. Her breathing was soft and slow.

"Faye," I said, taking a seat on the bed and shaking her.

"Hm," she grunted.

"Faye," I repeated, "who is the man?"

"The what?" she asked in a sleepy voice.

"The man in our house."

"Mm," she said, her eyes still closed. "He watches...you sleep. Stands right there...every night." She pointed a lazy hand at the ground next to the bed. "So I took them. I don't like it... when he watches."

"Took what, Faye? What did you take?"

She yawned and rolled over.

"His eyes."

My fiancée and I have since heard a long list of medical and psychiatric explanations for her night terrors, all of which would have been satisfying to a person who has never seen what I've seen. But now, I sometimes ponder the supernatural causes of these events. Maybe Faye, and others like her, can access a dimension of reality that most people cannot fathom. Maybe there is a place between the waking and dreaming worlds, and maybe she can slip through its cracks on her way to sleep.

After that night, we came up with a simple solution to the problem. I now wear earplugs to bed. Faye still talks in her sleep, but thankfully, I don't hear a word of it.

Long Live the King
Colin J. Northwood

On the banks of the great river, under a shroud of mournful thunderclouds, amid a ring of jagged peaks, King Madighan IV was slain by an arrow. For twenty years he had led the armies of Korrigan Vale against hordes of invaders from the plains beyond the horizon; and on the very day that the war was won, the man was lost.

A solemn procession began. The body, strewn with garlands by his beloved soldiers, was carried back from the frontier. For leagues they carried their fallen king through all corners of his realm, and allowed the peasants to pay their respects.

Madighan had been good to his people. Despite the war, his kingdom had prospered, and was stronger than ever before. Industrious craftsmen had flocked to its markets, and the arts had flourished under royal patronage. So esteemed was he that even his enemies in the plains sent their condolences when they learned of his passing.

The mourning ceremony continued for one week, after which Madighan's coffin was laid to rest among his ancestors. It was time for a new monarch.

Madighan's wife, Elanda, had died in childbirth. Their son, Prince Erdred, the heir to the crown, was vain and heartless. The business of war, courtly life, and stewardship of the kingdom had consumed all of Madighan's time; thus, he had fallen short as a father. And now, dressed in glorious robes and standing haughtily at the gate of his ancestral palace, Erdred was ready to ascend to the throne.

Erdred had a wife, Millicent, who was chosen in order to secure the support of her father as a political ally. The couple were rarely seen together. However, she bore him a daughter, Celia, who was now nine years old. The extinction of the male line weighed heavily on the minds of the court, who would not entertain the rule of a queen in her own right. Erdred, though, neglected his wife in favor of a succession of mistresses, each of which was banished to avoid embarrassment when she became pregnant with his latest illegitimate child.

The coronation was magnificent. On the steps of his palace, surrounded by his courtiers, Erdred was crowned by Roderick, the high priest of the Vale. The new king basked in the adulation of those who were once his peers. Though he had grieved sincerely, he was eager for the chance to emerge from his father's shadow.

The preparations for the big event had been stressful, but it was in the end a happy day for Millicent, too. She enjoyed the company and attention of the guests, and was particularly glad to be visited by her parents and siblings. They were beaming with pride for the new queen, and also for Celia, whom they had not seen for two winters.

From all around the realm, gifts came to the palace: ornamental furniture, superb musical instruments, imported silk robes, and exotic songbirds in jewel-encrusted cages. But above all these, there was one gift in particular that caught the fancy of the court.

A small mirror, ordinary in appearance, was causing quite a stir. A crowd had gathered to take turns looking at it, and rumors were now spreading like wildfire. One after another they told the same astonishing story. In the silvery surface of that mirror was a window to the future.

Looking into the glass, the guests saw older versions of themselves looking back. Few were happy with what they saw, but still they could not avert their eyes. A mysterious enchantment was at work. No one thought to ask where the mirror had come from or who had brought it to the palace. It was only later that this became a topic of discussion, and in the end, no one seemed to know.

When the royal family heard about the commotion, they insisted on seeing the mirror for themselves. Celia was the first to look, and saw herself as a beautiful young woman in her twenties. Millicent looked too, and saw herself pregnant with a second child. The court rejoiced at the good tidings, and Roderick proclaimed it to be a divine omen sent from heaven to herald the new king's reign.

But when Erdred himself looked into the mirror, he saw his own skeleton, draped with bits of rotting flesh and impaled with a sword through the back. A pall fell over the celebration, and nary a whisper was heard in the throne room.

Erdred took the mirror in hand and retreated silently to his private quarters. The sight of his own decaying remains was seared into his memory; even when he took refuge in his favorite books, he could think of nothing else. Neither Millicent nor Celia was able to calm him. They too feared that his death was at hand, but his behavior made them worry that his sanity would evaporate long before his soul left his body.

That night, Erdred's dreams were plagued with inescapable death. A blade would pierce him from behind, thrust through his abdomen, and emerge from his chest soaked in blood. He would look down to see it twist and jerk skyward, creating a cleft through the front of his torso and releasing a torrent of gore. Finally, as Erdred felt the warmth departing his body, the blade would be forced upward through his heart. But every time this happened, his body would become whole again. And no matter which way he turned, some malevolent presence always lurked behind him, waiting to begin the cycle anew.

When Erdred finally awoke, drenched in sweat and gasping for air, the sun was just beginning to rise. He took another look into the mirror, and once more he saw only death in his future. For so many years, he had awaited his glorious reign. Only now did he consider for the first time that his power would one day inevitably come to an end.

But today, he was still a mighty king, and the commander of the legions of Korrigan Vale. If a dire fate awaited him, he resolved that it should not take him without a fight. The hand that held that treacherous blade would be a trophy on his wall. And since no foreign foe could breach the lines of his stalwart army, he knew exactly where to look. Erdred summoned his most loyal guardsmen and ordered them to round up every nobleman in the kingdom.

The king's court had by now all heard about the ill omen, and already were worriedly debating amongst themselves as they convened in the throne room. But when the king himself arrived with an unusually large escort of armed guards, all of their voices fell to a hush.

The entire group concurred that there was reason to fear that the killer was in their own midst, so they agreed to be searched one by one. They remained calm even as the guards restrained each of them and led them single-file to the ceremonial stone altar at the center of the room.

It was only when the first of the nobles was allowed to step forward that trepidation began to set in. For he was asked to lay his bare hands on the altar and remain still before the king as two guardsmen held him in place.

Erdred took one more look at the mirror, beheld his ghastly corpse, and spoke.

"Do it."

And with that, a third guardsman raised a gleaming sabre into the air and chopped the nobleman's hands clean off. An agonizing scream echoed through the room as the severed wrists became wellsprings of blood. In his trauma, the nobleman was unable to resist as his two chaperons carried him off – first to the blacksmith to have his wounds cauterized, and then to the dungeon, for his loyalty could no longer be presumed intact.

Panic began to break out among the remaining noblemen, but the guards kept them under control. Erdred looked into the mirror and was disappointed to find that his fate had not changed. *No matter,* he thought. *The show must go on.*

"Next!"

And so, every nobleman in the kingdom lined up to have his hands cut from his body. With each amputation, Erdred would look again at the mirror, despairing that he had not yet found the traitor in his court. Even when every one of his guests had been maimed, the face of death still mocked him from within that dreadful mirror. He frowned at the pile of hands laying before him and the horrible stains on his altar, knowing that his task was not yet done.

Next came the workmen of the palace, whose loyalty was proved as each one lost his hands and still the shadow of the king's death remained. Their severed hands were tossed unceremoniously into the corner of the throne room, mementos of Erdred's incipient reign of terror.

The maidens of the palace, noble and peasant alike, followed in the footsteps of their male counterparts, for Erdred feared that they too might have been plotting against him. Not even his own family escaped; Millicent and Celia too were mutilated. And still, the king's skull stared back at him from the mirror, gnashing its teeth behind disintegrating lips.

Roderick, the high priest of Korrigan Vale, was caught trying to escape the palace. Erdred held him in special contempt for this cowardice, and for having heralded the mirror's unusual property as a miracle. And so, rather than remove Roderick's hands, Erdred ordered the guards to break his bones mercilessly. His limbs were shattered, then wrenched into diabolical positions more worthy of an insect than of a man. His face was bludgeoned until every recognizable feature was crushed into oblivion and he could scarcely force his breath past his swollen tongue. And there on the altar they abandoned him, a quivering mass, slowly choking on his own distended flesh.

Erdred didn't care to check the mirror this time. He merely sighed and retreated to his study, exhausted yet satisfied that he had done a good day's work.

That night, his horrible dream returned. Again and again, his sacred body was defiled by the same accursed blade, wielded by the same unseen hand. What had frightened Erdred the previous night now filled him with rage. *I have sacrificed so much,* he thought, *and still the scoundrel evades justice!*

In spite of this indignation, Erdred faced the morning with renewed determination. No one, inside or outside of the palace, could now get past his guards. The killer, Erdred surmised, must be within the ranks of the royal guard itself.

And so, one by one, he commanded his guards to arrest and execute one another. With unfailing loyalty, they complied with his orders until only Erdred's personal retinue still drew breath. And so great was the loyalty of these men that, upon seeing their king's reflection taunting him from beyond the grave, they too bowed their heads before the sword. Erdred thanked each of them for their service and slew them all by his own hand.

When the young king looked upon his reflection that evening, he beheld the fruit of his labor. The sword that had impaled him through the back was gone. But alas, he found no relief, for his reflection now showed a spear through his chest and a noose around his neck.

Erdred flew into a rage and threw the mirror to the ground, but it would not break. He tried to smash it with all manner of weapons, but the glass remained unscathed. Finally, he resolved to climb the highest watchtower in his palace and cast the wretched thing to the rocks below.

Up and up the stairs he went, hurling curses at the heavens, until at last he reached the top. There, looking out over his domain, he saw the advancing armies of the plains. And so despondent did he become that, even when he tossed the mirror from the side, he was not soothed. Now, he saw the error of his ways. Too late, he saw the true shape of his doom.

With no one to oppose them, the warriors of the plains stormed the palace. Erdred, who was found hiding in the stables, was executed at the point of a spear. As a message to the people of Korrigan Vale, their king's body was hung by the neck from the watchtower. His reflection, which had not suffered a single scratch, still gnashed its teeth, hidden in the rocks below.

Cold Shoulder
Felix Blackwell

"You *bastard!*" I scream, shoving him aside.

He shouts something from the hallway, but I don't hear it. Instead, his voice is lost in the jungle of agonizing fantasies that play out in my head: *she passionately kisses him; they tear off each other's clothes like ravenous animals. He runs his fingers through her fiery blonde hair, and begs for her.* I try to shake these dark thoughts, but they take possession of me entirely. My heart is pounding in my ears, blocking out his protests. The putrid scent of unfamiliar perfume overwhelms me as I storm into our bedroom. I furiously heave pillows to the ground and rifle through the lumpy bed. If only I could find a lipstick stain, or a strand of hair...any tiny shred of evidence. This familiar rage consumes me, and everything becomes blurry. The room spins, and the foul taste of vomit creeps up the back of my throat. Even amidst my chaotic rampage, I can feel Chris watching helplessly. I can sense the guilt that wracks his conscience.

"Heather...did you take your medicine today?" he asks, gently. *Condescendingly.*

I whip around, scowling at him through teary eyes.

"Don't even try to make this about pills, you son of a bitch," I reply, striking a pillow. "I know what you're doing,

Chris. I know exactly what's going on." I square off with him, a bull before the charge. A desperate glaze clouds his eyes, and he backs away wordlessly, disappearing into the living room.

Everything is a mess now. Lately, he just smokes his cigarettes and I just paint my pictures.

One of the few things that used to calm me was standing on the balcony of our old apartment, watching the city lights of New York. They were like billions of glittering gems, each illuminating a room someone was in – maybe even someone just like me. Switching medications resulted in the loss of my job, however, and so we lost our home too. This new place is a squalid hellhole. A puke-green ramshackle nightmare that feels more like a prison than an apartment.

Since we moved in, Chris and I have become totally detached from each other. He stopped telling me I was beautiful, so I stopped wearing makeup. Or maybe it was the other way around. I can't remember. All I want, all I dream of, is to rekindle the old flames that once blazed between us.

And now, he's sneaking around with another woman.

After I inspect the room thoroughly, I give up and crawl into bed, defeated. I cover myself with the starchy sheets and bury my eyes in my pillow, sobbing. The bedroom light flicks off suddenly, and in tiptoes Chris. I hear him set a bottle of pills on the nightstand, next to that vase filled with old, dead roses he got for me months ago. I couldn't bear to get rid of them. They were the last gesture of his withering affections. Then he softly climbs into the sheets behind me. He doesn't say a word. I remain as still as death, but the stink of that vile perfume radiates from his body. I start to cry again. My brown, stringy hair is matted to my face. Now I wish I were blond like her.

Hours pass.

Suddenly, I'm jerked from a deep slumber. In a nightmare so vivid it shook me to my core, I shattered the vase over Chris's head as he slept, while screaming, "*Is she prettier than me?*" The dream soaked me in the cold sweat of terror. Now I find myself gasping the stale midnight air. The mustiness of the apartment, and of our broken love, is closing in on me. I'm drowning.

Teeth chattering, and distant screams still ringing in my ears, I lean over and wrap my arm around Chris. His warmth soothes me, and I whisper, "I'm so sorry for everything." He touches my hand, but doesn't say anything back.

I wake up early the next day, and creep quietly out of the house. It's raining outside, but I'm glad to feel the icy drops lick my skin. I want to buy fresh roses for Chris, to help our old love blossom once more, so I walk a few blocks across town. When I get home, he's still asleep, so I replace the dead flowers with the new ones and head into the kitchen to cook him his favorite breakfast, cinnamon French toast with strawberries.

"Chris...honey, come watch some TV while I make us something to eat," I call out in a melodious voice. Two forces tear me in opposite directions: the thrill and excitement of renewing our relationship, and the covetous rage inspired by vivid thoughts of his affair. I try to bury the latter in the darkest part of my mind. My blood courses through my veins like molten lava. There will be time to fight later. Right now I just want to see him look at me with joy.

As I dance into the living room with two plates in hand and a big, plastic smile on my face, I find him sitting motionless on the couch, vacantly gazing at the screen.

"I...honey...I made your favorite."

He doesn't look up. I begin to smell the faint reek of that perfume, and feel my nostrils flare in anger. I try desperately to suppress the furor boiling within me.

"Chris, you haven't even *showered* yet? You stink, and you're beginning to look pale. What is the matter with you?"

He doesn't say a word. He's ignoring me again. A lightning bolt of rage strikes my heart, and I shatter the plate against the table, spattering warm syrup and bread pieces all over both of us. The pig doesn't even flinch; he's trying to give me the cold shoulder.

We don't speak for the rest of the day. He watches a few shows and then gets into bed while I'm in the shower. I have no words to say anymore. My dream of a perfect life with the man I love has been ripped away by a hurricane of exotic perfume, and all the tears I can cry will never bring it back. And this goes on, for two more days, before I decide he's had enough space.

"Chris…" I whisper into his ear from behind, as he sits at the breakfast table. "I need to forgive you. And…I need you to forgive me. Can we do that for each other? Can

we talk?" Once again, silence is the hole that sinks my ship. I reach out to put my arms around him, but his back muscles are taut with anxiety. I recoil, and tears begin to drip down my face, washing away the shred of hope I desperately cling to.

Despair anchoring my footsteps, I sulk into the living room and drop heavily onto the couch. The tight grip of my sadness drags me ever downward, and I fall asleep with the television on. Wild dreams drift in and out of my mind, and then there is nothing.

As I come to, I hear familiar voices nearby. I crack open my eyes, and I'm greeted by the TV's relaxing glow. It's my favorite movie. The one about the professor who has an affair with his student. I remember it so well that it almost feels real:

She passionately kisses him. They tear off each other's

clothes like ravenous animals. He runs his fingers through her fiery blond hair, and begs *for her.*

Oh, how I love this movie.

And then, I experience another fleeting moment of clarity.

No matter how much I pretend that Chris is still here, I can no longer do this to myself. I can move him into any room, or dress him up in any clothes. I can tell him how much I love him, or kiss his cold, stiff face. I can tell him, "I was wrong," over and over. But I can never, ever hear him say, "I forgive you, my darling...I still love you." I can never bring him back.

I will never forget to take my medicine again.

inbetween
Felix Blackwell

"These little ones are baby universes."

That is what she said to me. That's what she said as she placed the blue things into my hand and smiled. I said nothing, because at the time, I didn't know what to say. Now, I know I was right not to say anything, because there could be no words to describe or relate what was about to happen to me. I said nothing at all. I just walked away, out of the meadow I found her in, out of the woods I'd wandered through to get there. I didn't look back. I just assumed she crawled back into the soft soil hole where she lived. I briefly imagined her in the grasp of voracious roots, becoming ensnared beneath the earth and periodically running her black, twiggish fingers through her oily hair. I imagined her falling back to sleep, dormant for another eon.

When I got home, everything had changed. I was alone. Most of the elegant furnishings of the house had fallen into disrepair or had gone missing, as though my world had shifted toward another dimension but had gotten stuck halfway there. The sun was visible through my window, but it was suspended lifelessly, and emitted a dry, purplish light that cast the room in an uncomfortable glow. There was no way to tell what time of day it was – or for how long

the sun had been stuck there in the empty sky.
Everything was still.
Still.
So still that a whisper would fall, clattering to the ground before anyone could hear it. No one was around. There was nothing but stillness.

My body was cold. My limbs were marble slabs that scraped and thudded loudly across the tile floor as I drifted aimlessly around the house, looking for something just beyond recollection. I was like a ghost, searching hopelessly for someone to haunt. All the food in the refrigerator had melted or rotted, but even if it was edible it would be of no use to me. I was busy chewing on broken bits of the grandfather clock that had died some time ago. Its pieces were strewn about the living room. The wooden pieces had little oxygen bubbles in them, which assisted me in breathing as I waded slowly through the hallway. This hall was completely filled with water and had smiling fish floating in it. The fish were unmoving, unblinking, and they stacked perfectly together into complex geometric shapes.

While observing their stacks, I had forgotten to continue chewing, and therefore ran out of air. As I struggled to escape the hallway, one of the many hundred doors on either side creaked open, and all of the water rushed out, draining me and all the shapes into a featureless void of black.

Everything was still.
Nothing was still.
The abyss.

I worried that I had ceased to exist, and became concerned that this was now a permanent state. I felt a drop of blood trickle from my neck and down my spine, so I reached my left hand back to touch it. In doing so, I realized that my finger had been in my ear, and now that it was removed, I could hear a little. I could hear blood dripping all around me. I touched my back and felt the blood, then removed my right finger from my right ear. Now I could hear well. Blood was splattering and sloshing all around me. My breathing sounded so mechanical it was as if it did not belong to me. It frightened me that I could not see what I was hearing. The void was so dark and endless.

With both hands free, I could rub my eyes. When I did so, I saw tiny slivers of pale light. I realized now that my eyes had been closed, which had cloaked me in darkness. After a brief pause, I opened them.

I was not in my house, nor in the void. I was in the woods, at the bottom of a steep gully. It was not blood that splashed all around me, but rain. And the rain made mud. Lots of mud. I floundered and struggled there in the pit, trying desperately to escape it, but the slick mud imprisoned me down there. I looked up and witnessed the awesome storm clouds which darkened the world and mercilessly drenched me. I cried out and reached up for branches; they cut my hands and arms. This time, I bled.

If I couldn't get out, I'd drown in the rainwater. I feared for my life, and I had no more clock bits to chew. So I resolved to live. If I could not escape by climbing out, I would escape by digging in. I used my hands, which now looked more like black claws, to strip mud and earth away from the ground. My inky hair clung to my face and blinded me. I didn't care. I was going to live.

I tunneled for hours. I burrowed like a sightless mole through the earth.

Finally, I erupted from my chthonic prison. I saw the bright, sunny sky, and heard the birds chirping gaily. I felt the breeze coming through the hills and down into the meadow in which I stood. In the distance, a boy was waiting for me. He hesitantly approached.

I looked at him, and paused for a moment – then

reached my hand out, and gave to him a few blue things.

"These little ones are baby universes," I said.

He said nothing, and walked away. He walked out of the meadow he found me in, out of the woods he'd wandered through to get here. I climbed back into my soil hole, ran my fingers through my hair, and fell asleep amidst the tender strangle of the cool, wet roots.

Kismet
Colin J. Northwood

Day One

Shelter.

I absentmindedly scratched the back of my neck as I checked my email. Nothing. Again. This dating website is worthless. No, not the website. Me. I'm worthless. Not worth a goddamn email.

Amy had been gone for two months now. We were going to have children together. We were going to finish each other's sentences.

I thought about what the television had said to me last week. "More fish in the sea." The biggest cliché in the world. It's hard to believe people still say that.

Fish. In the sea. Of course there are fish in the sea. But the sea is a vast abyss with a little life clinging to the edges. Maybe it's not such a bad metaphor for my existence after all. I snickered at the thought, and the movement of my tongue reminded me again of the metallic taste that I had grown to hate so much over these last few weeks.

With a sigh, I pulled the gun out of my mouth, wiped the barrel on my pants, and tossed it back into the drawer beside my bed. What a coward I am. Next time, I'll do it. I know I said that last time. But still, next time.

We had bought the gun for self-defense, back when this apartment had someone worth defending. Now it's an instrument of self-destruction. Amy would appreciate the irony of that, if I pointed it out to her. Maybe I will, if I leave a note. I'll try to remember that next time, with the whiskey's permission. I'm going to have a wicked headache in the morning.

Shit. I have to work.

It took me a while to get comfortable enough to sleep. Comfortable with my thoughts, but also comfortable with this damn pillow. I think I need a new one.

Day Two

Awareness. Home.

I felt like a hammer was smashing my head when my alarm clock went off. 6:30 AM. I need to quit drinking. So I don't kill myself. But mostly so I don't have to endure headaches like this. I can barely move my head, let alone get up. But I need to get to work. In case I live through the week.

Although my head still hurt and refused to move much, I felt a little better when I got up and dragged my feet out the door. I wore the costume of a civilized person, and reassured myself that, with minimal effort, I could still fit in with other humans.

I played a good impostor on the train. So good that I could detect no suspicion in their glances. When I got off the train and headed for the office, they still seemed bored. All of them. They probably wouldn't notice if I just shot myself right here and now. Maybe I'm just not that interesting.

Hannah did notice my condition, though. I could dress up and walk like a real man, but I couldn't hide the scab on the back of my neck. I didn't remember where I got it, but I humored her with a story about a kayaking accident.

"Yeah, Hannah. I'll be more careful." I sported a fake and glassy smile. She was cute, but married. A little older than I like, but I still want to fuck her.

She wasn't happy with my answer, but I changed the subject. It's an easy thing to do, once you figure out how much people love to talk about themselves. I turned back to my desk and started typing again while she went on and on about her kid. She frowned a little bit, patted me on the shoulder, and went back to her desk. Patronizing bitch. I've already got a mother.

She was right about my neck, though, and now it was beginning to swell up. When I applied a little pressure, there was a pain that didn't feel like my own. What the hell did I do last night? Okay, no more booze. For real. Unless I need some extra courage.

When I finally called the clinic to make an appointment, I felt a twinge of fear. I don't know why. Maybe I'm ashamed of the state of my life. I guess I resent having to be under scrutiny, even if it's just a medical exam. They'll probably give me some good painkillers, though, so I'm nervously looking forward to it. Pity has its advantages.

Day Three

Am I...?

I didn't drink last night. I slept pretty well, thanks to my exhaustion from the previous night. It's Saturday. And there's an email. A woman who wants to meet me for coffee. I hate coffee, but I'm in no position to refuse. Yes, tomorrow is fine.

For the first time in weeks, I noticed the sun peeking through my blinds. Maybe the weather had been shitty, or maybe I just hadn't taken the time to notice when it wasn't. I tasted my breakfast – also for the first time in weeks. It pleased me to notice that my toast was burnt. I stretched out a bit, reveling in my rediscovery of dim sensations. I had something resembling a thought about all of this, but it wasn't fully formed. Like the primal cooing of an infant.

I laughed at how stupid I felt. Months of loneliness had gone up in smoke. How could I have taken myself so seriously? No wonder Amy never did.

On my way to the clinic, my inarticulate bliss continued. I had felt so alone for so long, and it was gone so suddenly. I whistled to myself, and felt almost like it echoed inside of me. Maybe I don't need those painkillers after all.

But when I stepped inside the clinic, I felt inexplicably confused. Nervous. Betrayed.

The nurse seemed concerned about my neck. The scab was healing normally, but the swelling had not subsided. When touched, my lump responded with a pain that echoed like my whistle. She left the room to get another nurse.

Why are we here?

What...?

The other nurse wasn't much help to my neck, and wasn't much to look at either. She made an appointment at the hospital next week for me. It's probably no big deal, she told me, but if it gets any worse I need to notify the doctor whose number is on the appointment card. She gave me an ice pack, but no pills.

Day Four

Good morning, John.

From an unusually vivid dream, I finally awoke. Or at least, I think I did; I can never be sure when I'm on these...wait, no, I didn't get any pills. I didn't even drink. Maybe this is what sobriety feels like. It's been so long I can hardly remember.

4:30 AM. Goddammit.

I yawned and checked my email. One new message. A reminder from that woman to meet her this evening for coffee. Yes, I remember.

In the shower, I felt a spasm of pain from the back of my neck.

Sorry, John.

What the hell was that? The words seemed to come from everywhere at once, just like in my dream.

I spun around in a panic and almost slipped.

"Who's there?"

No answer at first, but then...

John, don't be frightened.

Now I knew it wasn't a voice. It was inside my head. Maybe I had quit drinking too suddenly.

Then, another surge of pain from the back of my neck. It's time to call the doctor. I scrambled for the card I was given yesterday at the clinic and snatched up the phone.

Two rings later, the doctor's receptionist answered.

No, I won't hold.

I began to incoherently sputter out my concerns. My depression, my drinking habit, the crazy talk in my head, and this damn swelling on my neck.

John, please...

I froze, feeling a mixture of shock and, inexplicably, guilt. I was so caught up in reacting to the emotion in those words that I nearly forgot about the receptionist who was still on the phone. I interrupted her mid-sentence. "Um, sorry. I need to call you back."

I tossed the phone to the floor and felt my head spin with confusion. What the hell is wrong with me?

I mean you no harm.

Still panicked, I rushed back into the bathroom to wash my face, talking to myself all the way. "Whoever you are, get the fuck out of my head!"

Not your head.

Suddenly, I had a horrifying thought. I turned my back to the mirror and saw that the swelling had begun to creep down my spine.

Hello, John. Nice to meet you.

Then the world went black.

A familiar metallic taste revived me, but this time it wasn't my gun. It was blood.

For a moment, I struggled to remember how I ended up on the bathroom floor. I guess I must have bitten my tongue on the way down.

My memory didn't fully reassert itself until I heard the voice again. Or rather, regained awareness of thoughts inside my head that weren't my own.

Please be careful, John.

This can't be real. There's no way this is real.

I crawled out of the bathroom on my hands and knees. I'll never look in that mirror again. I must not be fully awake yet. I laid face-down on my bed, quivering and unnaturally cold.

After some time, my nerves began to calm. As this happened, I became increasingly aware that I was experiencing a second set of visceral sensations to accompany my second set of thoughts. I touched the back of my neck and yelped in response to the sharp pain that greeted me.

I'm here, John. Please be gentle.

My face reddened, and a few tears threatened to emerge. This time, it was pity that I felt. I had pitied myself for so long just for having ordinary problems, but this was...

I fumbled for the drawer next to my bed. Maybe it's finally time.

John, you're scaring me.

I slowly opened the drawer, retrieved my firearm, and

put it back inside my mouth. That's its home. It belongs in my mouth. The bullet belongs in my brain. It's meant to be. And my brain is meant to be a glorious splatter on this wall.

But then, something else overtook me. I've spent so much of my life feeling joy and sadness, excitement and boredom, fear and pity – and always for myself. But this time was different. This time, I could feel the fear of a second mind and the pity of a second heart.

A mad laughter erupted from my mouth at this thought. All that time with Amy. All the other ones before her, too. I even told some of them I loved them. Maybe I meant it. But this was different. After all of that time trying to connect with other humans, I had never achieved the level of intimacy I was now sharing with a parasite living on my spine.

I tossed the gun back into the drawer.

I'm sorry, John. Please understand.

"What is there to understand? You're a worm living on my back."

Not a worm.

I felt a little bit of guilt, and then scolded myself for it. This thing is a parasite, not my friend. It may be able to invade my thoughts, but – wait. "How the fuck are you even talking to me? How am I having a conversation with a tapeworm?"

I live inside your body, John. I communicate using your internal network.

"Internal network?" I began to laugh again, but slowly fell silent as I realized what that must have meant. I remembered the sudden episodes of pain that had struck me earlier, and now it all made sense. This thing wasn't just on the surface of my spine.

"This is insane. That's invasive, and just...evil. But you know what? I'm going to see that doctor in a few days, and I'm going to tell him exactly what's going on, and he's going to rip you out of me if it kills us both. And frankly, I don't mind if it does. You picked the wrong host, you son of a bitch."

I'm afraid, John.

"You should be afraid!" I began to laugh again, and allowed myself to slip into a lucid calm. In some small way, I had asserted control over my life. But no smile and no words of determination can fool a thing that sees into your lizard brain.

Just then, my alarm went off, as if to usher me back into real life. I grabbed a turtleneck and tried to remember what a human is supposed to eat for breakfast.

I couldn't help but laugh out loud at the dull faces on the train today. Ho-hum. Going to work at your stupid job. Reading the stupid newspaper.

Hey Hannah, how are your stupid kids? Oh, a cold. You don't say. Fascinating.

Hey, Desk. Hey, Laptop. Good to see you, too. Do you have any stupid kids to whine about today? No? Excellent. You're wonderful people.

Do I have any kids? Why yes, I do. On my spine. I call him Joey, because he reminds me of those ugly red worms that crawl out of a kangaroo just to prove that Mother Nature is disgusting.

Hey Joey, what do you think of that?

A name?

Yeah, a name. I'm gonna call you Joey.

And you think of me as your own child?

And with that, I burst out laughing again. I could no longer keep it to myself. The whole office fell silent and stared at me. I guess you all want an expression of shame? You're gonna be waiting a while. Get back to work, dipshits.

But yeah, Joey, I guess I'm your surrogate mom. Hannah and I can sit around yapping about mom stuff, now.

I'd knit you some little mittens if you weren't a worm.
Not a worm.
Yeah, I know. Not a worm.

I didn't get much work done that morning. Just talked to Joey. Made sure he knew who was boss. Just like my father did. But my father never spent this much time with me. And I never listened to him anyway. Probably because my life didn't depend on it. But Joey's did.

When I stood up for my lunch break, the pain returned. Knees weak, teeth grinding. Sitting back down, but it's still getting worse.

Fuck, it's too much. Don't you tell me you're sorry again.
John, it's my growth cycle. I can't control it.
I'm gonna kill you.
I know, John. You can kill me if you want. I'm at your mercy.
At least you listen. Amy never did that.
I have to listen, John. You're the entire world to me. I'll die without you.
You'll die with me, too.
Maybe so, but it doesn't have to be this way.
Listen. It's nothing personal. But this has to stop.
So you're going to the doctor, then?
What else can I do? I can't live like this.
John, I need a host, but...
But what?
...but it doesn't have to be you.

On the way home, I thought about my upcoming date. Coffee with the woman from the website. Joey didn't have any advice. Surprise, surprise. It turns out that parasitic worms don't know much about dating. Watch and learn, Joey. This one's gonna be a slam dunk. This one had better

be a slam dunk.
Promise me you'll go through with it.
I promise.
Good. Now watch and learn.
I know how to do this, and I showed it all to Joey. Father to son. The birds and the bees.
First a smile, then coffee. A gentle look to lure in the prey.
She doesn't know you're trying to mate with her?
She knows. She just isn't allowed to act like it.
Why not?
She has to pretend to not be a slut, and I have to play along. It's part of the human mating ritual. When she gives in, she's supposed to say that she doesn't usually do this.
Soft laughter. A touch of the hand. The deal is just about sealed now. All I have to do now is keep steady, and keep listening to her yammer.
John...
Yeah?
Do you think she'll let me in? Can you convince her?
Fuck no. You're gonna have to get her the same way you got me. Wait until she's out cold. Until then, you have to stay hidden. Or else you're gonna ruin my chances. And yours too.
Cigarettes. Touching her hair.
Why do humans smoke cigarettes?
I dunno. Why do you ask so many stupid questions?
Two glasses of wine. Call a cab. Bring the bottle. Yes, you can stay.
Close your eyes, Joey. This part's not for kids.

Day Five

Alone again. Always alone again.
She got up this morning and didn't say a word to me.

Just got up, grabbed her stuff, and went right out the door. But I saw the scab on the back of her neck. Enjoy your new pet.
 I feel a little bad about it. Not for her, but for Joey. Maybe I should be proud that he's leaving the nest and spreading his wings. But just like a real parent, I'm feeling a little bit useless without him. No one needs me anymore. Oh well. Life goes on. Time to get up and get on with it.
 Fuck you, toaster. Stop burning my goddamn toast. I need a drink. Or four. To kill this headache. To kill this...
 No. No no no no NO. You promised.
 John, I'm sorry. I didn't know.
 Didn't know what, exactly?
 I thought I could—
 But just as I can no longer lie to Joey, he can no longer lie to me. We've grown too close. He wasn't trying to move to a new host – he was trying to reproduce. And now I know that he was using me all along. A parasite using its host. Who would have thought? It's the most obvious thing in the world. Kids use their parents, parents use their kids, and Joey used me. It's the cycle of life. The snake swallows its own tail.
 Well, guess what else you're about to swallow?
 John, please. Put the gun down. I can explain.
 I bet you can.
 —Click—

174

Spike
Felix Blackwell

"It's a wolf," Camilla said, whacking the old wooden fence with a stick. A strange groan resounded from the other side, like a human's cry of pain escaping from an animal's throat.

"No," said Ethan, "it's a bear." He tried to peer between the slits in the fence, but he could only make out a rough shape. It sulked away, back to the house it came from.

"It's got a long tongue. I can hear it." Camilla leaned toward her big brother and spit her tongue out of her mouth, wiggling it all around. She managed to lick his ear before being shoved away.

"Gross!" Ethan yelled, loud enough to embarrass himself. His sister had lost a tooth earlier that morning; he worried that her mouth would smell like blood.

Camilla laughed at her brother's squeamishness and walked across the yard toward the tree house. "Maybe we can see it this time?" she speculated, climbing up the boards.

"We can never see it," Ethan said. "Not from there."

Camilla conceded and jumped off the second step. The wood creaked as she did. The nails in the board were coming loose from years of heavy use.

Behind them, Dad slid the glass door open and came

out onto the patio.

"Who...wants...hot...dogs?" he asked in a Frankenstein voice, holding up a bottle of mustard and lurching stiffly toward the kids.

Ethan and Camilla bolted across the yard, screaming in excitement as they went. They made their way into the kitchen, where Camilla snatched a hot dog off the plate and plowed mouth-first into it. Ethan washed his hands for sixty seconds and then carefully chose a hot dog.

"You are the most stressed-out eight-year-old I've ever met," Dad said, patting his son on the back. "You must get it from your mother."

That night, the kids lay in their bunk bed with full stomachs. Ethan drew in his sketchbook while his sister, high above, fidgeted around and spoke her every thought.

"You're shaking the bed," Ethan said. "Stop it."

Camilla purposely flipped around onto her stomach, causing the whole frame to shudder. "I think he's lonely," she said.

"Who's lonely?"

"The thing in the neighbor's yard."

"Nobody cares," Ethan replied, annoyed with his sister's babbling. He began shading the lunar landscape he'd drawn.

"That's why he's lonely, stupid," Camilla said.

As if on cue, a gruesome howl erupted from beyond the bedroom window. It wafted in with the cricket songs from far away, and set off a half dozen dogs throughout the neighborhood. Now the night air was raucous with frenzied barking.

"He's hungry," Camilla persisted. "That old witch always leaves him out there."

"Shut up, Camilla!" Ethan replied, trying to dissuade another one of his sister's bad ideas.

"He's probably cold, too!"

Ethan dropped the sketchbook to his lap and let his head go limp on the pillow.

"Will you please just go to sleep?" he said, sighing. "Just for once?"

Camilla jolted straight up in bed. Ethan felt his mattress sway.

"Let's give him some hot dogs!" she chirped. Her voice was so shrill with excitement that Ethan immediately shushed her.

"*Do you want dad to hear?*" he whispered angrily.

It took Camilla a half hour of pestering to persuade her brother into joining her – a new record time. Despite Ethan's opposition to his sister's troublemaking, she was intractably persistent and knew exactly how to wear down his will. The two snuck downstairs, careful not to disturb Mom and Dad, who were cuddling on the couch watching a boring grown-up movie. They snuck to the fridge and grabbed the mostly empty packet of hot dogs.

"You think this is enough?" Camilla asked, dangling the package close to her brother's face. It dripped cold hot dog water on his shirt. Ethan slapped her hand away and pushed her toward the sliding glass door.

"Just keep quiet," he said.

It was cold outside. Fall had arrived a few weeks ago, and the night air was starting to bite. The kids moved across the yard, careful not to activate the motion-sensing lights on the left side of the patio. As they approached the back fence, another lonely howl seeped through it.

"Toss 'em over and let's go," Ethan whispered.

Camilla obliged. She whistled softly, trying to get the animal's attention. It gurgled and trotted over. Its form brushed against the fence as it passed.

"Got you a little present," she said, barely able to

contain her excitement.

She carefully slid a hot dog out of the package and tried to lob it over. It bounced off the fence and fell back down onto her face. She burst out laughing, immediately inciting a loud "*shhhh!*" From Ethan.

"You throw like a girl," he said, yanking the package out of her hand and pulling another hot dog out. "Do it like this." Ethan catapulted the meat up into the air. It twirled and flew in a perfect arc, landing in the grass on the other side. The animal grunted and trudged over to the new object. It sniffed for a bit, then made a grotesque slurping noise. All the while, the creature groaned in misery.

"Jeez, what the heck is wrong with that thing?" Ethan asked, more to himself than to Camilla.

"Let me try!" she said, stealing back the package. She flung one much softer this time. This one fell dead on the lawn before it even reached the fence. Ethan failed to contain his laughter.

"Shut up, idiot!" Camilla shrieked. Ethan shushed her again. A dog barked in the distance, and a light turned on in the house beyond the fence.

"You're gonna wake her up and she'll come over here and tell Mom and Dad," Ethan whispered into his sister's ear. "Keep your mouth shut!"

Frustrated, Camilla fished the first hot dog off the ground. She wound up and pitched it hard, sending it flying well over the fence and across the neighbor's yard. It smacked with a wet *thunk* against that house's sliding glass door. The kids exchanged glances of terror and froze in place, too afraid to make a sound.

Indiscernible shouting erupted from inside the woman's house, growing louder as she approached the glass door. It slid open and crashed against its frame, inciting a frightened yelp from the creature in the yard.

"Spike!" a woman screamed, loud enough to set off all

the neighborhood dogs again. "Get in here!"

Camilla and Ethan listened as the thing shuffled obediently into the house, groaning as it did. They held perfectly still in the dark, praying that the woman didn't know where they were.

"Leave him alone, you little brats!" she yelled across the yard. A sheet of phlegm crackled over her voice; she must have been a lifelong smoker. She slammed the glass door shut and continued her shouting inside the house. After a moment, the racket died away and the gentle sounds of the night resumed.

"Satisfied?" Ethan whispered, glaring down at Camilla.

"I gotta see," she replied, ignoring his anger. "I have to."

Against her brother's protests, Camilla retrieved a chair from the patio. She climbed onto it and reached up to the top of the fence. The dew-covered wood slipped under her hands, but she managed to hoist herself up a few feet. Her eyes rose just over the edge, enough to allow a quick glimpse into the neighbor's yard.

"What do you see?" Ethan asked, tugging on his sister's shoe.

"It's dark," she replied. "There's...stuff everywhere. Gross stuff."

The neighbor's yard looked exactly the same as Camilla's, except the patio had a bunch of mud all over it. In fact, the dim light in the house revealed mud all over the carpet too. The dog – or whatever it was – must have tracked it in every time the woman called its name.

"I think I see him," she whispered.

"What?"

"Spike."

Camilla adjusted her grip on the fence. As she did, something sharp slid deep into her pointer finger, immediately causing her to let go. She cried out in pain and tumbled down to the ground, smashing against her

179

brother's feet as she did. Ethan picked her up and examined her hand as she held back tears.

"I think it's a splinter," Camilla said, barely able to maintain her composure. A single trickle of blood ran down to her palm and dripped onto Ethan's fingers. He jumped back, throwing his sister's arm away as he did. She winced in pain.

"It's uh, it's...it's gonna be fine," Ethan said, hyperventilating. He paced around in a small circle with his tainted hand outstretched, trying to distance himself from the blood. "Let's go back inside." As usual, Camilla was amused by her brother's phobia, and tried to reach for him.

"It's okay," she said with mock sympathy. "Hold my hand, you'll feel better!"

Ethan bolted back to the house. His sister followed behind, cackling with delight.

The two grabbed some bandages and snuck up to bed. That night, Camilla lay awake, nursing her sore finger and entertaining thoughts of what kind of strange creature lived next door. She had to know. Below her, Ethan slept well, certain that their adventure was over.

By morning, the children had mostly forgotten about last night's escapades in the yard. They watched cartoons and rode bikes, trying to make the most of their waning Sunday. Just as the sun touched the horizon, they agreed to a game of hide-and-go-seek with the neighborhood kids.

"Seventeen...sixteen...fifteen...fourteen..." a little girl chanted, covering her eyes with both hands. The other children scattered; Camilla tore down the block and leaped into a hedgerow for cover.

"Camilla!" Ethan yelled after her, unable to keep up. "That's out of bounds!"

"Nine...eight...seven..." the girl continued.

Ethan looked frantically in all directions. He gave up

and slid between a trash can and a recycling bin sitting at the edge of a driveway. He held his breath and instantly rued the filthy hiding place.

The chase was on, and the little girl blazed after two boys she'd flushed out of an open garage. Ethan took the opportunity to sneak back to the base (the street lamp where the girl had been counting) and tagged it, ensuring his own safety. He watched the drama unfold from afar, feverishly trying to brush the trash can's germs off his shirt. The children played new rounds until it was completely dark.

When he heard Dad's voice from down the road wrangling the kids up for dinner, Ethan realized he hadn't seen Camilla in a long time. She had never come back from her hiding place during the first round. Ethan assured his father that he'd go get her and be home in a few minutes.

"Cammy?" the boy called out, poking around in the bushes. He walked up and down the street calling her name, but received no answer. He turned right on the road just past the hedges where he'd last seen his sister; it looped around toward the mean woman's house.

A wet, lazy barking sound echoed through the neighborhood, momentarily silencing the crickets.

"You didn't," Ethan muttered, fearing that his foolish sister had again tried to get a peek at the strange animal. He stood before the woman's house and considered knocking on the door to apologize for the recent string of annoyances. He took a deep breath and marched up the empty driveway. As he stepped onto the welcome mat, something sharp slid up through his shoe and burrowed deep inside the arch of his foot. A lightning bolt of pain exploded up his leg and into his skull, and then the world went sideways. Ethan caught a glimpse of the stars and heard the *smack* of his body against the porch. Then, the darkness of the night sky embraced him.

Ethan woke up in a pile on cold cement. For a moment he thought he'd awoken right where he'd fallen, but there was no welcome mat anymore. There were no stars, no front door. Instead, there were walls and wooden support columns. A tiny amount of light trickled into the room from a slit high up on a far wall.

A basement, Ethan thought. It was big, just like the one in his house, but this one was dark and unfurnished. The air was warm and heavy with humidity, and an odd stain blackened the floor. Worst of all, it stunk like nothing he'd ever smelled before; not even Dad's feet reeked this bad. It was foul and acrid, like metal and the sickly sweetness of rotting chicken.

Ethan's heart hummed in his chest. He pulled himself up to his feet, but was dragged down by the heaviness of his head and the acute pain in his foot. He poked at the injury; for some reason his shoes were missing. Ethan realized then that he'd felt this way before. Two years ago when he'd woken up from a tonsillectomy, it felt sort of like this. Dull. Disoriented. Numb.

"Hello?" he called out. His voice sounded strange in the air. The room tilted slightly, as though he were on a boat.

Another sound rang out in the darkness: a tiny whimper. Ethan instantly recognized it as Camilla.

"Cammy? Where are you?" he whispered. There was no response, so Ethan crawled forward. At the end of the long room a pair of little feet came into view. He squinted through the gloom and recognized his sister.

"Cammy!" he said, grabbing her foot and shaking it. She uttered a weak moan. Camilla was sitting propped up against the wall, half-conscious and white as a ghost. Her arms lay heavily at her sides. As Ethan drew nearer, he noticed blood caked around her neck. She'd been bitten. Even in the obscurity of darkness, he could barely stand to look at it.

Something moved nearby. Ethan looked into the corner and saw more people, some sitting against the walls, others face-down on the cold cement. They were withered and lifeless. One of them reached a shaking hand out toward him, but it dropped down to the ground soon after.

"Wake up, Cammy," he said, shaking her again. Tears dribbled down his face. "Please, get up." His heart thudded even faster.

Cammy's lips quivered in response, but she was too addled to speak.

"I'll get help," Ethan said. "I promise." He hoisted himself up again, ignoring the pain and leaning a hand against the wall. He followed the dim light that seeped in from the other side of the room, back from where he'd crawled. It led him to a small wooden staircase. At the top, the bright outline of a door glowed. Ethan shuffled up the steps, one by one, grimacing in pain as he went.

When he neared the top, his injured foot came down at an angle on a rusty nail. It shredded the swollen wound from earlier. Blood exploded from it, and Ethan screamed in agony. He tumbled backwards down the stairs, but managed not to smack his head this time. Instead, he landed on his arm.

The boy squealed and cried. His noises elicited the whining of an animal from the other side of the door. It scratched at the wood and groaned.

"Who's down there?" a woman called out playfully. "What do you hear, baby? You wanna go down there?"

The door creaked open.

Ethan bit down on his lip and withdrew from the stairs into the shadows. He hid behind one of the load-bearing pillars and peeked around it.

A tall, ugly woman with a waxy face descended the staircase, dragged by a dog on a leash. She looked like something from a nightmare; her hair was frazzled and burnt from years of obsessive grooming, and her skin bore the texture of a fresh corpse. Bones jutted from every inch of her gaunt form, and her eyes bulged so wide Ethan could see their whites in the dark.

The dog that led her was unlike anything Ethan had ever seen. It was big and probably weighed as much as he did, and it made sounds he'd never heard from any other dog. It sniffed at each stair excitedly, no doubt aware of the boy's presence. It immediately scampered toward the pillar he sat behind, but the woman yanked on its leash.

"This way, silly," she croaked. The animal yelped and turned reluctantly toward the far end of the room, where Camilla lay.

Ethan watched the pair as they moved further into the dark. He caught a glimpse of the dog up close, and forced back a scream. Huge patches of skin were missing from all over its body, exposing the sleek muscles beneath. Blood soaked its fur, and as it trotted past, it left little red pools on the ground. Its jaw hung slack but there were no teeth; instead a half-dozen syringes erupted through its gums, surgically placed in a row of needled "fangs." Their plungers stuck out from the dog's snout and jaw, affixed to long tubes that ran all the way to the wounds on its back. A mechanical apparatus dangled off the dog's neck from the collar; it appeared to control the syringes. The sight was so grotesque that Ethan nearly passed out again.

"No no," the woman said, "this one. This one!"

Ethan could barely make out their forms across the room, but he listened as Camilla whined in pain. The apparatus made a whirring sound, and the woman cooed, "Good boy, Spike. That's a good boy. Momma loves you."

Terror overwhelmed Ethan and compelled him to his feet. He snuck through the darkness and hobbled up the stairs as quietly as he could, careful not to draw any attention to himself. He avoided the rusty nail and stepped into the light of a short hallway.

The walls were bright white and adorned with a few landscape paintings. Were it not for the years of bloody paw prints across the carpet and glossy crimson streaks along the baseboards, the house might have looked well-appointed. The vivid reds and sickly browns assaulted Ethan's brain. He forced back the simultaneous urges to puke and faint and scream. He limped to the other end of the hall, crusty carpet mashing under his bare feet as he went. Fresh red prints appeared behind his injured foot.

He came upon a living room with white furniture. The seats of the couch were a nauseating rust color, no doubt stained beneath Spike's ghastly form as he lay with his "mommy" each night. Macabre smudges lined the windows and door that faced the front yard; some of them were prints made by human hands. The entire house reeked of decomposing blood.

Ethan choked back a wave of vomit and dragged himself to the front door. Sweat slicked his entire body and made him feel as dirty as the loathsome house he moved through. He grabbed the knob and instantly felt a searing pain shoot up his forearm. He clutched his hand and screamed; a needle had been fixed into the knob and now stuck out of his palm. As he slid the needle out, the muscles in his hand cramped and his fingers flinched uncontrollably.

The woman's voice rang out from the basement in response to Ethan's cries. He couldn't make out what she said.

The front of the house was booby-trapped. Instead of risking another injury, Ethan doubled back to the other side of the living room and entered a large kitchen. Its countertops were lined with hundreds of bottles of prescription pills, some of which bore labels that had yellowed with age. Pills were scattered all about the counters and floors, and some unidentifiable food rotted in the sink. The trash can overflowed with bottles of rubbing alcohol, sanitary wipes, and dozens of used syringes. Their needles jutted ominously in every direction, reminding Ethan of his mortal peril. Despite his terror, he remembered Camilla's pale face, and summoned new courage within himself. He reached for the telephone and dialed 911, but the moment he pressed the phone to his ear, he heard a loud pop, followed by a dizzying ringing in his own head.

The boy dropped the phone and caught himself on the counter as he careened toward the floor, barely averting another blackout. His arm, injured from the earlier fall, throbbed with pain. Blood trickled out of his ear and down his neck. His eardrum had burst. The phone dangled from its cord nearby; a single needle gleamed from its earpiece.

Ethan's heart rate slowed. Warmth flooded back into his limbs. For the first time in his life, he felt like he was going to die. He *knew*. And for some reason, this feeling overrode the electric sensations of fear that coursed through his body. His mind alternated between thoughts of rescuing his sister and thoughts of his own death, and his head grew heavy again. He pressed onward, looking for another way out.

Spike and his wretched master stomped up the basement stairs. Ethan snuck past the hall before they spotted him and limped up a staircase to the second floor. The laws of gravity were unmade by the pain in his ear, and the entire house swayed to and fro in an attempt to throw him off his feet. But Ethan pressed on, knowing that a loss of consciousness would doom his sister, if she wasn't already dead.

"You little shit!" the woman screeched from the kitchen. "Where are you?!"

Ethan slogged over the putrefied carpets of another hall and found a door with bloody paw-streaks all over its lower half. He pushed it open, careful not to touch anything that could conceal a needle. He found himself in what must have been the master bedroom; a huge bed occupied the room's center, flanked by two nightstands. The comforter was white and matched the rest of the décor, but on one side it was stained reds and browns and blacks and held all the textures of a decade of dried blood. Syringes and spare needles lined one of the nightstands, and on the other rested a stack of magazines from before Ethan was born. Dangling from the lamp was a dusty ID card that read:

Dr. Joan Richards, veterinarian
Toluca Falls Animal Hospital

"Get back down there!" the woman screamed from behind him. Her voice was dry, and it cracked through the air like a leather whip. Ethan spun around in time to see the hideous woman lunge at him, her calloused hands striking at his throat and pulling him forward. "You little shit! How dare you put your filthy hands on my things!" Horrible scars lined every inch of her arms, and beneath the mask of cheap makeup on her face, Ethan could see a hardened layer of old cuts and scratches. She looked like a man Ethan and his father once saw at a bus stop – a "dope fiend," as Dad had said.

"Get away from me!" the boy screamed, clawing at her face. The woman shrieked and threw him into the nightstand; one of the syringes pierced into his lower back as he landed against it. She was on him like a wolf, thrashing him back and forth and beating him with open hands. Ethan yanked the syringe from his back and slipped it between her flailing arms, jamming it into her neck.

The woman howled in pain, and somewhere behind her, the dog howled in response. She screamed a string of curses and pummeled Ethan with a fist. One of the strikes landed on his bloodied ear, and all went black. This time, he could not fight the darkness.

 The boy stirred. He opened his eyes, but could not see anything at first. It took a few moments for his vision to adjust. Eventually he could make out a faint wooden beam in the gloom. The coldness of the cement finally registered on his skin, and the familiar stink of death awoke his sense of smell. Across the darkness he could barely make out the form of his little sister. He inched toward her, feeling his heart fail in his chest. There was Camilla, or what remained of her, propped against the same wall. She was ghost-white, and her dry eyes were locked with his. Her mouth hung open, her lips stiff. She was nearly gone. She weakly reached out for her brother.
 Ethan tried to scream out in horror and despair, but whatever drug coursed through his veins prevented him from making much more than a squeak. He wanted to reach out and hold his sister's hand, to feel her one last time, but he recoiled from the sight of her – not just the dried blood that now covered her neck and clothes, but the nearness of death to her. Sadness washed over her face, then disappeared, leaving her expression blank and lifeless. Her hand fell to the ground, never to move again.
 The mournful sound of wet paws rose behind Ethan, and he turned his aching head in time to see a dog's snout. A ragged tongue dangled from Spike's mouth, shredded from running over all those filthy needles where his teeth should have been. The creature sniffed a few times, then bit down on Ethan's neck. The same mechanical whirring noise rang out, and suddenly the cement felt much, much colder. Ethan's eyes rolled back, his limbs twitched, and everything warm and living escaped his body into Spike's gory maw. The icy feeling ran up the boy's legs, up his fingers, up his arms. When it reached his head, the feeling

passed, and disappeared with the world into a soothing darkness.

Six Steps Forward
Colin J. Northwood

"Ms. Patel, I presume?" The voice carried the confidence that comes with already knowing the answer, and a little more confidence as well.

Sita turned her head to see a tall woman in an expensive white business suit entering the room, and suddenly felt a twinge of embarrassment. Casual attire was common in the tech community, but perhaps it wasn't the best choice for this interview. No matter – there were important questions to be asked, and she wasn't going to be intimidated so easily. She sat up a little straighter.

"Yes. Are you Ms. Harper?"

"Call me Cheryl." Her posh accent pierced the soft ambiance of the lobby. "How do you do?"

The company bosses must have known what was coming, Sita realized. It made sense in light of their recent infamy. They wanted a softball interview, and Sita was going to have to battle to get anything else. Maybe that was why they invited such a novice, she thought. But her determination returned and she pushed her self-doubt to the back of her mind.

"I'm very well."

Sita had been blogging about the latest developments in the tech world for a few years, with a special focus on artificial intelligence. She had recently been hired as the tech correspondent for a larger news site. This was her first major insider interview.

"Lovely. Now, I'll not waste any more of your time. I know you're here to see the new model, and I'd love to show it to you." Cheryl beamed. They were off to a great start.

"See it? Oh...I didn't realize it was ready."

"Well, it's not quite ready for production, but the prototype is up and running. It'll be a surprise sneak preview, just for you!" Cheryl nodded toward the back door. "Right this way."

Sita had thought the Ucritech spokespeople would show up prepared only to talk in generalities about the new model, so it would be easy to turn the tables on them with some tough questions. But this was too good to decline.

As she stood up and followed Cheryl into a long corridor, she began to notice the conspicuous absence of security personnel. It seemed strange for such a high-profile private research facility to be unguarded. Corporate espionage had been rampant in the past few years, but perhaps the famous robotics company had other solutions. Sita made a mental note to ask about it – later.

"Miss...uh, Cheryl...I'm really grateful for this opportunity. I suppose I should confess that I had other topics in mind when I arrived."

Cheryl didn't skip a beat. "Oh, we're well aware of the ongoing public interest in the URSA incident, but I'm afraid there's nothing more to say about it. It's a tragedy, but we're a tech company. We have to keep moving forward."

They *did* know. Sita sighed. "Then perhaps you could kindly answer one question for me. How has the incident informed your development of the new model?"

Cheryl turned around with a smile too steady to be

sincere. "I'm glad you asked."

Again, they were one step ahead.

"You see," Cheryl continued, "many of our competitors have gone along with the accepted wisdom on the subject. They think the AI was too ambitious, and the tasks were too complex for it. They've scaled back their efforts. They've resigned themselves to making machines that don't even attempt something as bold as autonomous surgery."

Sita raised an eyebrow. "You can hardly blame them, in light of what happened."

Still, Cheryl was unfazed. "Of course. We in the industry have to be sympathetic to public concern about the safety of our products. Now, I'm sure you know that the nature of that incident is in dispute. I won't rehash that any further. If you aren't satisfied with our previous answers...well, I'm afraid that's still where it stands."

"That's not very reassuring."

"I'm sorry, dear, but I'm not here to reassure you. I'm here to show you the new model."

They rounded a corner, and the end of the corridor came into view. A large open space lay beyond that.

"You still haven't answered the question." Sita was growing frustrated, though in the back of her mind she was secretly gratified that the interview was beginning to meet her expectations. "How does the URSA tragedy inform the development of the new model? Everyone in the world knows that a major course correction was in order after that, but it sounds like you're doubling down."

Cheryl maintained her confident stride. If not for her occasional pauses, her fast pace would have left Sita lagging behind like an errant child. "You're right, Ms. Patel. I haven't answered your question yet, and I can understand why you might have misgivings about our operation's ethical standards. But let me assure you, we *do* have an answer for you, and I think you'll leave here satisfied with that answer."

"How can you be so sure of that?" Sita snapped. "Your company is at the forefront of public concern about AI, and you know those concerns are reasonable. The URSA incident proves it. This kind of lip service didn't satisfy the families of the victims, and it won't satisfy me." Sita frowned. "So, tell me. Tell the world. Why should we look the other way while you flout your responsibilities? Haven't you learned anything from your mistakes?"

Cheryl stopped at the end of the corridor and turned around, glaring down at her interlocutor. "Ms. Patel, perhaps I owe you an apology. I may have given you the impression that we aren't taking these kinds of questions seriously. It's just that—"

"Stop toying with me, Ms. Harper. Are you going to answer the question or not?"

A draft of cold air spilled out from the room ahead. In her restless state, it was almost enough to make Sita shake.

"—it's just that we've given up on AI altogether."

Sita's jaw fell slack, and there was a long moment of silence before she finally found her voice again. "Given up?..."

Cheryl's smile returned, and this time she meant it. "I told you, love. We at Ucritech pride ourselves on thinking big."

"But how's..." Sita's thought trailed off while Cheryl politely waited.

"If our competitors want to fool around with second-rate AI, we're happy to let them. We're not trying to follow the crowd. We've been on top of this industry for a while, and it's because we're not afraid to take bold action. We *have* to be bold. We're the future."

"Then what are we here to see?"

"As I said, Ms. Patel...come right this way."

They entered a cavernous room, several stories high and lined with doors on every side. There were many windows too, but they only showed labs and offices. Perhaps to combat the feeling of confinement, there was quite a lot of live vegetation everywhere. The walls were overrun with dense vines, and several vigorous trees sprouted from enormous boxes of soil. The ceiling was painted to resemble a cloudy sky and lit as if by natural light.

"This must be a relaxing place to work."

"Yes. It's important to us that all our employees feel comfortable in their work environment."

There were several teams of machinists working on various projects out in the open. Laughter and casual conversation filled the air.

"It must be very expensive to maintain all this."

"Innovation is worth any price."

Sita couldn't believe that such a secretive company was fostering such an open environment. Even the air smelled fresh. "Aren't you worried about security? I haven't seen a single guard or camera anywhere. Couldn't someone just walk out of here with a stockpile of confidential data?" She turned toward a crew of gardeners trimming a hedge.

"We have security," Cheryl insisted. "But we'd be fools to make it obvious, wouldn't we?" She paused to wave to a man up ahead, who gave a thumbs up in response. "We keep the tightest ship in the business," she added. "No one gets in or out of this building without our knowledge. We haven't had a leak in years."

As far as Sita knew, that was true. "So, automated security then?"

Cheryl didn't answer, but directed her attention to the man as they approached. "This is Wesley Reynolds, the project manager." He stood in front of a large, tarp-covered

object which was flanked by two more men.
"A pleasure to meet you, Ms. Patel."
All three men were dressed informally, and Sita felt a little better about her flannel and blue jeans. It was Cheryl in her business attire who stood out here.
"Nice to meet you, Mr. Reynolds."
He turned his glance from Sita to Cheryl. "Ready?"
Cheryl nodded, and the men pulled the tarp away, unveiling a machine the size of an automobile. Along its sides were six short, metallic pillars, and on the near end were several apertures similar to the camera fixtures from earlier models. The whole thing rested lifelessly on the ground in a slightly asymmetric position.
Sita folded her arms and took a few steps toward it, then turned to Cheryl. "I thought you said it was up and running."
"It is, dear."
Sita walked around to the back. "But no AI?"
"No AI."
Now Sita took a closer look and saw a logo depicting a stylized red and blue bull. It held its chin in the air, puffing itself up into a position of self-importance. The parallel with Cheryl's wardrobe did not escape Sita's notice. "Is it a vehicle?"
Wesley pulled a hand from his pocket and took a step forward. "This is TAURUS."
The animal branding of these devices was not endearing to Sita. It seemed insensitive after the infamy of URSA, but she admonished herself to be professional. "What does it do?"
Wesley scratched his head. "Telecognitively Activated Unit for Rescue, from Ucritech Systems." He nodded in agreement with himself.
Sita rolled her eyes. "That's awkward...wait, did you say telecognitive?"

Cheryl interjected. "I think you'll find TAURUS to be anything but awkward." She signaled to Wesley, who scuttled off into a nearby door and disappeared from sight.

"So it reads minds?"

"Something like that. You'll want to back away, love. The show's about to start."

Moments later, the muffled whirring of circuits began, and the cameras lit up. The central body of the machine began to lift itself off the ground, and the pillars revealed themselves to be its supports. As it ascended, two hydraulic joints unfolded from inside each pillar, and broad plates emerged at the tips. The entire sequence took only a few seconds.

Sita was at first slightly alarmed at the speed of TAURUS, then deeply unsettled at its lifelike motion. She backed away a little further, but Cheryl stood her ground.

Now towering over both women, TAURUS stretched its limbs slightly and shook its feet as if waking from a much-needed slumber. It swiveled its cameras from side to side, eventually pointing a few of them at Sita. As if to display the nightmarish imaginations of its creators, it now exposed two telescoping arms on its underside, each tipped with a floret of articulated claws. With a series of rapid and mystifying movements, one of them reached toward a nearby shrub, plucked a single white carnation, and held it before Sita as an offering.

Any charm that the gesture may have been intended to evoke was lost on her. She briefly glanced down at the flower, then back up at the glowing red eyes just in time to see one of them spinning wildly. "This thing is a monster!"

Cheryl scowled. "Not in the slightest, love. This is the future of search and rescue operations."

TAURUS swayed in agreement and insistently presented the flower to Sita, who snatched it and threw it to the ground. Her face was flush as she turned back to

Cheryl. "After what happened to all those people...this is *unbelievable*. This thing is terrifying. How can you sleep at night?"

The cameras turned away from her indignantly.

"What happened to those people was an earthquake," Cheryl explained. "If TAURUS had been there, it might have rescued every last one of them." She placed a hand on a spindly metal leg and stroked it like a pet. "Isn't that right, Wesley?"

TAURUS tilted up, then down, punctuating Cheryl's words with a sense of finality.

"What the hell is going on here?" The way Sita sputtered out her words rendered them more profane than anything she could conjure with curses alone. "Never mind. I don't care anymore." She spun around, trampling the flower, and marched back toward the entryway.

Cheryl furrowed her brow and TAURUS shrugged, but neither followed.

Sita weaved her way around several groups of workers as she retraced her steps. On any other day, she would have been embarrassed to have caused a scene in front of so many people; today, though, she shot spiteful glances at anyone in her periphery who looked her way.

Despite stepping over cables and around the devices connected to them, she kept up a swift pace. She proceeded into the corridor, rounded the corner, and headed for the lobby.

She grabbed the door's handle, relieved to be on her way out, but when she attempted to yank it open, it would not budge. With a grunt, she pulled harder, but to no avail. As she struggled with it, she was overtaken first by anger, then by panic, and finally by despair. She kicked the door one last time before sitting in an adjacent corner with her head in her hands.

After some time, she heard footsteps from the hall, and

looked up. It was Wesley. He stopped to greet her with a sheepish wave.

"Hey. I'm sorry if I scared you."

"Yeah. Normally I would say I wasn't scared, but I guess when you're operating a robot that can read minds, it isn't much use lying to you."

"Huh? Oh, no. It doesn't work like that."

Sita sighed and resolved to make the most of the ordeal. After all, she had come here to get some answers. Wesley stepped forward and offered her a hand. She didn't take it, but stood up and brushed herself off.

"Alright, then. How does it work?"

"C'mon. I'll tell you all about it." His relaxed tone was a relief to Sita, even under these circumstances. They began to walk slowly back down the hall.

"Why was that door locked? You can't just keep me prisoner here."

Wesley glanced back at the door as they were about to round the corner. "Oh, I'm sorry about that, ma'am. The door handles recognize fingerprints. Only employees can open them. It's a security precaution." He stopped and turned toward Sita. "If you really want to leave, I'll let you out."

Sita paused to consider this, but decided against it. "It's alright. If I've got any future in journalism, I'm gonna have to get used to uncomfortable situations."

Wesley dipped his chin and fidgeted.

"I didn't mean you," Sita reassured him. "But if I have to spend one more minute with that woman..."

He smirked. "Alright, then. Just you and me."

They turned the corner and continued down the corridor toward the main room.

"So, it's 'telecognitive' but it doesn't read minds?" Sita asked.

"It sorta does. It's controlled by thought."

"Oh. Ms. Harper made it sound like something revolutionary, but lots of other companies have developed machines controlled by thought."

"They have, but not like this. It's like virtual reality, but...not so virtual."

"So is that why she called it by your name?"

"Yeah. When you're operating TAURUS, it completely replaces all the sensations of having a human body. It's like you *are* the machine."

They returned to the lush environment of the main chamber. The feeling of being outdoors while deep inside the building was increasingly disconcerting to Sita. She had to remind herself it was just an illusion, even as she stepped over a column of ants.

She turned her attention back to Wesley and asked, "How do you achieve that level of immersion?"

"Through sensory deprivation. TAURUS can only be operated from its control room. It's totally silent in there and the climate is regulated to minimize disruption. And once you start up the machine, the rest of the room goes pitch black."

"And you wear goggles?"

"No, just a helmet. It bypasses the human senses and interfaces directly with the brain. The use of your eyes would interfere with your concentration. You really have to feel like TAURUS's body is your own."

Cheryl was standing by TAURUS and talking to one of the other workers. She turned toward Wesley expectantly as she heard them approach. He shook his head at her. She looked quickly at Sita, who made a point not to reciprocate, then turned back to her conversation.

TAURUS was lying on its side like a sleeping dog. Sita grimaced at it before moving on toward the far end of the room, where she could see the door into which Wesley had gone earlier.

"This is the control room," he said, and pulled the door open. It looked like a recording studio, with soundproofing all around and a large computer console taking up the entirety of one wall. In front of that sat a single plush chair with a design that was reminiscent of space operas and baby baskets. In the chair was a helmet, connected to the console by insulated wires.

As the door closed behind Sita, the fresh air of the room outside gave way to a stifling atmosphere. She stood in place, getting an eyeful of the room. "So, search and rescue, huh? What kind of engineering challenges are involved in that?"

Wesley picked up the helmet, sat down, and placed it on his lap. "You have no idea. It's been in development since even before URSA." He looked at the ceiling and began counting with his fingers. "It has to be sturdy enough to withstand a building collapse, but light enough to climb up the side. It has to be strong enough to break down doors, but gentle enough to put a person with a broken neck onto a stretcher. It has to be large enough to carry people around, but flexible enough to fit through doors and windows. It has to have sensitive instruments, but be able to withstand harsh environments. It's fireproof, waterproof...you name it."

Sita fixed her gaze on Wesley. "Do you have any documentation of all this? The last thing anyone wants is to see this thing fail out in the real world when people are relying on it."

He grinned, showing the crooked teeth he had been hiding until now. "I can do better than documentation."

"Oh really?"

He stood up, walked around Sita, and opened the door to yell outside. "Hey, everyone! Hey! Everyone, clear out! Yeah...I'm gonna let her take a test drive!"

Suddenly, Sita was glad she hadn't been able to escape

earlier.

Wesley closed the door and gestured at the chair. "Go ahead."

As Sita turned to look at the chair, she soaked in the eerie silence. Every footstep was deafening in this environment.

"I should warn you, though." Wesley held up his hands. "The first time is a little weird, so just take it easy."

Sita picked up the helmet and sank into the chair. "I'm ready," she said.

"'Attagirl."

When Sita placed the helmet on her head, she wondered for a moment how to start it up. She turned to Wesley, but before she could say a word, the lights began to fade out, and her consciousness with them. She had the distinct sensation of falling.

And then she woke up in her new body.

TAURUS knew it had left its human body far behind, but every time it awoke as a newborn, it paused to appreciate the fact that its master was resting in a cradle.

One by one, its cameras came online. Infrared, sonar, and visible light. It looked in several directions, not yet having learned how to focus its instruments. It hadn't yet realized it was capable of stereoscopic and panoramic vision simultaneously. That would come with time.

The feeling of having so many limbs was strange for TAURUS every time it was born. It would have to learn how to stand again. Walking was out of the question.

TAURUS took an inventory of its body. Many retractable appendages and hidden compartments were tucked away under its tungsten alloy exoskeleton. It extended a tube and involuntarily released a blast of cold gas. A fire extinguisher, perhaps.

It stretched its wobbly legs and tried to stand, but only managed to sit. That was good enough to survey its surroundings. Nearby were some crates and a tall tree. A mouse was visible in the infrared spectrum, hiding beneath a hedge.

A little farther away were some humans. Some of them were speaking, but their voices were drowned out by the constant pulsing of sonar. TAURUS realized it was equipped with a smoke detector when it caught a light whiff of cigarette smoke from a jacket that one of them was wearing.

And then, just as suddenly as it was born, TAURUS was caught up in a spell of fatigue and collapsed to the ground.

The lights in the control room were back on, and Wesley was leaning on the console. He pulled the helmet from Sita's head. "So, whaddya think? Pretty cool, huh?"

She was too disoriented to answer. Neither meditation nor drugs had ever made her mind feel so disconnected from her body. It was as if she had lived an entire lifetime in those circuits and was leaving it all behind with an aching sorrow.

Wesley patted her on the shoulder. "It takes some time to get used to it."

She looked at him in silence.

"I'll get you some water. Be right back. Don't go anywhere." He set the helmet on the ground and left the room.

Sita mourned the loss of her electronic senses and wondered for the first time if her fleshy eyes were equipped to experience true beauty.

But Wesley was right. By the time he returned with the water, her brain had recovered and she felt like herself again. The whole episode was fading away like a dream.

He handed her the glass. She took a sip, then set it down.

He smiled at her again. "It's really hard to describe, isn't it? It's like being someone else."

"Yeah. I guess I've got my story."

On her way out of the room, Sita took one last wistful look at the console, then stepped back out into the main chamber. It felt like stepping back into real life. She didn't dare look in the direction of TAURUS, for fear that the sight of it alone might imperil her sanity.

Wesley escorted Sita through the main chamber. The sounds of busy engineers seemed a million miles away to her. It was as if the stifling silence of the control room had followed her. Wesley picked up on this, and began to speak.

But he was interrupted by a scream from behind. The two of them spun around just in time to hear a sickly crunching noise. The source of the disturbance was not visible until TAURUS began to climb the wall. Even at this distance, it was obvious that a man was impaled on one of its limbs. Panic spread quickly through the room, and people began to flee in all directions.

Cheryl dashed down the aisle and approached Wesley, shaking. "Reynolds! What the hell is happening?!" Just then, TAURUS leaped from the wall and out of sight. Another scream rang out, and Cheryl cringed at the sound. "Who's driving that thing?"

"I don't know. I was just in the control room a minute ago. No one should be in there."

"Well someone is bloody well in there!"

Wesley stood still for a second, then took a deep breath and began to run toward the control room. Sita just stood and watched until her trance was broken by Cheryl.

"Run, you twit!"

The two of them headed for the entrance corridor. Even in her stylish shoes, Cheryl was able to maintain a good pace. Every few seconds, another sound added to the chorus of calamity behind them. Trees shook, crates tumbled around, and people screamed with their final breaths.

Then, silence.

Cheryl and Sita kept running until they made it to the corridor, then turned around. Despite some visible wreckage, the courtyard was evidently at peace.

Sita put her hands on her knees and caught her breath. "Wesley must have shut it down."

"There's nothing to shut down. I told you, there's no AI." A few beads of sweat lingered on Cheryl's forehead, shattering her invincible aura. "Someone was driving that thing."

And just then, a metal claw curled into the door. Sita shrieked, but Cheryl didn't have time. In a fraction of a second, a clamp closed around her neck and ripped her head from her body. For a moment, her headless frame remained standing, hands on hips, until it collapsed to its knees. When it finally fell forward, shoulders to the ground as if in worship, the blood formed a tidy river and pooled off to the side, leaving the clean white suit largely untouched. Cheryl would have wanted it just that way.

Sita wasn't sure if TAURUS had been unaware of her presence or had simply lost interest. In any case, she stood there in shock and watched it scuttle off across the courtyard, perhaps in search of other prey.

She stumbled a bit further down the hallway before realizing she would be unable to escape. She tried some doors anyway, and had to stifle a strong urge to shout profanities when, as expected, none of them would budge.

So now, here she was, a sitting duck. If TAURUS came back, she'd be trapped in the hallway with nowhere to run, nowhere to hide, and no way to fight back. She wasn't sure she'd fare much better outside, but she had to try. Maybe she could find an employee who could help her get out through one of these damn doors, she thought.

And so, back into the courtyard she crept, trying not to draw attention to herself. She felt some relief when she heard the sound of glass shattering in the distance. She had at least a little time to figure out what to do next.

A few pairs of hedge clippers, abandoned by a team of fleeing gardeners, sat by Sita's feet. She glared at the tools for a moment, considering whether they would have any use at all against an armored enemy. Maybe she could damage its cameras if she got lucky. Or maybe...

Sita grabbed a pair of hedge clippers and ran back into the hall. She positioned them around Cheryl's forearm, closed her eyes, and squeezed the handles together. The steel blades were not sharp, but they were strong. They punctured the tender skin of Cheryl's arm, and produced a few small splatters from the soft flesh within.

"Sorry about the suit," Sita mumbled under her breath. She gripped the handles harder and pushed them together with all her might. Cheryl's bones cracked and splintered. After a brief struggle, Sita managed to cut through the arm completely, and picked up the severed hand by the wrist.

She wrapped Cheryl's fingers around the nearest door handle and, just as she had hoped, it opened. This was a closet full of cleaning supplies, but now she knew she had access to the doors and could escape if she wished. However, an unexpected doubt lingered in her mind. The control room was just across the courtyard, and TAURUS was distracted...

Sita couldn't believe she was considering such a foolish idea. She had a good chance at a clean getaway, and was risking her life even by standing here thinking about it. It was crazy.

But maybe there were worse things to be than crazy. Sita had been following the URSA story for years, and had come here because of her concern for public safety. There was no way she could live with herself if she fled just when her fears had been validated. She turned around once more and began to walk briskly through the foliage, Cheryl's severed hand still in her grip.

The pace of TAURUS's rampage seemed to have slowed, if the noises coming from across the courtyard were any indication. Sita knew she had to act quickly to have a chance of making it to the control room. She darted from tree to tree, staying behind cover whenever possible.

Halfway across the courtyard, Sita spotted Wesley lying on the ground, staring at the ceiling. His clothes were shredded and his skin had fared no better. She dashed to his side and whispered his name.

No response.

She shook his shoulder, but could not awaken him. A scream rang out from across the room, then a heavy metallic clank, then silence. Sita knew she had to keep moving. She drew close to Wesley's ear and said to him, "You're gonna be okay. Stay here." Then she was back on her feet and running.

When the control room was in sight, Sita scanned her surroundings to make sure the coast was clear. She froze when she saw TAURUS fifty paces behind her – near enough to rapidly close the distance if it noticed her. It had the posture of a sniffing hound, and was slowly advancing. Much to Sita's dismay, she realized that Cheryl's severed hand had left a trail of blood all the way across the courtyard.

But it was too late to hesitate now. Sita dashed for the door and was relieved to have made it alive. She turned back just as TAURUS looked up and began to bound toward her. In a panic, she wrapped Cheryl's hand around the door handle, yanked it open, and jumped inside.

The room was empty and dark.

"Who's in here?!"

No reply.

Sita banged on the console and the lights came on. Still, no one was visible. The chair was empty and the helmet was on the floor, just where Wesley had left it.

Outside, TAURUS had arrived. Even the soundproofing of the room could not entirely muffle the loud crashes it made as it battered the wall with its limbs.

TAURUS managed to dent the door. Sita knew it wouldn't last much longer, and that she was going to be easy prey in this room. "Goddammit! I knew that bitch was lying!"

She kicked the helmet at her feet, rolling it over. And just like that, TAURUS came crashing to the ground and the pandemonium outside ceased.

Sita looked down at the floor. There, in the exact spot where the helmet had been sitting, was an ordinary spider. It returned her gaze, and lifted two of its legs at her in a threat display.

"Fuck you," Sita said to the spider, and crushed it beneath her foot.

Poor Richard
Felix Blackwell

The workload of grad school is enough to give anyone thoughts of death. Suicide is uncommon in graduate students, but it does happen – and the university knows it. So they relentlessly advocate that we make room in our schedules for relaxation. But all of that quiet reading, quiet writing, quiet grading – all of that sitting we do – never made me tired. It made me angry. So I jogged and went to the gym every other day, religiously, lest I explode from all the potential energy humming inside me.

And there's another kind of decompression one must learn to survive graduate school. The overwhelming daily stress causes tension to build up not only in the body, but also in the mind. Some of my cohort members depressurized with rounds of drinks at downtown bars on Friday nights; others picked up vices of varying appeal. As a lifelong teetotaler, there was only one thing that ever really worked for me: nature walks.

Behind Westmaple is a state park called Walder Ranch. Out there, a labyrinth of mountain biking trails crisscross the landscape, cutting between brilliant emerald groves of redwoods for miles and miles. I spent several months walking them all, giving them names, and mapping the area in my head.

One of the trails was particularly beautiful. I named it *Brightwood Loop*, because of the way hundreds of shafts of light fell on it from the canopy. From the road, a narrow path cut directly into the woods, met up with a few broader trails, and then snaked along little cliffs and valleys and looped right back around to the starting point. At a lollygagger's pace, one could be back to the car in under two hours. So, once a week, I'd grab my iPod and a water bottle, and spend some time in the great outdoors.

The best thing about walking the loop was that it required zero brain activity. I could shut off the analytical part of my mind, get lost in the music, and let my thoughts run wild. With the golden glow of sunbeams piercing the woods here and there, the songs of a thousand birds, the breeze that makes the whole forest come alive, this lush little world carried me away. As a graduate student, this was exactly the medicine I needed. Most of my "lazy hikes," as I came to call them, were uneventful – and thankfully so. Then, one day, I found something in the woods.

It was nearing winter break, and all of the undergraduates were busy studying for finals. None of them had time to hike. Local mountain bikers had also abandoned Wilder Ranch because of the early sunsets and the intermittent rain, so I was utterly alone. There was nobody around for miles; no longer did I pass an occasional friendly face during my travels.

It was gloomy that day. The dying light was scattered by the fog, so everything was dim and gray. No birds sang, spare the crows. I'd completed a little more than half the loop and was just arriving at one of my favorite parts of the trail: a narrow, leaf-covered path that followed the ridge of a steep downhill slope. From here, on a clear day, I could see the entire redwood valley stretching out to the next town. But today, the fog made it seem like the world simply ended five yards off the path.

Something caught my eye up ahead. At the base of a large tree, just a few feet from the trail, something was sticking out of the ground. At first glance I thought it was simply the knuckle roots that grow out of the soil beneath redwoods – the kind that knock mountain bikers off their bikes. But as I approached, the unmistakable shape of hands came into view. Two hands – *human* hands – were jutting out of the earth. They were filthy things, caked with flecks of dirt and mud. I stopped dead in my tracks ten steps away and yanked my noisy earbuds out. The silence of the forest washed over me, amplifying the oddness of the sight. A lone crow called out from far away as I stood there frozen, trying to figure out whether or not my eyes were playing tricks on me.

I walked forward a couple of steps, crunching the brittle leaves beneath my feet. I looked over my shoulder and all around me, acutely sensing how isolated I was from the rest of the world. As I shuffled closer, the hands came into clearer view. They were withered, ancient things, the skin pale and patchy, the flesh hard with death. They were as motionless as the trunk of the tree behind them, frozen wide open, as if to sign, "Hallelujah!"

I must have stood there for several minutes, just staring. The tiny cries of A Perfect Circle still murmured from the earbuds dangling around my neck. Someone had either buried a statue out here as a practical joke, or someone had buried a corpse. And in such a remote location, I didn't think anybody was trying to play a trick.

"What the hell..." I blurted out. My voice carried on farther than I'd expected, provoking the cry of a crow. I gathered the courage to get closer, and knelt down to examine the hands. The nails were cracked and rotten, the skin peeling off and receding around them. The knuckles were beaten and bone-dry, and what looked like the tan line left by a wedding band circled the ring finger.

"How did you get here?" I asked, sorting through a mixture of disgust and curiosity. As I leaned even closer and bent down on all fours, one of the hands suddenly twitched. I screamed and leaped backward onto my feet, then tripped on a root and fell on my ass. A flock of noisy crows erupted from the woods behind me and flew away, cawing in anger at the disturbance. After a while, the forest was still again. The fog began to thicken.

I sat there on the ground, too terrified to move, my gaze fixed on the hands. The soil around them was undisturbed, littered with dead autumn leaves that must have accumulated over several weeks. Everything about the hands told me they'd been here a long time, but I had walked through here on a half-dozen occasions in the last month. It was as though they'd just popped up out of the ground overnight. I imagined them as evil flowers blossoming on dreary days, their roots reaching all the way down to Hell.

As I sat there, mortified, one of the hands began to move. It slowly closed, then opened, and repeated this a few times. As it did, the brittle bones crackled. It was *waving* at me. My whole body went cold. My teeth clattered behind my lips. I didn't know what to do. I wanted to run away, but I was still hypnotized by my own morbid curiosity. The hands resumed their stillness, as if awaiting a response.

"...Hello?" I called out in a cowardly voice. The hands didn't move.

"I can...I can get help," I said. I began to doubt my sanity. "Who are you?"

No reply.

I sucked in a breath and clambered up to my knees. A dead leaf fell out of the tree above me and landed on the back of my neck. I jumped.

"Uh, are you alive?" I asked. It was a ridiculous

question, but my wits were hardly with me. The hands remained unmoving for another minute. Then, one of them slowly waved again. Perplexed, I picked my own shaking hand up off the ground, examined it, and then waved back. One of the ugly things slowly balled into a "thumbs up" expression in response, then returned to its regular position.

Nope.

I jumped to my feet and took off running, sending leaves and dirt flying behind me. I passed by the hands, keeping far enough away, and strained to see down the trail ahead of me through the fog. Only a few moments after passing them, there was a loud clacking sound from behind. I whirled around to see if anything was following. The sound repeated, and echoed through the entire grove. Wisps of fog drifted by, allowing me a momentary glimpse at the hands. Somehow, they were still facing me from their little plot of soil.

One of them snapped its fingers at me, the way one would snap at a dog. I squinted through the mist and watched as the hand made a "come hither" gesture. With a rotten, bony finger, the hands beckoned me to return to them. My stomach leaped into my mouth; everything I'd eaten came up to the back of my teeth, then sloshed back down into my guts. I practically flew down the trail, my body on autopilot. It took me only minutes to get back to the car at that speed, and I peeled out without looking back.

That night I couldn't sleep. I tossed and turned, alternating between ripping the sheets off during hot flashes and burying myself in them when my skin froze. Each time I shut my eyes, visions of those hands invaded my mind – visions of a dead man hoisting himself up out of the ground and chasing me through the woods, of thousands of corpse hands popping up along the trails, of the trees themselves becoming gigantic arms that reached longingly into the dead sky. When I did temporarily slip into unconsciousness in the early morning, a nightmare sent me right back out of it. I dreamed that I returned to the hands, and helped to unearth them. There beneath the surface, a foot or so down, was a hideous creature – a demon. It smiled up at me with jagged teeth, and blinked the soil out of its jet-black eyes.

The next day I thought of calling the police. After rehearsing what I planned to say, I changed my mind, knowing they'd institutionalize me before I could finish my sentence. Instead I called my buddy Richard over. We hadn't known each other very long, but he was a member of my grad cohort, and we got along pretty well. He showed up in his typical dress shirt and jeans, sporting a perfectly manicured five o'clock shadow. His undergraduate students were powerless to that hipster charm.

"I'm not saying I don't believe you," he said, stretching out in my computer chair. "But dude, come on."

"I'm *not* lying," I retorted, sitting down onto the edge of my bed. "You know me. I don't even take cold medicine anymore. This wasn't a hallucination or a mental breakdown. This shit is real. I think someone was fucking with me. And if they were, they should get an Academy Award. I really felt like I was about to get axed."

Richard straightened up in the chair and scratched his sandpaper chin.

"I know you're not lying," he said, trying to appease me. "Just take me to see it."

The mere thought of going back to that place made my stomach flip over, but I thought about it for a while and eventually agreed. It would be good to prove that I wasn't making it up, but it would be even better to find evidence that someone was just messing with me. A small part of me had to know if my dreams were omens. I needed to know what was buried there. What those hands were attached to.

How they moved. How they *saw* me.

The next morning, Richard and I had breakfast at our regular bacon-and-eggs spot downtown, then headed up to Wilder Ranch. I was feeling better now, and almost no longer believed that the hands had ever existed. Being around all the people in the bustling city, exchanging funny stories about our students, and just plain laughing, chased away the thoughts of death that had possessed my mind.

I parked my car boldly in front of the trailhead as a tiny "fuck you" to my waning fears, then hopped out with Richard and headed onto Brightwood Loop. The sun was beaming proudly onto the woods; there wasn't a cloud in the sky. The world was bright and green again, and a crisp winter breeze seemed to push us along the path.

"Nice out," I said, trying to convince myself that today would be a normal day. Richard didn't respond.

An hour passed. We talked about random things: our most annoying students, which members of our cohort were unlikely to finish the Ph.D., our mutual financial woes. The closer we got to the area where I'd found the hands, the more stiff and feigned the conversation felt. I found myself forcing up laughter, and offering one-word responses to nearly everything he said. Fear began to creep back over my mind, along with a morbid curiosity that suspended my urge to turn back.

The place I dreaded was only a few minutes away now. The path narrowed and the branches hung low over it. We passed a moss-covered "DO NOT ENTER" sign that dangled from some ancient barbed wire. I'd seen it a dozen times before and had never given it a second thought, but now I realized that it may have been put there for a reason. Wilder Ranch weaved between plots of private land, and occasionally you'd run into tattered wooden fences or "KEEP OUT" signs, but most people just ignored them. I wondered who owned this property, and whether they knew what was buried out here.

"...So I might as well, you know?" Richard said. "I found out about a month ago."

I snapped out of my fearful reverie and nodded my head as if I'd been listening. A crow squawked high above us. The feeling of doom welled up within me from some place deep inside.

"Up here," I choked out, trying desperately to maintain my composure. My stomach felt like I'd swallowed ice. Our power walk slowed to a cautious pace. Richard laughed and slapped me on the back.

"Chill, dude," he said. "Relax. Seriously. You're freakin' me out."

I could see his breath. The air was rapidly getting colder. The place where I saw the hands was right up ahead, on the north-facing slope of the trail. That little bend was shrouded entirely from the low-hanging sun, darker and colder than any other part of the woods.

"It's creepy here," Richard said, noticing the darkness too.

"The sun barely comes up over the treetops this time of year," I replied, pointing through the canopy. "It's like permanent twilight on some parts of this trail."

A lump formed in my throat as we pushed through a net of dangling twigs. Richard stepped ahead of me and kept an eye out as we moved. I watched the back of his black jacket in an attempt to regain my calm.

"Where'd you see 'em?" he asked, scanning the wall of trees to our left. The sun glinted from between them now and again, lighting up his face momentarily. "Do you know if—"

Richard halted, and I stumbled into him from behind. His gaze was fixed directly ahead, far down the trail. I moved up to his side and saw his shocked expression. His eyes led me to them – those awful hands, jutting out of the leafy ground. I could feel the blood draining out of my head. Everything went out of focus.

"Holy shit," he muttered after a half minute of silence.

"It's them," I whispered.

"Those look real," he replied. "Holy shit, that's amazing!" Richard started cracking up, then looked all around us. "Somebody's messing with you, Felix. This is good. This is really clever."

He started off toward the hands, moving in front of me as he did, but then stopped in his tracks again. This time, he didn't say anything.

"What?" I asked, jogging over to him.

As the hands came into view over his shoulder, I saw that they had moved. One of them was pointing directly at us. The fingernail was black and split up the middle. The skin on the knuckles was frayed like old cloth, exposing the bones beneath.

I strafed a few steps to the side. The pointing hand followed me. I moved back to Richard. It followed me back.

"Alright, who the hell are you?" Richard called out, unzipping his jacket like he was about to kick somebody's ass. The hands didn't seem to respond.

"Probably some engineering students," he continued. "They make robots all the time. This would be easy for them."

As I'd done a few days ago, I slowly waved. The open hand waved back, while the pointing one curled into a "come hither" gesture.

"There's got to be a camera out here," Richard said, examining the trees in a circle around us. I looked up and down the trunks, in the branches, and along the forest floor, but could not confirm his suspicions. There was nothing here but the hardened soil, a bed of crumbled leaves, and ten corpse fingers sticking into the air. My friend grew frustrated and walked straight up to the hands, tapping one with his shoe. They didn't move; they simply praised the sky in their dormant state.

"They're real," I said. "Look at them."

"Then I say we dig this guy up and beat him to death," Richard said over his shoulder, "then bury him in the same spot with his hands sticking out. A lesson in irony."

I swallowed hard and made my way toward Richard, but one of the hands abruptly pointed right at me again. It sat there, twenty feet away from me, silently condemning me with a rotten finger.

Why does it only point at me? I thought. Deep inside, I knew the answer.

"It's one of them," I said softly.

"Who?" Richard asked, tapping the hand again with his shoe.

"The cold people."

A bunch of crows shrieked all around us, as if in recognition of the phrase. The sound javelined through me, heralding my death.

"The cold what?" he said.

I watched as Richard dropped down to his knees and slapped at the hands.

"Come out of there or I'll start breaking fingers," he said. He smacked them a few more times.

Like lightning, one of them grabbed his hand and yanked it down toward the ground. He pulled free and backed away, emitting a surprised laugh.

"Son of a bitch," he said.

"Don't!" I called. My feet were frozen to the ground. "It's not a trick, man."

Richard began brushing leaves to the sides in big swipes, trying to unearth the hands without touching them.

"Come help me with this," he said. He leaned over them as he worked. Suddenly, the hands snatched up the dangling part of his jacket and yanked it hard into the ground. Richard fell right on top of them. He tried to escape. He squirmed and writhed as they grabbed at his clothes, tearing them up and reaching for his arms.

"Get off of me!" he yelled. "Felix! Get over here!"

I'd heard the expression *scared stiff* before, but it had never happened to me like this. My legs might as well have been tree roots jammed ten feet deep. They didn't let me help or flee. I could only watch in horror as the hands pulled at Richard's collar. While one of them held him tight, the other violently clawed at his face. His screams grew louder and more desperate, until he was crying.

"Help me!" he screamed, "please, help me!"

The urgency in his voice only compounded my terror. My teeth diced up the words I tried to spit out: "L-let- go of him!"

Richard managed to flip over onto his back in a final effort to escape. As he turned, I could see his face. It was horribly mangled; deep cuts ran across his cheeks and forehead. His nose had been clawed off. Bloody pulp dangled out of the hole. He cried, and mumbled something to me through trembling lips. The sound was lost behind the din of my heart pounding in my ears. The hands reached up from behind his head, one at a time, and wrapped their wicked fingers around his throat.

I could do nothing but watch. It was almost as though I'd lost consciousness but had not yet fallen over; not a single part of my body responded to my brain's commands to run over and help. I knew I was next. Richard reached a weak arm up toward me, begging, then it collapsed back onto the ground. The few parts of his face that weren't streaked with red began to turn purple. Gurgling sounds escaped his mouth. His legs twitched rapidly, then slower, and finally stopped.

For just a moment, Richard's body was splayed out on the ground, unmoving. Then it began to jerk. The hands were pulling him under. They bent his head back in a horrific way; the bones in his neck crackled and crunched. His head was the first part of him to disappear into the soft dirt, followed slowly by his torso. Tears dripped down my face, leaving cold trails on my skin, but I could not cry out. I watched the last parts of my friend disappear into the earth, and then there was nothing. The hands were gone too. In a moment, I was alone with the crows.

I could move again. The hypnotic spell of my terror was broken the moment Richard was gone. I wobbled a few steps, blinded by my tears, then found the strength to run. I tore through the woods, shrieking and crying hysterically, shouting "Oh my God...help me!" over and over. After dashing a few dozen yards I came to a fork in the trail and slid to a stop. I was so freaked out that I didn't recognize even this familiar place. My heart bashed against my chest like a baseball bat. My head spun. I puked.

Okay, which way, which way, I repeated in my head, looking down both paths.

Suddenly, the corpse hands erupted from the soil beneath me and grabbed onto my ankles. They pulled me downward with their inhuman death clutch, but the power of fear gave me super strength as well. I dove forward through the air, kicking my legs free, and landed hard on the dirt. I jumped up and darted away, watching over my shoulder as the hands sank back into the ground.

I rounded a corner and flew down a hill, twigs and leaves jumping up in the air behind me. The meadow was up ahead. I could see my car in the distance. As I moved toward it at full sprint, a long, rotting arm thrust out of the knothole of a big tree and nearly grabbed my neck. I ducked and flailed as I avoided it, my hand barely grazing the bicep. The skin was cold and taut with death. I looked back and saw it withdrawing into the tree, making that same "come here" gesture before disappearing into the dark.

I made it to my car and jammed the key into the lock, scratching the shit out of the door as I did. I peeled out and swung a wide U-turn, leaving tire tracks all over the little road. I went home, got into the shower, and curled up in a ball on the tile, crying as burning-hot water pummeled me.

That night I lay in bed next to a sleeping Faye, staring up at the stripes of moonlight on my ceiling. I imagined Richard's helpless body sinking into the blackness, rotting and transforming into the same sort of ghoul that brought him there. I heard his cries at the edges of my memory, and tried to force them down into the oblivion just beyond. Sleep eventually came, and with it, a calming silence. I would never speak of him again. It was the only way. I had to forget poor Richard.

Maternal Instinct
Felix Blackwell

My fiancée still suffers from night terrors. There were a few major incidents over the years, culminating in a dream that brought a man into our basement. About nine peaceful months after those events, it started happening again. Faye had been promoted and was now under a lot more pressure at work. She'd also turned twenty-nine, and was beginning to worry that her maternal clock was ticking. We didn't make nearly enough money to have kids yet, so any talk of starting a family became a tense and depressing affair.

It didn't help that she had just received a baby shower invitation from the neighbors, Dan and Kristen, another young couple like us. Dan probably made three times as much money as I did. Faye was always spending time with Kristen – talking about babies, no doubt. She'd always come home with tears in her eyes. It absolutely crushed me. I felt like such a failure for not being able to provide her with the joy of motherhood, but I didn't know how to make her feel better. She began to grow despondent whenever the subject was brought up, or whenever she heard the neighborhood kids playing outside.

Stress and depression are the most common triggers of Faye's night terrors. When her grandmother was near the end of her battle with cancer, my fiancée would sometimes get up in the middle of the night to go check on her in the guest room – despite the fact that her grandmother was on the other side of the state. I'd wake up to Faye's muffled laughter and storytelling, or tearful promises that she'd take care of herself. I'd go to the guest room to retrieve her, and she'd wake up confused and disoriented. Naturally, maintaining Faye's happiness was one of my highest priorities.

I got her a dog. It was a little Boston Terrier puppy, so cute that even I, a cat person, found him irresistible. He was brown and white with a little black nose. He'd stick it into everything and jump if he didn't like what it touched, so we named him Boop. Faye fell in love with him instantly, and her troubles seemed to melt away over the first week we had him. She transitioned from her concern about having a baby to an obsession with buying doggy accessories. In a way, Boop became her child.

Because of the new distraction, I was surprised when Faye resumed sleep-talking. About eight days after I'd adopted the dog, Faye nudged me in my sleep.

"Huh?" I asked, yanking the earplugs from my ears.

"The baby's crying," she said.

"The what?" I replied. I nearly fell back asleep waiting for her response.

"...He's crying," Faye said. "Your turn."

I sat there for a moment, trying to make sense of her words, but my sleepy brain couldn't muster the power. I nodded off.

That morning, Boop woke us up with his cute little snorts and tiny paw-pokes. The moment Faye opened her eyes, she smiled and pulled him in for a hug. My plan appeared to be working; every day she was happy when she woke up, and happy when she came home from work. I brushed the strawberry locks out of her face and kissed her forehead, then made my way out the door to administer a test at the school.

When I got home around 4 PM, there was a cheery message on the machine from Arianna, Faye's best friend.

"Faye! It's me! Call me back! Call me back right now!"

Boop scrambled up to me, delighted at my arrival, and wagged his tail-less butt back and forth. He was wearing a tiny Christmas sweater. I rolled my eyes.

That night in bed, Faye was unusually snuggly. She kept peering deeply into my eyes as I read, until I got the point.

"What's on your mind, babe?" I asked.

She sighed.

"Arianna's having twins," she replied. Her emerald eyes looked wet and slick. "It's so sweet. I'm happy for her."

The voicemail played in my head.

Great.

"That's wonderful," I said, running my fingers through her hair. I so desperately wanted to avoid an argument. Or a waterfall of tears. "We'll have to drop by."

Faye put her hand over the book I was reading and pushed it down to my lap.

"I hope we can have a family someday too. Hopefully not too far from now."

My mouth hung open slightly, crammed with a few possible responses. As if on cue, Boop leaped heroically onto the bed and sauntered up to us, then licked Faye's mouth. She burst out laughing and pushed him away.

"See?" I said. "We've already got a little family!" I reached over and scratched the dog's head. "Where's your mommy, Boop? Is this your mommy?"

We fell asleep, all three of us, in a big pile around 10 PM. But not long after that, Faye started up again. I awoke to her sitting straight up, eyes wide open, looking at the door that leads into the hall.

223

"Do you hear him?" she asked.

"No," I replied, putting a hand around her forearm. "Go back to sleep, baby bear."

"He's hungry," she said, a bit louder. "He sounds like that when he's hungry."

Faye swung her legs off the bed and got up, then stiffly made her way to the door and peeked out. Typically, I tried not to wake her during a sleepwalking episode, because she would get confused and upset. Instead I'd let the event run its course and prevent her from hurting herself, or I'd lead her back to bed and try to soothe her into a deeper slumber.

"Where'd you put him?" she asked. "God, it's so loud. He won't stop crying."

My fiancée disappeared into the darkness of the hallway. I got out of bed, calling her name. The last thing we needed was for her to fall down the stairs and break something.

"Faye," I said into the dark. Boop brushed past my foot and went after her. I felt around the wall for the light switch, and flicked it on. The hall was empty.

The moment that light came on, screams erupted from the guest room. Deafening, terrified screams. They boomed down the hallway and slammed into me, almost knocking me back in fear. Boop came racing out of there and ran all the way back to our bedroom. I bolted toward the sound and threw the door open, almost knocking Faye over. I turned the light on in the guest room and found her standing there, hands over her mouth, looking all over the walls and ceiling at something I couldn't see.

"Faye," I said, grabbing her gently and pulling her into me. I hugged her tight and rocked side to side. "Wake up, sweetie. Wake up. It's just a dream."

"What is that?" she asked, hyperventilating. "God, it's everywhere!"

Faye screamed a few more times into my shoulder, then fell silent and went limp in my arms. A moment later, she regained consciousness, and stared into my eyes.

"I had such a bad dream," she said, tears streaking her fair complexion. We sat down on the little bed together. She rubbed the sleep from her eyes.

"What was it?" I asked.

She shook her head.

"I don't want to tell you. It was awful."

We walked down to the kitchen together and got Faye a big glass of water, then returned to bed. She tried to calm down as I rubbed her back, and eventually fell asleep with Boop nuzzled up against her legs.

Around 3 PM the next day, Faye called me from work and asked if we could go out to dinner to get her mind off of her dreams. I obliged, and we ended up at a local Italian joint with plates of chicken parmesan in front of us. She twirled her pasta with a fork and dragged her thousand-yard gaze around the room; it landed on everything but me.

"Look," I said, reaching for her hand, "why don't you just tell me what happened in the dream?"

She evaded my touch and rubbed her face.

"It's terrible. Maybe the most graphic one I've ever had."

The hallucinations during night terrors are often impossible to distinguish from reality. As such, they can traumatize her, and can affect her for several hours or even days afterward. This event was likely going to stick around in Faye's mind, and catalyze more episodes over the next few days. I'd seen it all before.

"We had a baby," she said. A tear dripped off her face into her food. "And I did something to him. There was blood everywhere. Covering everything. I was painting the walls with it." She held up her hands and examined them. They were shaking.

Jesus Christ, I thought. I tried to keep the revulsion from spreading across my face.

"Listen. These things..." I said, stumbling through my words, "these things happen, Faye. I don't know why they happen to you. But lots of people have night terrors. They're actually pretty common."

She looked into my eyes, waiting to hear something more consoling.

"...And lots of women have dreams about losing their babies, or hurting them," I continued. "That's even more common. And do you know what it means?"

She shook her head and sniffled. A waiter walked up, but when he saw her face, he turned around and left without saying a word. Nearby, a little kid smacked his fork against a water glass over and over.

"It means you're afraid of anything bad happening to your child. That thought terrifies you. It should terrify any good parent." I took her hand and caressed it. "It means you're going to be a great mommy someday. Trust me."

Faye smiled and put her other hand over mine.

"I hope so."

The candle on the table burned out. We finished our dinner and left.

Back at home, Faye sat on the couch with the dog on her lap, both of them wrapped up in a blanket. I was on my laptop at the breakfast table nearby. A movie played on the TV.

"I would never hurt our baby," she blurted out.

"What?" I said, looking over at her.

She tossed her hair out of her face and ran her fingers across the dog's back. He relished her attention.

"I wouldn't do it," she said. "I'm not like my dreams."

I didn't know what to say. Maybe it was the low light, or the dream she shared with me, or the fact that I was busy writing a horror story when she said it. But the image of

Faye holding Boop and promising never to be violent unnerved me a bit. I returned my attention to the laptop.

"Okay."

All night long I dreamed of bad things happening to the dog. He got trapped in places, crushed under things, I came home to find his body in the kitchen. And in each dream, Faye was there. I got out of bed after midnight and snuck into the bathroom, careful not to make any loud sounds that could trigger a night terror.

I splashed cold water all over my face and stared at myself in the mirror. Was Boop safe with Faye? Could she harm him during one of her midnight strolls? She had never become violent in the past, despite having scores of night terrors, but her dream was so unsettling to me that my mind kept returning to the dog's wellbeing. And the way she tried to reassure me that she wouldn't hurt our child – it seemed more like she was trying to reassure herself.

When I opened the bathroom door, I saw Faye sitting up in bed. Her spine was rigid. It was another episode.

"Is he okay?" she asked. "Bring him to me." She extended her arms up toward the hallway. She didn't seem to notice I was standing on the other side of the room.

"Faye, honey," I said, trying to speak gently.

"Oh, look at you," she cooed, giggling and wrapping her arms around an imaginary child. She held it there and hummed.

"Faye," I called, louder.

My fiancée craned her neck toward the sound of my voice. Her eyes were closed. She licked her lips and put her arms down to her sides.

"*Boooooop,*" she called.

The dog's head popped up from the fluffy bedspread. A bit of moonlight seeped in through the curtains and glinted in his eyes, giving them a creepy glow. Boop climbed over

Faye's legs and stood there on her lap. She picked him up and held him at arm's length, examining him with her eyes still closed.

"What..." she said, her voice quivering. "Why are you..."

Suddenly, Faye exploded in tears and began screaming. The dog recoiled in fear and flailed his little legs, trying to escape. She shook him as she screamed, and turned her head away in disgust.

"Faye!" I yelled, running over to the bed. "What the hell is wrong with you?" I snatched the dog away from her and turned the light switch on with my elbow. Boop squirmed out of my grip and tumbled to the floor, then scurried out of the room.

The light woke Faye up. She glanced around the room, puzzled, then covered her eyes with her forearm. I walked over and sat on the bed next to her, grabbing her by the shoulders.

"Faye, you have got to see a doctor," I said. There was zero patience left in my voice.

"God, can't you hear that?" she asked, wiping tears out of her eyes.

"Yes," I said. "I hear you screaming. All the fucking time. I'm about to call an exorcist."

She glared at me with a mixture of anger and fear. I reminded myself that however annoying her night terrors were to me, they were horrific ordeals to her.

"I keep hearing a baby crying," she said. More tears welled up in her eyes. "Can't you hear it? It's not a dream. I'm hearing it more and more."

For once, I stayed up and talked with Faye about her experiences, rather than trying to usher her back to sleep as quickly as possible. We laid there in bed with a few candles lit, holding each other, talking about our happiest and scariest dreams. The hours drifted by and the candles melted away. When I woke up, the sun was burning through the curtains and Boop was whimpering to be let out. It was almost noon.

We spent the day walking the trails in the woods near our house. Boop excitedly chased squirrels, leaped at butterflies, and splashed in the puddles of last weekend's rain. It was his first time on a hike.

"So what about last night?" I asked. Faye was a few steps ahead of me, taking photos of the scenery with her cell phone.

"It was really nice," she said, and smiled over her shoulder at me.

"No, I mean, the dream."

"It was just...it didn't make sense," she said. I could tell she didn't want to talk about it.

"You can tell me."

She stopped walking and put the phone in her pocket.

"I dreamed Boop died," she said flatly.

This took me by surprise. I looked over to the dog. He was running up and down the trail frantically, trying to understand the squirrels in the trees above him. They chirped angrily at him.

"...Ah," I said, trying not to sound upset.

"It's nothing," she continued. "I just want to forget about it."

The day went by too fast. Yet again, I found myself dreading to lay down in that bed, dreading what terrible things my fiancée might conjure up in her sleep. I stayed downstairs watching a movie long after she had retired for the night. Boop was curled up on my lap. He kept looking up at me, into my eyes, as if he wanted to tell me something.

"What is it, buddy?" I scratched his chin.

He blinked a few times.

"Momma scarin' you?"

He buried his nose in the blanket.

"Yeah, me too," I said, laughing.

I shut off the TV and headed up to bed around midnight. I drifted off quickly. Tonight, the dog slept on the floor.

In my dreams, I saw his death. I was sitting in the same position Faye had occupied the night before: straight up in bed, arms out, holding Boop's little body in front of me. It dripped blood all over my lap. It was too dark to make out how he had died, but across the room, I could see ghastly stains all over his doggy bed.

The nightmare jolted me awake. I threw the covers off my body and tried to wipe away the blood, but everything was dry. My senses slowly returned. The clock read 3:03 AM. I moved a hand across the bed in search of Faye's warm back, but I found only the cool sheets. She'd been gone for a while. In the distance, there was a noise.

It was a cry. Not the familiar sobs of my fiancée, but an unrecognizable shriek. It sounded almost like a dog. My eyes darted over to Boop's bed. It was empty. The door into the hallway was closed.

"Boop?" I called out. He didn't come scampering out from a hiding place. I leaped out of bed and followed the cries into the hall. As I pushed the door open, the shrill noise invaded our bedroom. It wasn't a dog. It was an infant.

There was a baby in my house.

This realization confused and horrified me simultaneously. I waded through the black hall, hands out, feeling for the light. Sheer terror caused me to forget the layout of my own house. As I neared the stairs, the crying grew louder.

What the hell is going on?

"Faye?" I called out. My voice barely rose above a timid whisper.

By the time I got to the bottom of the stairs, the baby's

deafening wails had shaken me to the core. I could hardly see anything, but a few yards ahead, moonlight poured in from the sliding glass door and lit up the living room. Someone was in there.

I moved forward, trembling violently with each step. My jaw locked shut. The glass door was open, and a gentle breeze pushed the curtains around. The screaming grew louder and more fervent as I approached. There was a figure sitting on the couch, facing away from me. From where I stood, she was entirely silhouetted by the pale light.

It was Faye. Her hair fluttered in a gust of wind. The air was so cold it bit down hard on my skin, making me shiver more.

"What are you doing?" I called out. "Faye!"

The crying ceased, and she turned her head to the side for a moment, listening. Then she looked away, and the noise resumed. I stormed up to her, fighting to stop my rubbery legs from giving out. I looked down into her lap. She was holding something in her arms, cradling it. Boop flashed into my mind.

"What have you done?" I asked, circling the couch and walking over to the light switch on the far wall. My fear was momentarily replaced with anger. "Where is the dog?"

I flipped the light on and spun around to see what Faye was doing. Her body was rigid like a department store mannequin, and she cradled something wrapped in a blanket. She wasn't looking down at it. Instead, she looked straight forward. Her eyes were rolled back in her head, and she was making the crying noises herself. She imitated the cries of a baby with impossible accuracy, and persisted even after the lights came on.

"What the fuck are you doing?!" I shouted, loud enough to wake the neighbors.

She stopped the noises once again, and her head jerked

toward me. Only the whites of her eyes showed, and her lips peeled back into a deeply eerie smile.

"Wake up, Faye," I said. Anger and fear hung on my voice. "If you hurt that dog I swear to God—"

Just then, Boop came flying around the corner, issuing a brave and tiny growl. He ran up and stood between my legs, barking at Faye. Relief momentarily flooded my body. He was alive.

Then what the hell is she holding?

I walked straight up to my fiancée and stole the bundle out of her hands. It was heavier than I'd expected. Maybe she'd grabbed a bag of flour from the kitchen. I unwrapped the blanket and screamed in shock when it came off.

It was a baby.

A real baby.

But its skin was hard and gray; its lips and eyes were dry. This infant hadn't been alive for days, maybe weeks.

I tried to scream again, but nothing more came out of my mouth. I tried to inhale, but there was no air in the room for me to breathe. Boop kept up his incessant barking. When I managed to rip my gaze from the child in my hands, I saw Faye standing in front of me, white eyes piercing into me.

"We have to give him back," she said. She slammed her palm into my temple, staggering me, and then yanked the corpse from my hands and darted out the sliding glass door. I fell to one knee, clutching my head.

"Faye," I called out. Spots twinkled across my vision.

When I managed to stand, I wobbled over to the glass and watched as Faye stood in the grass of our backyard. She was half-naked, clutching the child's body against her chest as if protecting it from the cold. She looked back at me with those hideous eyes, then down at the ground.

A few yards away, something was jutting from the grass, just barely lit up by the moon. When the static in my vision finally abated, a new terror coiled itself around my throat. The breath went out of me, as if strangled by a python. It was a pair of hands. Rotten hands, as dead and gone as the child itself. They sat motionless, frozen in a "Hallelujah!" pose. I recognized them the moment I laid eyes on them.

Faye walked up to them, her movements stiff and alien. As she did, the hands came to life and reached longingly toward her. I stood there immobilized behind the glass, watching as she carefully placed the corpse into the hands. They twitched in excitement as the body lowered onto them, then gingerly receded into the earth, dragging it down with them. Even the blanket inched its way underground and disappeared. An owl hooted in the tree above the yard.

Faye then dropped herself down into the wet grass. She sat there, spine rigid, as if meditating in her sleep. Her expressionless face squared with mine, her eyes still rolled back in her head. The soil churned around her. Fingers and hands angrily poked up out of the ground in a six-foot line between us. Too many hands. Faye smiled.

Something climbed up out of the ground. Something had been living there, patiently waiting beneath the flower pots and manicured grass. Waiting for God knows how long. It was a creature from beyond my darkest nightmares: a human head erupted first, followed by a writhing torso with a dozen arms jutting from it like the legs of a centipede. The arms unfolded themselves and dragged the creature up out of the earth, clawing and crunching as they went. Its putrefied skin matched that of the baby, but this creature moved with a terrifying liveliness. It clambered out of its tomb of soil and gasped wheezing breaths, no doubt its first in ages. Its many limbs suspended the foul thing a few inches off the ground. One of its hands slowly pointed in my direction.

Faye leaned over and placed her face near the creature's head. It met her halfway. Through quivering lips and blackened teeth, it whispered something in her ear. She paused for a long time, then slowly turned toward me, the whites of her eyes glowing in the moonlight. The creature's gaze mirrored hers until its yellow eyes fell upon me. Its hand hung in the air, pointing at me as it mouthed words I could not hear. They both studied me, then Faye dropped her head back down and whispered something in response. The arachnoid thing smiled. It tore its horrible eyes from me and sulked back into its hole, the many hands working to cover itself with the soil it had displaced. In a few moments, it was gone.

The wind intensified and rustled the trees around the edge of the yard. Faye collapsed into the grass. She fell backward and lay flat, eyes finally closed, snoring all the while. Fearing she'd be dragged down too, I broke free from my terror. I rushed over and scooped her up. As I carried her inside and laid her down on the couch, she woke up, and was confused as to why we were downstairs.

"What are you doing?" she asked. Her voice was innocent and sleepy. Boop nuzzled her hand as it dangled off the couch. I had no words at all to offer her, so I just shook my head in dismay. Rage and fright and hopelessness swirled inside me and welled up in my throat, pushing tears out of my eyes. I dropped down on the floor and leaned against the couch, sobbing into my hands. Faye shifted behind me.

"Felix," she murmured, swatting me with a hand. "Don't wake me up. Baby shower is tomorrow."

Icarus
Colin J. Northwood

It was easy to get enough skin. The small bones were the difficult part. Such a delicate balance to achieve, with so much variation in materials.

Matthias hummed a cheerful tune as he put the finishing touches on the wings. He couldn't wait to finally experience true freedom. This was like Christmas morning.

Too many years in this dreary town. Too many years among these ungrateful wretches. No more. The voice in the walls had promised him the power of flight, should he dare to construct the necessary implements.

Over and through the needle goes. Tedium in its dying throes.

When finally they were done, Matthias took a moment to savor his anticipation. The wings stretched across an entire wall of the wine cellar, their grand stature promising Matthias the bounty he craved. The armature was both intricate and sturdy. The membranes radiated both beauty and mechanical precision.

A job well done, Matthias told himself. The voice in the walls agreed, and praised his craftsmanship. In order to guarantee that he was ready to leave his humanity behind, the voice explained, Matthias would have to craft his wings from real human skin and bones. That seemed sensible enough.

He had spent a few weeks gathering the materials. Having never worked on such a challenging project, he wasn't sure in the beginning whom to collect. At first, he was tempted by the easy targets: vagabonds, streetwalkers, invalids; but the quality of their parts was dubious. That simply would not do. Only the best for *my* wings, Matthias promised himself. With a little greater ambition, he improved at his errand and gradually reaped a magnificent harvest.

Outside the cellar's tiny window, a gentle snowfall had coated the ground in immaculate white under a full moon. It seemed that heaven itself had blessed this occasion. To commemorate his last night as a workman, Matthias kissed a bottle of wine, then shared a toast with himself and a few laughs with the voice.

It was finally time.

His heart raced with joy as he stripped naked and wiggled into the embrace of the attachment mechanism. It was a perfect fit. His eyes moistened as he fastened the clasps tightly around his ribs and began the incantation. Tears began to escape as he felt the first tremblings of life stir and mingle with his own.

The clasps tightened further and further, digging into his tender sides until they drew blood. The two spines of the apparatus, from which the great wings erupted on either side, caressed his back like an eager lover before grinding their way into his bones.

For a brief moment, Matthias considered that he may have made a terrible mistake, but this was no time for hesitation. And soon, his patience with the pain was rewarded, as the bones fully merged with his own and settled happily into his frame. Strips of shorn skin remained where the device had forced its way inside.

An eye for an eye, Matthias opined with a droll

satisfaction. The law of man had touched him for the last time. The resulting scars would be a wonderful memento.

Now, he alternately folded and stretched his wings, finding them nimble and sensitive. The extra time he had taken to gather superior parts had paid off.

Matthias could wait no longer and dashed out into the street. The glimmering stars showered him with crystalline light that sparkled off his bleeding wounds. The hallowed silence of the night was broken only by the crunch of his exultant steps through the snow. The sleepy town was empty – just the way he wanted to remember it.

And here, he caroused like a child, discovering the dexterities of his new parts through trial and error. He rolled in the snow and shook it off his wings, giggling at the way it made him shiver. He waved them up and down in a cheerful greeting to his reflection. He crouched by the gargoyles at the cathedral and grinned at the resemblance.

What a majestic night to behold, and what a fortunate thing am I. What a heaven in which to break free, and what a life I will live in the sky.

The final test beckoned. Matthias stood on top of a rock and jumped, flapping vigorously...and fell. But he felt it: the wings were going to hold. It was his own awkwardness and inexperience that kept him from flying.

So he tried again. *Calmly, calmly.* And again, he fell.

Again.

And again.

And again.

After several tries, he could glide a bit. After several more, he could turn from side to side. And after several more still, he could drift comfortably on the low breezes. The voice in the walls had been wise. Perhaps he would return to the cellar and thank it someday.

More, and more, and more. Higher, and higher, bolder and bolder. Until—

Success!

With mighty flaps, Matthias rose into the sky until he could see the entire town below him. A gentle breeze licked his naked flesh and chilled his exposed ribs.

Glory! Glory!

No more could the brutal Earth contain him in its cage. No more would he be a slave to gravity's dictates.

Free! Free! I am free at last!

Matthias traced lazy circles in the sky. No man had ever seen such sights. And so it would remain, for Matthias was no man. No longer.

The sky's proximity was intoxicating, and Matthias was its new paramour. He admired its curves and fondled it sweetly. Deeper and deeper into the firmament he rose, and deeper he fell under its spell, until he no longer knew up from down. No matter, he thought; it is not in the nature of heavenly creatures to concern themselves with such things.

And when even the clouds were far below him – when he felt that he had achieved the ultimate freedom – Matthias learned of a freedom greater still.

For so great was his body's wanderlust that his very skin wished to be liberated from his flesh, and finally saw its chance. It had been fastened to him too tightly, for too long. Too many years encumbered by this useless meat.

And so it began to emancipate itself.

It crawled free of his bleeding thorax. Free of his thrashing arms and his squirming legs. Free of his rigid skull.

Matthias commanded his skin to stay, but it would not listen. He tried bargaining with it, but he had nothing it could not already take. Finally, he pleaded with it pitifully, but to no avail. For just like Matthias, his skin was resentful of such manipulation.

I have become like the jailors who caged me.

Matthias was a principled man, and realized he had to let go. His skinless body departed its husk, leaving his precious wings behind. He savored this display of altruism, proud to have given the ultimate gift.

As his handmade wings flew off into the distance, piloted by his wayward skin, he admired their elegant silhouette against the milky moon and jeweled sky. A job well done, indeed.

And as he plummeted back toward the ground, always looking up, he marveled at the way the wind felt against the barren flesh of his back. He watched his blood form spirals above him, the droplets descending at a leisurely pace as they bid him farewell. *Goodbye, friends.* His eyes watered again, but this time in gratitude. How lovely it was to experience such vivid things.

Icebreaker, part II
Felix Blackwell

My grandfather, Martin Blackwell, left that horrible Soviet ship in 1968, but it never left him. For years after, he suffered nightmares and long bouts of insomnia that slowly wore him down. He complained to his wife of feeling watched. He heard whispering in the halls of his home at night. On more than one occasion, Martin claimed to have seen terrible beings in his dreams, and they persisted even after he awoke. Each dream was different; he sometimes saw the creatures travelling across a vast abyss into our world. Other times, they climbed up through tunnels of ice deep beneath the sea. They were always looking for him, and always wanted the same thing: to drag him away, back into the dark.

Martin's visions slowly drove him mad. He continued pursuing his old hobbies, but they took on a corrupted and sinister nature. Once an amateur landscape painter, he began painting scenes from his nightmares: a dark corridor, a frozen hatch, an arctic midnight. At the end of his life, he gave all of his works and writings to my father, who kept them tucked away in our garage. My dad hoped that it could all be buried and forgotten, along with the pain of watching a loved one's grip on reality wither away. But my grandfather's descent into psychosis weighed heavily on my dad's heart, and began to haunt his sleep too.

I remember sneaking into the garage one night as an impetuous child and uncovering the paintings. They'd been hidden beneath a stack of old blankets that had since become the home of many spiders. A cold, morbid exhilaration pumped through my veins as I flipped through the canvases. They were glimpses through the eyes of madness, each more surreal than the last. Martin had devoted years of his life to perfecting these grim creations, and now I gazed down on the masterpieces of a mind entirely conquered by Hell. Most of them are now blocked out of my memory and lost forever, but the few that remain still haunt me. One depicted his wife's rotting carcass sitting dignified in an armchair, swirling a glass of cabernet. Another showed the passageways of a ship constructed entirely of flesh; a dark figure stands at the far end watching the observer. Another showed a person's head frozen in a block of ice, the eyes screaming helplessly. Several were of a Soviet admiral without a face.

The painting that stood out to me most, however, depicted a Dali-esque dreamscape before a rising moon. In the foreground, surreal growths jut from the earth, clawing at the night sky. A strange entity stands at a frigid shore, staring out into a dark sea. Its body is composed of gnarled driftwood formed into a skeletal structure; something glows within it. In the distance, stars gleam down on a massive, shadowy icebreaker approaching from the horizon.

Beneath the stack of paintings was something I had not expected to find. It was a leather journal, tattered by decades of handling. As a child it was a meaningless thing to me; I could not read the strange language of its contents and could not see how it was connected to my grandfather's art. But in the years to come, its significance to my family and the curse we suffer came to light.

Martin snuck Admiral Petrov's journal back to the United States and stashed it away for nearly a decade. He feared that the government was watching him, so he kept it secret as long as he could, afraid that it contained military intelligence that could get him imprisoned. But when the darkness overtook him, it compelled him to treat the journal as a puzzle to be solved, and the prize was his life. He searched through libraries and visited universities, hoping someone could help him read it. It turned out that some of the entries were not written in Russian, but rather in a coded form of the language that no one could break. Translating the journal, he believed, was the key to stopping the insanity that deteriorated his mind.

But help never came, and many of the words faded from the old pages. Martin withdrew from his family and spent his time alone. Then one day he simply disappeared, just after finishing his painting of the old icebreaker. To my father he left the journal, the paintings, and all of his crazed scribblings about dreams and curses and dead people who walk around in the dark. My grandmother believed he had decided to take his own life somewhere far away. A search party scoured the woods behind their home but never found any trace of him. It wasn't until years later that my dad found a clue: while moving Martin's possessions from one house to another, he noticed a little string of words written in pencil on the back of the painting of the ship. It read, "I'm going back."

My dad reported the disappearance to my grandfather's old military contacts, but they all pretended that the mission and the icebreaker had never existed. Some strange men came to our home one night and encouraged my father to drop the issue and move on with his life. To this day, the ultimate fate of Martin Blackwell remains a mystery.

Eventually, my dad decided to rid himself of the eerie

paintings. He kept the journal, probably because he knew how much it meant to his father. As far as I know, my dad never made any attempts to translate it, and instead kept it in a safe with a few other priceless family heirlooms.

"Out of sight, out of mind" did not apply in the case of my family's dark secret. My father began to lose his grip on reality, much in the same way that his father had. Terrible dreams wracked his mind with increasing frequency, and he became paranoid that he was being watched. He often refused to sleep. On a few occasions as a child, I remember waking up to the sound of his cries. Once, I got out of bed to see him with his ear pressed against a closet door in the hallway. He mumbled angrily and appeared to be having an argument with something inside it. Unlike Martin, who told his wife everything, my dad handled his psychological deterioration in a more private way: he avoided all conversation about his strange night terrors and refused to open up about his insomnia.

My father's death is difficult for me to talk about, but I feel that it's time to share the truth. In the last year of his life, he barely recognized me anymore. He looked at me like I was a monster, and eyed me with suspicion most of the time. We became strangers living in the same house, and eventually we ceased speaking altogether. He would barricade himself in his office all through the nights, furiously writing and talking to himself. We drifted worlds apart, and my mom began the process of divorce.

In the summer before I entered high school, there came a day when my dad suddenly changed. In our backyard he built a huge bonfire with everything he'd ever written. We watched as it burned; a satisfied and relaxed look rested on his face the whole time. He wordlessly hugged me and walked away, then spent the rest of the evening watching movies.

When I came home from a friend's house the next day,

he was face-down in our pool, dead for hours. At first I thought it was an accident, but then I found an envelope on my bed. It contained a letter, thousands of dollars, and a scrap of paper with a number written on it: *80117*. It turned out to be the combination to the safe in his office.

In the letter, my dad tried to tell me everything about our family's dark visitors. It rambled on about my grandfather and the unfathomable place from which his tormentors came. But mostly it read like a bad sci-fi novel. Against my better judgment, I got rid of it.

The journal came into my possession at age thirteen, but I was powerless to translate it until I was much older. For years I did what both my father and grandfather had done: I tucked it away in a futile attempt to avoid the despair it caused in me. I knew even at that age, however, that my family's illness – or curse – had festered deep within me, and by age fourteen I was already beginning to see "them" too. I never spoke of those experiences with my mother for fear of breaking her heart; I didn't want her to think she'd lose me the way she had lost her husband. Thankfully she never realized the centrality of Petrov's journal to my father's death, and so she never asked about it.

The limited resources of high school made it impossible to crack the mystery of the journal, but in college, I met Jessica Vorhaus, a professor who specialized in the history of Soviet espionage. After giving her an edited version of my family history, she agreed to translate the journal to the best of her ability. In a few weeks, I had a short summary of each entry: typical logs of conversations with other officers, philosophical musings about Stalinism and human nature, pompous autobiographical drivel. Petrov was an ordinary man in every sense of the term, despite his prestige. He never documented any critical information about the *Spear of Kutuzov* or its mission, spare brief mentions of coordinates and references to other top-secret ships.

About halfway through the pages, however, the writing changed. It became frantic and paranoid. The admiral's coding became unreliable, making it extremely difficult to decrypt. In the parts that Professor Vorhaus was able to translate, the words read exactly the way my father used to speak.

In his contemplations, the admiral surmised that he was going stir crazy from being at sea for so many months. He detailed the various sounds he began hearing: the whispers of his deceased mother, otherworldly animal screams, a loud metal banging. But within days of that entry he lost the ability to assess his own mental stability altogether, and soon after he described horrifying dreams of his men dying. At one point, he whimsically remarked upon the coming of "the cold people," and how he barricaded himself in his chamber because he couldn't take the "bothersome screaming" anymore.

In the final entry, Yuri Petrov wrote in plain Russian:

We let them in. I can hear them in the lower levels of the ship. Their footsteps ring out all hours of the night. The children are screaming too. There are no children on board but they scream anyway. They cry and beg for help. They call my name. We let them in.

Scribbled at the bottom of the page was what looked like a poem, written in a language that Professor Vorhaus had never seen before. I took it to every language department on campus, and no one could identify it. I scoured the internet, contacted professors at various universities across the world, and never moved an inch closer to translating the words. It wasn't until my final year of graduate school that I could read the text.

Four years later, while working on my Master's degree, I attended a symposium on the cultures of Iron Age Europe. The keynote speaker was a professor of linguistics from England named Magnus Farmer. We corresponded via email a few weeks after we met, and I introduced the poem to him, hoping that he could finally put an end to the mystery. He recognized the script as a language spoken by a people called the Cwenlins. They were annihilated by neighboring tribes in Gaul and their culture died out, but their oral traditions were recorded by emissaries educated in the Roman Empire. With great difficulty, Magnus translated the document as follows:

In the most ancient aeon,
When the World was born,
The stones and the waters sang to the rhythm of the Only Pulse
And the spirits of creation looked proudly upon their work:
The Age of Unity.

But the song did not end
When their task was finished,
And for the first time, without a shared vision to guide their energies,
The spirits knew not what to do next; and in their confusion, they quarreled;
The Birth of Discord.

The symmetry of the World was broken
As the schemes of individual minds
Pulled the World in many directions, and the Three Thousand Evils spread
Like cracks on the surface of a frozen lake, ever

weakening the center,
Each encouraged by a mind of its own.

The spirits despaired
Of their conflict
And in their sorrow, they pried open the Eye of the Master,
Whose righteous anger flooded the world with warm light, warning them of wrath;
The First Day had begun.

But with only one eye to keep watch,
Half the World remained dark,
And the misfit spirits tried to take refuge in the night, bringing the chill of evil with them;
So the Eye forever spins around the World, leaving them no place to hide
And the spread of Strife is thus contained.

Having lost their prerogative,
And unable to remain hidden,
The Three Thousand Evils were imprisoned in the far North, where still they remain;
And so wicked are their hearts that their very presence brings permanent winter to those lands;
May their icy slumber never end.

The poem brought little to light for me. Its words were ambiguous and fantastical, like many of the creation stories I teach to my undergraduate students. As an academic, it did not differ to me in the slightest from a thousand others just like it. However, around the time of its translation, I began suffering from particularly disturbing nightmares. Whenever I close my eyes I see a barren tundra, glazed with ice. As I glide across it, there is a black chasm in the ground. I stand at its mouth, peering down into the yawning darkness, and hear voices deep inside. My grandfather and father are down there, crying for help. Their voices are joined by a chorus of children's screams. Their agonized babble erupts from the hole in a language I cannot begin to describe, and as I try to understand, my feet slip over the rim and I fall in. Before the endless dark completely takes me, I wake up.

My nights have been this way for over a month now. Last night in my dreams, while gazing down into the same chasm, I saw the hull of a distant ship. It was moving away into the darkness, and I felt a strange urgency to chase after it. It beckoned to me, like there was something on the ship that I needed to find. Like someone was trapped deep within it, silently calling to me.

Sleep comes to me less and less now. When it does, it is fitful and filled with unspeakable terrors. For reasons I can't explain, I feel pulled northward, into the snowy wasteland of my dreams. I want to understand my family's curse; I want to see the ship where it all began and the hole where it might end. And although I do not know how I will ever find either of them, or whether they even exist, I am more confident with each passing day that I must leave. My grandfather calls out to me now, even while I am awake, and he beckons me to the answers waiting in the dark. I have only to follow his voice.

About the Authors

Felix Blackwell emerged from the bowels of reddit during a botched summoning ritual. He is best known for his popular short horror series colloquially referred to as "Romantic Cabin Getaway." He writes novels and short stories in the horror, thriller, and fantasy genres.

Colin J. Northwood is made of twigs and barbed wire. He is allowed out of his cage only when Felix wants him to write. Otherwise, he doesn't get to eat. Someday, he hopes to become flesh and blood. For now, he just wants his stories to take your breath away – literally.

For more creepy things to keep you awake, visit
www.felixblackwell.com

Connect with the authors at
facebook.com/felixblackwellbooks